Sometime in Summer

KATRINA LENO

POPPY

LITTLE, BROWN AND COMPANY

New York Boston

Poppy
Hachette Book Group
1290 Avenue of the Americas, New York, NY 10104
Visit us at LBYR.com

First Edition: June 2022

Poppy is an imprint of Little, Brown and Company.
The Poppy name and logo are trademarks of Hachette Book Group, Inc.

The publisher is not responsible for websites (or their content) that are not owned by the publisher.

Library of Congress Cataloging-in-Publication Data
Names: Leno, Katrina, author.
Title: Sometime in summer / Katrina Leno.
Description: First edition. | New York ; Boston: Little, Brown and Company, 2022. | Summary: Fourteen-year-old Anna Lucia Bell expects the worst from her summer vacation in Rockport with her recently divorced parents, but everything changes with the arrival of new friendships and a magical comet that lead Anna to broaden her understanding of herself, love, and friendship.
Identifiers: LCCN 2021030793 | ISBN 9780316194518 (pbk.) | ISBN 9780316192057 (ebook)
Subjects: CYAC: Divorce—Fiction. | Books and reading—Fiction. | Family life—Fiction. | Love—Fiction. | Friendship—Fiction. | Time travel—Fiction. | Rockport (Mass.)—Fiction. | LCGFT: Novels.
Classification: LCC PZ7.L5399 So 2022 | DDC [Fic]—dc23
LC record available at https://lccn.loc.gov/2021030793

ISBNs: 978-0-316-19451-8 (pbk.), 978-0-316-19205-7 (ebook)

Printed in the United States of America

LSC-C

Printing 1, 2022

To Elliot
and Aaron,
two of my favorites

luck

really thought thirteen would be the year that changed my life.

People—grown-ups—put a lot of emphasis on thirteen.

It's the first actual *teen* year, which I guess could have some weighty significance, but it's also pretty universally acknowledged to be an unlucky number. Black cats. Broken mirrors. The number thirteen. All things people are taught to stay away from. I mean, half the buildings in Los Angeles don't even have a floor thirteen. The elevator jumps from twelve to fourteen, like we're all supposed to think that's going to save us from something. Like luck—good luck or bad luck—can be tricked with something as easy as misnumbering the floors of a building.

Like we all don't know that fourteen is really just thirteen in disguise.

Which is why, on the morning of my fourteenth birthday, I felt two things simultaneously: a light, floaty *relief* to no longer be thirteen, an age that had brought me nothing but the start of my period and the separation of my parents, and a slightly chest-crushing realization that fourteen was probably just going to be an extension of thirteen. Like the fourteenth floor in tall buildings, I was still as unlucky as I'd ever been.

My father, Everett Bell, didn't believe in luck. He'd owned a series of black cats growing up, all with cutesy, twirly names that belied their true superstitious nature: Mitsy, Buttons, Peri-winkle, Fluffy. (*How many cats did your family go through?* I'd asked him once, and smiling, he'd pretended to count on his fingers but didn't actually answer the question.) He'd bro-ken enough mirrors (and plates and cups and mugs) to fill a small garage with bad omens. And I regarded one of his big-gest vices as always, *always* opening the umbrella indoors before plunging out the front door into whatever pathetic rain-storm LA had conjured up in an attempt to stay relevant with meteorologists.

My mother, Miriam Bell, was luck-neutral. If she spilled salt onto the kitchen table as we sat down to our breakfast of omelets or quiche, she might lick a finger and touch it to the jagged crystals, pressing it to her tongue so as not to con-tribute to food waste, but she had never once thrown it over her shoulder. She only sometimes remembered to say *bless you* after a sneeze. If I wasn't looking where I was going and accidentally stepped underneath an open, leaning ladder, she might look up at it momentarily, as if contemplating its origin story, but then she'd shrug, and we'd continue walking as I'd mentally try to calculate how many extra years of bad luck I'd added to my tab.

Me, Anna Lucia Bell, I *did* believe in luck. It was *bad* luck that filled up the toilet bowl with blood the morning I'd turned thirteen, leaving me peering between my legs in a fuzzy, early-morning panic, knowing there was something normal about what I was seeing but unable to put a name to it until I walked into the kitchen and my mother saw my sheet-white face and took me by the hand and pulled me back down the hall to the bathroom and handed me a box of sanitary napkins. (*And you're sure it will stay where it's supposed to stay?* I'd asked, anxiety thrumming through my veins in a not-unfamiliar way. And Miriam had smiled and taken one out of its wrapping and said, *That's what these flaps are for. They call them wings. I know it's silly. I'll show you how to use a tampon tonight.*)

Now, a year later, I knew better how to track the monthly bloodletting, how to watch my body for signs of its coming, how to lessen the chances that I'd be caught unprepared, scrambling around for something absorbent to shove into my underwear.

Now, a year later, I understood that the only difference between thirteen and fourteen is the acceptance that nothing is really different at all.

I opened my eyes to the same pale purple walls (a color I picked out when I was seven and so far had both gotten sick of and grown fond of again in a steady rhythm of every six months or so). I rolled over in the same bed. I had the same body, only an inch or so taller. I had the same brown hair. The same brown eyes plucked from my father's head and replicated in mine. The same house, although Everett Bell had packed up (most of) his things and moved into a smaller house, a rental, just a few streets away. The same smell of pancakes—my birthday pancakes, with chocolate chips and bananas, an order that hadn't changed since even before I'd picked out the paint color—wafting underneath my closed door, drifting into my dreams before I'd even opened my eyes.

Yes, fourteen was here, and so far, everything appeared exactly the same.

I rolled over in bed again and opened my eyes, staring straight up at the popcorn ceiling. A half dozen glow-in-the-dark stars still clung resolutely to its surface. Occasionally, one would fall on me as I was sleeping, and I would wake up in a panic, positive the spider war had started, swiping blindly at miniature enemies that had chosen me as their first human conquest.

I took a deep breath. How many breaths had I taken since midnight? How many breaths as a fourteen-year-old girl?

I grabbed my phone off the nightstand and typed:

How many breaths does the average person take in a year?

Eight and a half million.

I'd taken eight and a half million breaths as a thirteen-year-old, and pretty much every one of them had sucked.

In the kitchen, Miriam was wearing her apron, the red-and-white-striped one that made her look like some sort of vintage magazine advertisement for kitchen appliances. Underneath it, she wore a sleepshirt that fell to her knees and dingy slippers that had once been pink and were now a fuzzy sort of brown. Her hair was clipped up on the top of her head, and it was messy, like she'd slept on it. She had pancake batter on her cheek. My mother was an excellent cook, but she was a messy cook, and the food got absolutely everywhere, like on her cheek, splattered on the top of the stove like a crime scene, even once, memorably, when she'd forgotten to put the top on the food processor, on the ceiling and overhead light fixture. My father called her a walking kitchen disaster. Miriam called herself inventive with a spatula.

I sat down at the kitchen table, and only when she heard the chair legs scrape against the tile floor did she realize I was there—she gave a little squeal and ran over to hug me, probably getting pancake batter all over my pajamas. She smelled like cinnamon—her secret pancake ingredient—and she held the hug for a beat too long. When she pulled away, her eyes were misty, and I groaned before I could help myself.

"Mom—"

"I'm sorry, I'm sorry," she said, fanning her face with two flattened hands. "I just—gosh, Anna, can't you *pause* for one freaking second?"

"If you're asking me to pause time, trust me, I've tried," I said. I moved my hands urgently, flipping fingers against thumb in the way of the middle sister from *Charmed*, but nothing happened.

She caught both of my hands in both of hers and squeezed my fingers hard. Her eyes were big and wet, but to her credit, she didn't actually start crying. Miriam was quick to tear up but excellent at not actually letting herself cry. I never cried. Everett Bell cried at basically every movie he saw, most TV shows, and certain commercials, like the ones about grandparents and life insurance and, sometimes, new cars.

"My beautiful fourteen-year-old," she said.

"Mom, geez."

"I'm so freaking proud to be your mom, kid."

"You're about to be so freaking proud of burning the pancakes."

She jumped at that, dropped my hands, and flew back to the frying pan, flipping a pair of pretty black pancakes. "They'll taste fine with syrup," she called over her shoulder. I had a tiny sip of her coffee, decided I still hated coffee, and leaned back to wait for my first meal as a newly minted fourteen-year-old.

"Fourteen is a meaningless age," I said, leaning on one elbow. "Thirteen is the first teen year. Fifteen you can be a lifeguard. Sixteen you can drive."

"You want to be a lifeguard?"

"If I did, I'd have to wait a year."

"You always get pouty on your birthday."

"I do not."

"You do. It usually burns off by lunchtime."

She got two plates from the cabinet and transferred the pancakes from skillet to plate with a neat flick of her wrist. One of them landed on the counter. She picked it up with two fingers, then yelped and stuck them into her mouth.

It was June 10. School had been out for two weeks. In the fall, I'd be a freshman. I was one of the youngest in my grade. All my friends were turning fifteen in a few months. *They* could be lifeguards if they wanted.

Mom set the plates on the table and sat down across from me. She dumped a sizable amount of syrup on her pancakes, then handed me the bottle. "So you want to be a lifeguard," she said.

"Not necessarily."

She took a bite of pancake, chewed thoughtfully, then pointed her fork at me. "You can work in a nursery. That's what fourteen-year-olds can do."

"With babies?"

"Not that kind of nursery, silly. A flower nursery."

"A flower nursery?"

"Like Dover Succulents."

"You want me to get a job at Dover Succulents?"

"I don't *want* you to do anything. Except what makes you happy."

"I already have a job."

"I know. And don't get me wrong, Anna, I'd love it if you stayed at the bookstore forever. But maybe it's time for a change, to *branch* out...." She paused, smiled, and added, "*Leaf* the bookstore. *Fertilize* a new dream."

"Okay, okay," I said. "I get it."

"I'm just saying. The world is your oyster."

Bell's Books. The bookstore my parents had owned since I was one, the bookstore I had been raised in, learning to walk next to bright-red copies of *Beloved*, cutting my teeth on a dingy paperback of *Pride and Prejudice*. I'd been helping them after school since I was eleven and could competently recommend *One Hundred Years of Solitude* to guests wanting something "a little magical," and now that it was summer, I was there almost every day, sometimes working, sometimes wandering around, sometimes lying down in the back room, amid boxes of unsorted books, breathing in their particular smell of must and ink and pages.

Miriam always said: *The right book at the right time can change your life.*

Pretty much everyone in our small, touristy, beachside town, at one point or another, had had a book recommended to them by Miriam.

If they were smart, they bought it on the spot.

If they weren't smart, my mother would somehow procure their address, wrap the book in brown paper, and have me drop it off at the post office.

We'd wait a few days, maybe a week, maybe two weeks, and then inevitably the door of Bell's Books would open and we'd look up and there would be so-and-so, my mother's latest victim, clutching said book to their chest with tears welling up in their eyes, sniffling about how they'd just finished it and walked all the way to 219 Olive Street to tell my mother that she was right and they should have listened to her in the first place.

Miriam always smiled. Always took their hand or put her

palm on their shoulder. Always nodded and said, "We all take different times to arrive at the same conclusions."

This was a very nice way of saying, "Yes, duh, you should have."

I'd seen Miriam recommend *Wuthering Heights* to the leather-clad leader of a biker gang rolling through town. I'd seen that same biker come back a month later with a fresh Heathcliff tattoo and red-rimmed eyes from crying.

I'd seen Miriam hand a tattered copy of *The Road* to a young, new father with eyes wide and unfocused from lack of sleep. I'd witnessed him return two days later, holding his baby with a new sense of purpose, a new protectiveness and pride that honestly made me roll my eyes a little (somewhere he couldn't see).

"I like the bookstore, though," I said, and it was the truth, even though (and this was something I knew Miriam considered a personal failing on her part) I had never understood the appeal of books. I read them on occasion, of course, mostly when forced to by school, and I knew their summaries because Mom herself had a disconcerting habit of reading aloud, her clear, large voice filling up the store like a familiar audiobook. And not to mention the *actual* audiobooks, which she loaded her phone with, playing them in the car whenever we pulled out of the driveway, regardless of whether we were going a few minutes down the street or a few hours into the mountains. Snippets of books followed me around my life like ghosts. I could recite the first lines of every Virginia Woolf novel (not to mention the last lines and quite a few of the ones in the middle), though I'd read none of them myself.

Mom smiled sadly. She sort of played around with her fork for a second, then laid it on the side of her plate. "I have a few things to tell you," she said in the exact same tone she used when she and Dad sat me down in the living room to tell me he was moving out and they were getting a capital-D-Divorce. My stomach turned uncomfortably, and I set my own fork down on my plate.

"Okay..."

"Your father and I have been discussing things—" (So far this was *exactly* like the capital-D-Divorce conversation, like, verbatim.) "And we've decided it's time to close the bookstore."

If I hadn't already put my fork down, I would absolutely have dropped it now. I kind of wished I were still holding it, because the clatter it would have made when it hit my plate would've been a very dramatic punctuation to what she had just said. As it was, there was only silence, and the silence was incredibly unsatisfying.

"You're whatting the what?" I asked.

"It's time, my love. We'll finish out the summer and close the doors at the end of August. It's just not bringing in as much money as it used to, and frankly, with the overhead and the expenses, well...It's barely breaking even."

The bookstore. My childhood. My nursery (baby, not plants). The smell. The ink. The words. The cramped bathroom with the door you had to hold shut. The time I fell off a step stool and smashed my nose against a copy of *Valley of the Dolls*. Miriam's book recommendations. Miriam's insistence: *The right book at the right time can change your life*. All of it. Gone. Donezo. Finished.

"Anna? Can you say something?"

But I couldn't say anything, because how could I say what I actually wanted to say, which was, *You can't close the bookstore, because you've never recommended a book to me; a book has never changed my life, and I need that, I need you to do that, I need that to happen*!

"Well," she continued, still smiling sadly, biting her lower lip in a way that meant, I knew, that her heart was breaking. "I'm sorry, Anna. But I have a bit of good news, too."

I made myself look interested; I made myself fix an expression on my face that I thought might give off some small sense of hope. I made myself say: "Okay?"

"We're going to go away for a little bit. A nice vacation. Just the two of us. Well, your father will come for a week or so, but mostly just us two. What do you think?"

"A vacation? To where?"

"The East Coast. My aunt's cottage, by the sea. Remember?"

I'd been there once when I was six. My great-aunt had died just a few months ago, but at her insistence, there had been no funeral.

"I used to spend every summer at that cottage," Mom continued. "And she's left it to me. In her will. I just thought... what a nice opportunity. To get away from everything."

"And the bookstore?"

"Your father will look after it. When he comes to join us, we'll have Luke take over for a week. I think this will be good for us. It's been a tumultuous year for you, Anna. And for me. It might be nice to have a change of pace."

A change of pace. Right now, my pace was: reeling. What might my pace be on the East Coast?

"When do we leave?" I asked.

"Tomorrow night. Red-eye."

I nodded. I felt...I didn't know how I felt. A little numb. A little sad. A little anxious. A little crampy.

"Thanks for breakfast, Mom," I said, because honestly, I didn't know what else to say.

She stabbed a piece of pancake with her fork. I did the same. We toasted across the table, clicking forks, pancake against pancake, a thin line of syrup dripping slowly to the table below.

"Happy birthday, Anna."

"I really thought thirteen would be the year that changed my life."

"Every year changes your life," she replied solemnly. "Although it can be hard to see, at first. Hindsight is twenty-twenty. I think you're an exceptional kid."

We took our bites at the same time, and the chewing provided a welcome bit of silence.

Then—a warm dampness between my upper thighs.

Bad luck or biology or a little bit of both—I got up to find a tampon.

bell's books

There were a few things about my mother that did not make sense.

The book thing was one of them, sure: her ability to sell Shakespeare to an uninterested middle schooler or Judy Blume to a distracted father.

But there were other things, too.

Her eyes, the impossible shade of lavender at dawn.

The way she knew—before opening it, before even touching it—whether a used book would have an inscription on the inside cover or title page. It was her true passion: finding books addressed to other people. A copy of *Little Women* to Jenny, love Mom. A copy of *Beowulf* to Mikey, who loves monsters. A copy of *The Secret History* to Amanda, I hope this book changes your life like it changed mine.

She loved finding these books that had once belonged to other people. The really good ones she kept on a special shelf in her bedroom. The others she'd resell in Bell's Books.

Bell's Books.

Another thing about my mother that did not make sense.

It was as much an extension of her as I was, so much so that I often referred to it as my sibling and didn't think I was that far off from the truth.

A bookstore that, while fairly unassuming and generic from the outside, held as many impossibilities as its owner.

In this small town, people had been known to go into Bell's Books on a Monday and emerge on a Wednesday evening, newly versed in Chaucer and speaking only in Middle English for a full month straight.

In this small town, people who had frequented Bell's Books every week for their entire lives suddenly found themselves in an aisle of the store they had never before seen, an aisle with bookcases that stretched upward into a ceiling so far away that it could hardly be seen through the clouds that gathered at the topmost shelves.

In this small town, my mother moved like a shadow in the corner of your eye, sticking close to the edges of your periphery, her nose often hidden behind the cover of a book so she didn't have to answer direct questions like "Is this store bigger on the inside than it has any right to be according to the laws of physics?" and "I swear last week you didn't have an American history section, but I just got lost for an hour in a labyrinth of books about the Civil War—what gives?"

Because she generally liked books more than people, my mother rarely walked from point A to point B without one, some broken hardcover or dog-eared paperback she'd probably read already, some of them three, four, five times, enough so that she could recite them without the burden of pages.

"But I like the smell," she'd say, and breathe deeply: the scent of paper, of ink, of dozens of years being passed from hand to hand to hand until they ended up in our store.

Which was why it was impossible to me, *impossible*, that we'd sell the bookstore.

Which was why I sat on the toilet, my pancakes getting cold, my stomach cramping uncomfortably, and cried. Even though I never cried, I cried now, balling up toilet paper and burying my eyes in a big pillow of it, letting the tears flow down my cheeks.

I know, I know—I've already admitted that I don't really like books.

And my mother loved me in the fierce, powerful way of mothers everywhere, since the dawn of time, but I also knew without a smidge of doubt: that was the one thing she would change about me. She would wiggle her nose and I'd suddenly be Matilda, carrying around stacks of books, eating words like honey, letting them drip down my chin.

But my not liking books didn't mean I wanted the bookstore to close. No, no, I wanted the exact opposite. I wanted to *live* in the bookstore. I wanted to never, ever leave it.

Trust me. I *wished* I liked books. I wished I was more like my mother in basically every way. I wished I had her lavender eyes or her thick, long hair or her one-dimpled cheek (the left), just something to mark me as hers. But alas, I was my father's child through and through: lank, frizzy hair, unextraordinary nonlavender eyes, flat chest, and undimpled cheeks.

A knock at the bathroom door. "Sweetie," she said, her voice gentle and soothing. "Are you okay in there?"

"I'm bleeding to death," I said, which was true.

"You sound sort of sniffly," she replied. "Why don't you come out here and finish your pancakes?"

"I don't want to sell the bookstore."

"I know, honey."

"Can't we do *something*?"

"It's just time to let it go. Your father's doing so well with his new business, he doesn't have as much time as he used to. And you know the bookstore was always my thing, anyway."

My father's new business was a tattoo parlor he'd opened up in town. His waiting list had quickly filled up to a year, with tons of famous people scrambling for an appointment. He was super talented, covered head to toe in tattoos, and basically the second-coolest person I knew (after my mom).

I got up from the toilet, flushed, washed my hands, and opened the door.

"Oh, kiddo," Mom said, wrapping her arms around me. "I'm sorry I told you on your birthday. To be honest...I've been putting it off. But since we're leaving tomorrow, I thought it could be kind of a good news, bad news thing."

"It's okay. I get it."

"What do you want to do today? Anything in the world."

"Let's go say goodbye to the beach. If we're going to spend all this time on the East Coast, I want to make sure the West Coast knows we're going to miss it."

She kissed the top of my head. "I'm so happy you were born. And born to me! All the wombs in the world and you chose mine."

"When you put it that way—"

"It's romantic?"

"A little gross, actually."

"All romantic things are a little gross." She let go of me and started walking back to the kitchen. "Do you want to invite Jennica?"

"No, that's okay. She's busy today."

As far as my mother was concerned, Jennica was my best friend. I'd met her only a few years ago, when she'd moved to our town from San Diego. We'd been in homeroom together, and she'd been wearing a shirt from a band I loved. We hit it off right away.

But now...

I didn't know.

Things had gone...wrong. We'd started fighting over little things, like what movie to see on a Sunday afternoon or whose house to sleep over at on a Friday night.

And then Lara Biltmore showed up last year and ruined everything.

Lara was new in town, super pretty, super cool, and Jennica had introduced herself to her right away.

"When I was new in town, you were the only person who talked to me," Jennica had explained. "It's hard to move somewhere halfway through the school year. This is the nice thing to do."

It was hard to argue with that logic, even though I didn't love the idea of Jennica making a new friend. I was basically her only friend, and if I was honest with myself...I kind of liked it that way. And I just had a bad feeling about Lara in general.

And, as it turned out, I was right.

Because within two months, Jennica wasn't speaking to me, and she and Lara were doing everything together.

But I didn't want to tell my mom that. She was friends with Jennica's mom, Amber. I would be *mortified* if she mentioned something to her.

So—I went on pretending. Pretending we were still friends. Pretending nothing was wrong. Pretending everything was fine.

More bad luck of the thirteen-year variety.

It was an eight-minute walk to the beach from our house, and usually we took the route that led us past the bookstore, but not today. Today, Mom took us on a gently roundabout journey, claiming she wanted to grab a coffee from a little café on the same street as Bell's Books, only three blocks down. I waited outside as she went to get it, standing on the very edge of the sidewalk to see as far down the street as I could.

Olive Street was a six-block stretch of little shops and restaurants and cafés and, of course, our bookstore—which wouldn't be our bookstore much longer. I could just about see the green awning that hung over its front door. A few blocks past it was my dad's new tattoo parlor, Lucia Ink, although I couldn't quite see it from here. It was a cool shop, with all matte gold counters and framed tattoo art crowding every inch of wall space. One day I wanted to get a tattoo from my dad, although I had no clue what. Maybe the number thirteen, right over my heart. Or a black cat with its tail winding around my wrist. Or a broken mirror, pointy shards of glass collecting in a shiny heap on my rib cage.

You get the idea.

Miriam came out with her coffee and a plus-one in the form of Suzanne Bridges, the woman who owned Walk or Run, the shoe store where Josh worked. I'd known Josh forever; we'd met in swim class when we were just toddlers. He'd been the best swimmer since he was in diapers, and now he went to meets all over the state. He was honestly more like a brother than a friend.

When Suzanne and my mom got closer, I could see that Suzanne had tears in her eyes. I tuned in to their conversation just as Suzanne said, "...don't know how you do it, Miriam. I *hate* scary stories, but I swear, that book just *changed my life*."

There was that phrase again, that phrase I'd heard a hundred million times in the past exactly fourteen years: *changed my life*.

"What book?" I asked.

"*The Stand*," my mom said with a wink.

"Stephen King, I mean, Stephen King! Who would have thought?" Suzanne continued, hardly even seeing me. "Miriam, how did you ever guess that? I just feel like he opened me up and peeked right into my brain, you know?"

"That's what a good book will do, Suz," Miriam said, winking again (my mom loved winking).

"You're not kidding, Miriam," Suzanne said. She blinked and looked around, glancing down the street and up at the sky and down at the sidewalk, like, I swear, she was seeing the world for the very first time. "I better get to the shop. Hi, Anna."

"Tell Josh I said hi," I called after her because she had already turned and was heading away from us, her footsteps light and airy, like she was walking on clouds or a trampoline or, perhaps, a trampoline made out of clouds. Miriam stood looking after her for a moment, a strange, happy smile on her face, then she ruffled my hair, took a sip of her coffee, and started walking again.

"Come on," she said.

"Mom, you *can't* sell the bookstore," I replied, jogging to catch up with her.

"Let's just enjoy the morning, okay?" she said, fixing her sunglasses over her eyes.

I wanted to fight with her, to press the issue, but something in her voice made me stop. I shoved my hands into my pockets to give them something to do and followed her west until the pavement gave way to sand and the sand gave way to water. I slipped off my shoes and let the cold rush of it soak the bottom of my shorts.

Behind me, Miriam sank to a seat and wiggled her butt a little, making herself comfortable.

I often thought of her like that—Miriam—in moments when it was starkly obvious that she wasn't just my mother, she was a real live human who'd been alive for twenty-eight years before she even knew me. In moments when she ceased being my mother (just for a second or two) and became something like a stranger, a creature whose innermost thoughts I couldn't even begin to guess.

I think I picked this up from my father, who often called her Miriam, like he was still, after all these years, pleasantly surprised he had the good fortune to have met her.

I turned to look at her again; she'd pulled a book of poetry out of her purse and was reading it. Coleridge. When she saw me watching her, she cleared her throat and read:

> *"From his brimstone bed at the break*
>   *of day*
> *A walking the devil is gone,*
> *To visit his snug little farm the earth*
> *And see how his stock goes on."*

"Dark," I said. "Are you saying the devil walks among us?"

"I'm saying that *Coleridge* thought the devil walked among us."

"But probably that was just the opiates speaking."

"Maybe they're one and the same," she said, and shrugged.

And she went back to her book, and I knew enough to know I'd lost her again, at least for a little while.

birthday
dinner

My father came over for dinner every Friday night, and my mother set out the good silverware and lit candles and put on music, just like she was trying to win him back, which she wasn't, and so it got a little confusing.

Eleven months ago, my parents sat me down in our little living room and held hands on the love seat across from me, and honest to goodness, I thought they were about to tell me they were having another kid and I was trying to figure out how I felt about having a sibling so much younger than me when Miriam said—

"We got married so young, Anna."

And my father said—

"But we wouldn't change *anything*."

"Not a *thing*," my mother echoed. "But we just think—"

"It's time we—"

"Took a step back."

"A step away."

My parents were the kind of parents who finished the thoughts that the other one started. They were the kind of parents who held hands when they told their only child they were separating. They were the kind of parents who had never once in my entire life gotten into an argument more serious than whether to have Thai or Indian or Italian for dinner.

Maybe it would have been easier if they had.

The transition from living with both of my parents, together, to living with both of my parents, apart, had been as seamless as possible. My father moved his things out so gradually that a month after the announcement, his guitars still hung on our living room wall.

"I think I'll leave this one," he said when he finally packed up the others. "So I can play it whenever I'm here."

The three of us agreed on equal custody; my father came over every Friday for a family dinner, and I bounced between the two houses on no fixed schedule at all, trying to make things equal but not worried if it didn't always end up that way.

The house my father had moved into was smaller, a two-bedroom ranch four streets over.

Where Miriam was a mystery wrapped in ink-stained clothes, my father was an open book. The only thing that didn't make sense about him was how he sometimes put mustard on his eggs and salt in his coffee.

Everybody loved Everett Bell, who was generous and outgoing and just the right amount of dad jokes mixed with seriousness. He was a musician, a tattooist, and a terrible cook. He'd met Miriam (née Forrest) when he was a teenager, and they'd had me fourteen years later, at twenty-eight.

"You still want lasagna, right?" my mother asked as we walked home from the beach. She was sipping the last dregs of her latte, which must have been cold by then. She could nurse a coffee for hours. She could sip a glass for wine for an entire night. "For your birthday dinner?"

"Yeah, that sounds great," I replied.

She'd prepared the lasagna the night before. When we got home, she put it in the oven, then opened the sliding doors to peek into the backyard.

"Is it too hot to eat outside? I think it's cooled off a little," she said.

"I think it's fine."

"Do you still *love* each other?" I had asked Miriam after the big separation announcement, after my father had gone to the backyard with a glass of wine, to give us time to be alone.

"Oh, Anna," she'd said, and stroked my hair and kissed my temple. "I will never love another man the way I love your father. Look what he gave me. He gave me you."

Which, of course, was the exact almost right thing to say, besides the even righter thing to say, which was, *You're right, and we're being foolish, and of course we're staying together.*

Everett Bell knocked on the front door at seven exactly and let himself in while he was still knocking. He was whistling what sounded like some Pink Floyd song and carrying a bottle of wine. When he saw me, he stopped whistling and flashed his customary Everett Bell smile, the kind that was a secret meant only for you to decipher.

I thought of him like that—Everett Bell—for the same reason I often thought of my mother as slightly-almost-not-my-mother. As slightly almost a stranger, albeit one whose face I knew as well as I knew my own.

"Everett, *another*?" my mother said incredulously, because the right sleeve of my father's jacket was rolled up, revealing a fresh tattoo, because my father got tattoos the way normal people got a new shirt or pair of shoes.

"Look, Miriam, you'll love it," he said, and placed his arm in hers. "It's your favorite quote from *The Odyssey*."

My mother read aloud: "*My name is Nobody*," and then she laughed, dropped my father's arm, and hit him playfully. "You're a strange man, Nobody, and pretty soon you're going to be more ink than skin."

It was true; my father was *covered* in tattoos. They were mostly things from his favorite books: the dragon Tolkien drew in *The Hobbit*, the tiny *Dawn Treader* from the *Chronicles of Narnia*, a quote from *The Color Purple* about time.

"Sure smells good in here!" Everett Bell said before scooping me into a hug big enough so anyone watching would have thought he hadn't seen me in months, when in reality he popped into Bell's Books yesterday on his lunch break and spent half an hour helping me organize the sales table. "How's my little birthday Worm?"

The most unfortunate nickname. The bookworm who doesn't read.

"It's lasagna," my mother said, proud of herself, retreating back into the kitchen to check on it.

"I'm good, Dad," I said. I took the wine bottle from him. "I'll go open this."

I went into the kitchen. Miriam was pulling the lasagna out of the oven. She had spaghetti sauce on the very tip of her nose, such a neat circle of it that it looked like she'd put it there on purpose.

"You smell this?" she asked. "God, I can cook. No matter what happens, Anna, we've got that going for us."

"Sure, Mom." I grabbed a dish towel and wiped her nose, then I found a corkscrew and followed her onto the patio. She placed the lasagna on a set of trivets on the picnic table. My dad took a big whiff, and I opened the bottle of wine and poured them each a glass.

"You know, the screw part of the corkscrew is called the *worm*," Everett said, a fun fact he had told me probably no fewer than four hundred times. "So my little Worm is using a worm." He laughed at his own joke and Miriam smiled along with him, and I just felt sad and disconnected, because nothing made sense, because these two weirdos not being together anymore was the opposite of *making sense*. Then Everett Bell gestured at the table, at the two of us, at the whole scene spread in front of him, and said, in another Everett-ism, "What's wrong with this?"

Absolutely nothing, I wanted to say, which was exactly the answer he was searching for, but I didn't, because there's something to be said for keeping one's cards close to the table.

"Happy birthday dinner. Fourteen, Everett. Can you believe it?" Mom asked, taking her seat and lifting her wineglass for a toast.

"I cannot believe it. Our daughter is still in diapers. Our daughter still calls the elbow a *belbow*. Our daughter—"

"You're making her blush," Miriam said happily. Everett picked up his own wineglass, I held my water, and we all clinked glasses.

"Miriam, this smells delicious," Dad said.

"This wine is excellent," Mom replied.

"Yeah, my water is great, too," I added.

Dad procured a small glass from somewhere—seriously, where had he been hiding that?—and poured me the most teensiest sip of wine.

Mom raised her eyebrows but didn't say anything.

I had a taste.

"That's worse than coffee," I said, sliding the glass away from me.

"We're safe for now," Dad said, and winked at Mom. (Another thing they had in common: winking. They both winked all the time—incessantly—a shared language of eyelashes and lids.)

Then Miriam dished out plates of lasagna, and for a while we didn't talk. After we'd satisfied the first pangs of hunger, the conversation landed on the trip, and I realized with a jolt of surprise...we'd be on a plane in just about twenty-four hours. And we were going, as it turned out, for *two full months*.

"Two months?" I repeated incredulously.

"Did I not mention that?" Mom said.

"That's a long time," I said.

"Oh, you're going to have a blast. A blast!" Dad exclaimed. "I'm so excited to come and visit you guys. I'll be there in about a month."

I took a sip of my water. I was kind of conflicted, because two months was a *very* long time, but on the other hand, what did I have to do here that was so important? Literally nothing.

Out of the corner of my eye, I saw my parents exchange a look, then my dad cleared his throat purposefully and said, "Are you gonna take your guitar with you?"

"Oh!" I said, remembering. "I got my first callus."

I held my left hand out to my father, who inspected the tips of my fingers with an expression that could only be described as gleeful.

"Worm! You've been banging the old ax?"

Dad translation: playing the guitar he'd given me.

"Yeah, a bit."

"That's great!" He leaped up from the table, ran into the living room, and grabbed the guitar from the wall. He pushed it eagerly into my hands. "Show me what you got!"

I put my left hand on the strings and made a G chord. I gave it one good strum, and you would have thought I'd casually composed a symphony the way my dad clapped and my mother set her chin in her hands and beamed.

"That's amazing, Worm!"

"Dad, I played one chord," I said. I took a deep breath and flexed my fingers, and then I played what I'd been working on that week. Just a simple four-chord progression: G–E minor–C–D. There was a melody in my head that went along with it, but I was definitely not ready to share that yet, so I just played the four chords a couple of times, then ended with a silly flourish of my wrist.

I thought Dad might actually get up and hug me.

"Well, excuse me while I call the Los Angeles Philharmonic," he said. "That was *excellent*."

"I haven't heard you practice at all!" Mom said, equally impressed.

Whatever you said about my parents, you couldn't call them unsupportive.

"I'm gonna bring it on vacation," I said, carefully setting the guitar on the bench next to me. "Maybe when you get there, we can jam."

"Oh my god, she said *jam*. Miriam, she's a real musician." Dad lowered his voice and whispered, in a true tone of victory, "I won."

He was mostly kidding, of course, but there was a vein of truth to it; I think secretly my parents both hoped I would gravitate to their chosen passions. Books or music, music or books.

"Pretty soon I'll have my first tattoo!" I joked.

They instantly cooled.

"When you're eighteen," Dad said.

"When you're forty," Mom countered.

"Unless you mean temporary tattoo," Dad added. "In which case, knock yourself out."

"I'll be eighteen in four years," I said, and Mom's eyes grew so wide I thought her eyelids were going to get stuck. Dad took an exaggeratedly big sip of wine and then choked on it.

"Pause," Mom said, clicking an imaginary remote. "Pause. Everett, it's not . . . It's not working."

"One birthday at a time, Worm," Dad said, putting his hand over his heart. Then he reached across the table and took my mom's hand and squeezed it and held it for just a second or two.

In those moments—Dad tearing up a little from choking on his wine, Mom pretending to pause me like a movie, the two of them holding hands across the table even though they had been separated for eleven months—it became glaringly curious: Why hadn't Miriam and Everett Bell *actually* gotten a divorce yet? I knew California had a mandatory six-month waiting period once you filed the paperwork, and I knew divorces could take much longer than that if they actually got complicated, but these were two of the least complicated separated people I had ever encountered. And forget the waiting period—they hadn't even *filed* the paperwork yet. Josh's parents were divorced, and I remembered his talking about how they couldn't *wait* to file the paperwork, to get everything over and done with.

I'd asked Miriam about it six months ago, after my father had lugged the last cardboard box full of his things out to his truck.

"Have you filed the paperwork yet?"

"Hmm?" she'd asked, distracted, wandering around the house with a dustrag, attacking any flat surface she came across.

"For the divorce. Have you filed the paperwork?"

She stopped then, turned around quickly, peered at me from over the top of a pair of reading glasses she seemed to only remember to wear when she wasn't actually reading. "Oh, Anna. That's nothing you need to worry about. Okay?"

"But I'm just wondering. Josh said it was this big thing. His dad had to send a lawyer to give the papers to his mom."

"It won't be like that for us," she insisted.

"So you've filed them already?"

She placed the dustrag down on an end table and took my chin in her hand. "Are you feeling overwhelmed, Anna? We're trying to do everything right."

"I was just wondering."

She took a deep breath. "No. We haven't filed the paperwork. There's no big rush. I expect we will soon."

But as Everett Bell removed his hand from Miriam's now and winked at her before returning to his lasagna, I couldn't help wondering...why the wait? Wasn't the most obvious answer that they just didn't *want* to get divorced?

Dad had another bite or two of food before he made a noise

in the back of his throat and threw his hands up. "I almost forgot!"

He removed a small, sloppily wrapped present from the inside pocket of his jacket (Everett Bell wore an old green utility jacket even when it was boiling hot outside) and handed it to me.

"Happy birthday, Worm," he said, winking.

"Are we doing presents?" Mom asked. "Let me get mine."

She pushed up from the table and went back into the house as I took the box from my dad and shook it gently.

"Open it, open it," he said, bouncing up and down in his seat. My dad *loved* giving presents.

I tore off the wrapping now, revealing a plain cardboard box inside. I removed the lid and gasped. There, sitting on a cotton pillow, was a little gold ring with a milky-white stone. I picked up the ring, and as I brought it closer to my face, I swear the colors in the stone shifted. I saw baby blue, pink, green, a whole rainbow of colors that kept changing as I tilted the stone in different directions.

"Did you know June has three birthstones to choose from?" Dad said. "That's one of them. Moonstone. I thought it was the prettiest."

"Dad, this is *so* beautiful," I said. I slipped it onto the middle finger of my right hand. It fit perfectly.

"Do you like it?"

"Are you kidding me? I love it!"

"I thought it was about time you had a nice piece of jewelry,

Worm," he said. I looked up at him, and he was beaming; I threw myself across the table, diving into his arms for a hug.

"Thank you, thank you, thank you!"

Mom came back, smiling when she saw us. "Your dad was so excited to give you that, Anna."

I settled back in my seat, barely able to tear my eyes away from how pretty the ring was.

"I love it," I said.

"I knew you would," Mom replied. "That's why I let him have all the glory this year." She placed a neatly wrapped stack of book-shaped presents in front of me. "I got you your summer reading books."

I managed not to groan as I picked up the books and held them to my chest. "I'll cherish them forever," I said.

Miriam smiled and had a sip of her wine. "I had the better gift last year," she said with a wink.

She was right—last year she had given me tickets to see one of my favorite musicians in concert. Dad had given me a lava lamp.

But also last year my parents had still been together, the bookstore had been thriving, and Jennica and I were still friends.

This year...well. The ring really *was* beautiful.

But I'd take a hundred more lava lamps if it meant a bad-luck reversal.

I'd take a hundred more lava lamps if it meant I could go back to the way things were.

goodbye,
los angeles

spent the next morning packing, which was honestly impossible. How do you pack for two months away? Mom kept sticking her head into the bedroom and reminding me that the cottage had a washer and dryer and that I should be *really* picky about what I brought, but still! The stack of summer reading books alone took up a chunk of the suitcase. I hadn't even bothered to unwrap them; I just set them in the corner and started piling T-shirts and shorts and bathing suits around them.

Josh came over around lunchtime, wandering in just as Mom was pulling a quiche out of the oven.

"You have a sixth sense for food," she mused as he settled himself down at the kitchen table and waited patiently for a plate. Josh lived a few doors down and had been popping into our house with clockwork regularity since we were kids.

"Hey, Josh," I said, taking a seat next to him.

"You're going away for *two months*?" he said. "Miriam just told me."

"I know. She's basically kidnapping me."

Miriam sat down across from us, balancing three plates of quiche in her hands. She distributed them among us and chose to ignore my comment.

"I wish I could come visit," Josh said longingly. "It's going to be super boring without you. And Cecilia's away most of the summer, too. She leaves in a couple of days."

Cecilia was Josh's cousin and the third member of our little trifecta. And because I'd known her just as long as I'd known Josh, I also thought of Cece more as family. They didn't really count in the same way Jennica counted. They would never stop talking to me because a new, cool girl moved to town. Plus, Cecilia was always super busy in the summer. She spent her weekdays as a junior counselor at a sleepaway camp, and she spent her weekends at the beach doing eight-hour stints at volleyball camp. She'd always been the tallest and most athletic girl in our school, and she could basically wipe the floor (sand?) with anyone who challenged her to a game.

"Yeah, that kinda sucks," I admitted. "You're going to be all alone, Joshy."

Josh stuck his fork into his quiche and looked forlorn. "Well, Suzanne just gave me a raise yesterday, at least. So that was nice." He looked up at Miriam suddenly, as if putting two and two together. "Actually, she kept talking about Stephen

King. . . . You wouldn't have anything to do with that, would you, Miriam?"

Josh was one of Bell's Books' biggest customers, even though he technically wasn't a customer, because he never paid. He used Bell's Books as more like his personal library, and my mom as his personal librarian. Besides her, Josh had read more books than probably any human alive.

"She needed a little horror in her life," Miriam replied with a wink. "Have you read *The Stand*, Joshua?"

"Of course," Josh replied.

Only Josh and Miriam were cocky enough to answer a *have you read* question with *of course*.

"I love that one," Miriam said, her face taking on the dreamy expression she reserved for when she was talking about books.

"Oh, me too. A classic," Josh said. He turned to me and added, "You would hate it." That was where he and my mom differed; Josh accepted the fact that yes, I would hate it. My mom remained convinced there was a book out there that would eventually change my mind about books.

"Well, congratulations on the raise, Joshua. You definitely deserve it," Miriam said. "You're a hard worker."

It dawned on me then, as I watched Josh demolish his quiche, that he didn't know. He didn't know the bookstore was closing. Aside from the swimming pool, there was no place in the world Josh loved more than Bell's Books. The news would probably crush him just as much as it was crushing me. Should

I even tell him? Should I ruin his summer just as I was about to leave him for two months?

I happened to glance up at Mom, who shook her head an almost imperceptible amount. Josh was oblivious, but the message was clear: Don't tell him.

She was right, I thought. Better to wait and tell him when I got back, when I was actually around to comfort him.

When we finished lunch, Josh suggested we walk to the beach to catch the tail end of Cece's practice so that I could say goodbye in person. As we made our way, Josh kept up a constant stream of chatter, thoroughly explaining the plot of one of his favorite comics, *The Elder's Incantation*.

"And what's wild is, you thought it was going to be the Man in Silver the whole time, but it was *Arcania*! I honestly didn't even see it coming. Do you remember in the fourth installment, where there's that whole subplot of Arcania's birthright? I mean, that was all just a massive red herring!"

Having never read a single issue of *The Elder's Incantation*, I could confidently say I knew more about the series than even its most die-hard fans, thanks to Josh.

But that was Josh for you. He was super passionate about the things he loved, didn't necessarily need that much input from you when he discussed them, and was happy to carry on a fully one-sided conversation for many minutes at a time.

Jennica was kind of the exact opposite of that, and as Josh continued rambling, my thoughts wandered to her.

When I'd first said hi to her in the homeroom we'd shared,

she'd looked like a deer caught in headlights: wide eyes, an almost frightened expression on her face, her pen half raised to her mouth. I could see the pen cap was already chewed, and not knowing what else to say, I'd blurted out, "Once, a pen exploded in my mouth."

She'd cracked a smile at that and came unstuck. "Hi," she'd said. "I'm Jennica."

Jennica was shy at first, but once you got to know her, she was super funny, one of those people who, when she finally did decide to speak, usually said something so witty and caustic it made me dissolve into endless laughter. She was a painter and a ceramicist, and her dream was to one day have a small store on Olive Street where she could sell her creations to tourists and locals.

"She's not even that *good* at pottery," I said now, the words exploding out of me as a wave of bitterness rolled through my body.

Josh stopped midsentence and looked sideways at me. "Were you not even listening to a thing I said about the Mysterious Red-Eyed Woman?"

"No, Joshy," I admitted. "I was not."

"That's kinda mean, Anna," he said. "Plus, Jennica *is* really good at pottery. I've seen her work."

"You've seen her work? When have you seen her work?"

Josh looked a little uncomfortable, but he recovered quickly. "This whole Jennica thing is..."

"Is *what*?"

"Nothing," he mumbled. We'd gotten to the beach anyway, so I let it drop. We waited for Cece, who was just finishing up her practice and saying goodbye to the other girls on her team.

"Hey, guys!" she said, running over to us. "This is a surprise!"

Cece had long blond hair; long, muscular legs; and long, toned arms. She wouldn't have looked out of place on the cover of *Sports Illustrated*, where I just assumed she'd be one day. She was all sweaty, so she skipped hugs. When I told her about going to the East Coast for the summer, she said, "Anna, that's incredible! You're going to have so much fun. This will be good for you."

"What do you mean 'good for me'?" I wondered, and she put on a sympathetic expression.

"You know you've been a little mopey," she said. Cecilia was not the type to beat around the bush.

"I would not describe myself as *mopey*."

"*I* would describe you as mopey," Josh said.

"I just mean," Cece added, "that a change of pace might be a really good thing for you."

"I will keep that in mind," I said.

"Don't get grouchy," Cecilia said.

"I'm not," I said grouchily.

We spent an hour or so at the beach, and then Josh and Cece walked me home. The rest of the day passed quickly in a blur of more packing and unpacking and repacking and freaking out and asking Mom for help and sitting and watching as she methodically went through my suitcase, gently suggesting that I didn't need *four* pairs of jean shorts, maybe two would suffice? By six o'clock, our suitcases were by the door, my backpack was ready for the plane, and my guitar was in its case leaning against the wall. The two of us sat at the kitchen table for what felt like forever, waiting for Dad to get there and drive us to the airport.

"How are you feeling?" Mom asked after a few minutes of silence, during which I picked frantically at a thread on the cuff of my sweatshirt.

"I dunno. Kind of excited. Kind of bummed. I'm going to miss Dad. I'm really sad about the bookstore. I'm still—" I was about to say, *I'm still really upset about Jennica,* but I managed to catch myself before the words came out. I sort of shrugged and added, "Just a lot on my mind, I guess."

"I hear you," Mom said with a sigh. "I hear you loud and clear. It's been a wild year. I hope this trip is a good idea. I just..." She sort of shrugged, too (I guess that's where I got it from). "I hope it is."

"I'm sure it will be great. I remember loving the cottage," I said. It was true, too—Aunt Dora's cottage was about as close to the water as you could get without being *in* the water. It had two bedrooms, a creaky front porch, and wooden floors so old and worn they were as smooth as glass. And even if it did feel a little scary to leave Los Angeles for the entire summer, well... What was so important that I had to stay here?

A quick honk from outside let us know Dad had arrived,

so we gathered up all our things, said one last goodbye to the house, and traipsed out to meet him. Mom kept up a steady barrage of reminders on the way to the airport ("Don't forget to water my plants!" "Don't forget to set the alarm at the bookstore!" "Don't forget to process payroll every Thursday!" "Don't forget to take the mail in!") as I stared wistfully out the window, watching the palm trees disappear behind us as we drove south to LAX.

"Miriam, give me *some* credit," Dad replied at least a dozen times. He kept meeting my eye in the rearview mirror and winking, a smirk on his face as Mom reminded him to turn the porch light on every few days to make it look like we were still home.

"I'm just feeling a little nervous," she admitted.

"I know," Dad said, resting his hand on her leg for just a moment. "You hate flying. This is how you get."

He put his hand back on the steering wheel and started whistling a tune I didn't recognize. I saw Miriam turn her head to look at the place his hand had been. The absence of his hand on her leg filled the entire car. My heart was breaking. I caught sight of the Pacific Ocean for the last time before the road curved inward and it dropped away behind the car. We'd be at the airport in a few minutes. It was all really happening.

I knew Mom was scared of flying, but to be honest, it had never bothered me. I hated all the waiting around that inevitably happened, but once we were in the air, I put on my headphones and stared out the window and let the sight of white puffy clouds lull me to sleep. Hopefully, I'd manage to snooze the entire way to Boston. We were renting a car there and driving to Rockport, the little town on the water where my great-aunt's cottage was. Mom had spent every summer of her youth in Rockport; it was where she met Dad, who was also an East Coast native. He lived in Gloucester, just a town over from the cottage.

I didn't remember a lot from the time I'd been in Rockport. It had only been for a few days, and I was much younger. I remembered a candy shop; a street packed with art galleries that led right to a long, rocky jetty; and a little circular window in a gate—when you looked through the circle, you could see a perfect slice of the harbor.

We were approaching the airport now; Dad slowed down to turn onto the ramp that led to departures, and I could practically feel Mom tense up watching an airplane taking off to our right.

"Breathe, Miriam," Dad whispered, pulling up to the curb and putting the car in park. "You'll be there before you know it."

Mom nodded. "Thank you for the ride, B," she said softly.

It was a nickname she used very rarely. I think it stood for *babe*, but I had never asked her. It seemed too private. Especially now, after everything.

"I'll get your bags," he replied.

We all got out of the car. Dad unloaded the bags from the trunk, then scooped me into a rib-crushing hug.

"I'm going to miss the hell out of you, Worm," he said, kissing my cheek.

"I'll miss you, too, Dad."

"See you both soon, okay?" he said, letting go of me and turning to Mom. I didn't know if they were going to hug or shake hands or what, but after a moment, Miriam held her arms out to him and he stepped into them. The hug lasted for 2.4 seconds (approximately), then he was waving and walking back around the car and slipping into the driver's seat and pulling away from the curb. We both stood there, not moving, just watching him.

"Mom?"

She blinked as if coming out of a dream, turned to look at me, and smiled what was probably the saddest smile in the history of the entire world. "Sorry, Anna. Let's do this, okay?"

Twenty minutes later, we were through security and camped out at the gate with forty minutes until boarding. I eventually filled our water bottles and bought a magazine, which she promptly stole.

"You know," I said after watching her for a second, "this will probably all go a lot smoother if you actually started breathing."

She took an exaggerated gulp of air, then squeezed me close to her. "I'm sorry, honey. I'll be fine once we're up there."

"It's an adventure, Mom."

She let me go after kissing the side of my head. "Everything is an adventure with you."

I let the cheesiness of that comment slide since she was in a very fragile state and the gate attendants had *just* announced the start of boarding.

It was a direct red-eye to Boston. In just about six hours, we'd be landing. It would be early in the morning over there; we'd file sleepily off the plane and trudge sleepily through the airport and pour sleepily into the rental car. We'd be coast to coast in half a day. Going to sleep west, waking up east. The start of a summer away from it all. And as we made our way down the skinny aisle of the plane and found our seats, I actually started to feel a little excited. Maybe Miriam was right. Maybe this was exactly what we needed, the chance to get away from it all. They say you can't run away from your problems, but maybe—for a couple of months, at least—we could.

rockport

B y the time we got our rental car and sneaked our way out of the city and onto the highway that would take us to the coast, Miriam and I were practically zombies: shuffling, speechless, sluggish creatures who pulled into the first gas station we passed for scalding coffee (for Mom) and hot chocolate (for me). The flight had been easy and smooth, and we'd both fallen asleep quickly, waking only when they raised the cabin lights for our descent into Boston.

The car ride was a fairly quiet one; we hadn't said more than ten words between us by the time we got to the two roundabouts that took us to Gloucester. You had to drive through the town to get to Rockport and the cottage, and I stared out the window as we passed quaint houses and small businesses and miles and miles of peaceful roads with hardly anyone on them at all.

"It's Sunday morning," Mom said, the first words either of us had spoken in forty-five minutes. "Everyone's either sleeping or at church."

The cottage was on a road called Atlantic Avenue, which ran flush against Rockport Harbor. We made our way slowly, peering at each house we passed, until finally Mom pulled into the driveway of a white cottage with pale blue shutters.

"Wow," she breathed. "It looks exactly the same."

The cottage was set on a tiny lot across the street from the water, with a tiny front yard and a tiny backyard and a tiny driveway. The windows were dark, and there was something sad about it, in general, as if you could tell from the outside that nobody had lived in it for six months. There was another car in the driveway, my great-aunt's old station wagon, and there was barely enough room for the rental car behind it.

"She didn't have any kids to take care of anything," Mom said. "I was her only niece. I should have done this months ago, but...I guess better late than never, huh?"

"We're here now," I agreed.

"God, this brings me back." She still hadn't made any move to get out of the car, and I followed suit, sitting quietly next to her as she peered through the windshield and up at the house she'd spent so many summers in. "It felt so much bigger when I was a kid. I remember that porch being monstrous, endless, but look at it—it must be barely twenty feet from side to side."

I knew what she meant, because even though I'd only been at the house once, it had also seemed bigger to me then, like maybe my six-year-old body had taken up such little space or maybe something about the house adjusted itself to however much room a person ended up needing. Maybe if Dad were here, it would seem bigger; it would swell open to allow us all room to get comfy.

I know that seemed a little far-fetched, but I'd seen Bell's Books do some pretty weird things in its day, so I was ready to believe a little more than your average person, as far as the laws of physics were concerned.

Eventually, after one or two more minutes of not moving, I saw Mom's hand reach slowly to the door handle. I let myself out of the car at the same time as her, and the first thing I noticed was the heavy, thick smell of the ocean, and the second thing I noticed was the heavy, thick heat, so sudden and present it took the wind out of my lungs. I swatted my hand through the air, and I swear the humidity was so corporeal it was like moving through water. I instantly felt ten pounds heavier, and I could practically feel my hair curling.

"Yikes," Mom said. "Hot."

I remembered now, being six and not understanding what *humidity* meant, how the same temperature in Los Angeles was so much more bearable because it was a dry, desert heat, while the East Coast heat felt like something you could cut with a fork and knife.

The ocean scent was another story entirely—I basically *never* smelled the ocean back home, not until I was waist-high in it, being knocked backward by waves. Here, it was an overwhelming, heady smell of brine and seaweed and fish. I remembered how it filled up the rooms of the cottage, how it clung to your skin, how in the shower, it seemed to shed off your body in great, dark blue flakes.

Mom had walked around to the trunk of the rental and was getting our things out; I went and grabbed my suitcase and guitar and backpack and dragged them onto the porch. There was a porch swing to the right of the door, just big enough for two people to sit, just big enough for Miriam to drape her body across, legs hanging over the side, and read a book for hours and hours. That was how she'd spent her last visit and, I imagined, how she'd probably spend the bulk of this one, too.

Miriam got her things to the porch, then dug through her purse and withdrew a set of keys I hadn't seen before. They must have belonged to Aunt Dora. They had a little anchor key chain on them that Miriam touched now, smiling a bit to herself, lost in a memory. Then she found the right key, inserted it into the lock, and pushed the door open. It gave a long, dramatic creak—like the house was saying hello to us.

The air inside the cottage was warm and musty. Mom flicked on the hall light and went around methodically opening curtains and windows. The first floor consisted of the kitchen, the living room, a bathroom, and a small, enclosed porch at the back. Up the narrow flight of stairs were two bedrooms and another bathroom.

I walked into the kitchen to the right. There was a circular kitchen table with four chairs around it, four matching place mats set out for company. The counters were bare and clean. The refrigerator was unplugged. I wondered—who had done all this for my great-aunt? Who had cleaned everything up? Had Miriam hired a cleaning company?

From the kitchen I headed back across the hall to the living room. The furniture was all wicker, with oversize, faded floral couch cushions and pillows. A bookcase in the back was filled with books and board games, their cardboard boxes swollen and soft from humidity, peeling and worn from years of hands grabbing and unboxing and stacking one on top of the other.

Through the living room was the enclosed porch, with a small coffee table and two chairs, a love seat, and more book-cases. These were crammed with books, not even an inch of space on their shelves. The three outside walls had large windows, which could be folded in to create a breezy, screened-in room. A door led to the backyard—hammock, picnic table, sad garden hose someone had curled up neatly and left next to the house.

Behind me, I heard a fan click on, and I made my way back into the living room to find Miriam angling an enormous vintage floor fan toward the corner of the room.

"This will get the air moving," she said. "Put your stuff upstairs and we'll go get something to eat. Aren't you hungry?"

"Tired," I said, yawning to prove my point.

"Food first, nap second," she promised, and I went back to the hall, grabbed my suitcase and guitar, and carried them up the stairs.

Miriam had taken the room to the right, which was slightly bigger and had belonged to my great-aunt, so I put my things in the other room, to the left of the stairs. Mom had opened the windows here and turned on a small window fan that gusted a surprising amount of air into the space. The bed frame was wicker, the nightstand was wicker, the dresser was wicker, and an armchair next to the dresser was wicker. My great-aunt definitely had a theme going.

I put my suitcase on the bed, debated changing my clothes, decided against it, and went back downstairs. Mom was waiting at the front door, half-in, half-out. Her hair was already slightly frizzy around the hairline, and her face was shiny from sweat. I imagined I looked pretty much the same, although she somehow carried it better. She already looked like an East Coaster again, in a hard-to-explain-exactly-why sort of way. Maybe it was the baseball hat she'd dug out of her suitcase and was now fixing on her head. Maybe it was the way she'd changed into jean shorts just a *little* too short, jean shorts I swear I'd never seen her wear back in LA. But whatever it was, she seemed almost younger, almost happier, definitely sweatier, as she held the door open for me and let us both out into the sticky air again.

"Gotta drop the rental car off tomorrow," she said. "And make sure that old station wagon still runs."

"Are we driving to breakfast?"

"Walking," she corrected. "That's the nice thing about this place. You can walk practically everywhere."

So we walked, the ocean both on our right and behind us. Rockport was at the eastern edge of the country and surrounded by the Atlantic on three sides. You could be almost anywhere in town and see water somewhere around you—and often in two completely different directions.

"I could go for some pancakes," Mom said, taking my hand when we reached the end of the road and steering us to the right. A few doors down was a café called Hula Moon. It was just past nine in the morning, and it was surprisingly busy inside, given how we'd passed exactly no one on the street. We sat down at a table right next to a wide window overlooking the harbor, and Mom wasted no time ordering coffee and pancakes. I chose a breakfast scramble with toast, and we settled down to wait for our food.

"That's Motif Number One," Mom said, pointing out the window, across a small wharf to a red barnlike building, the sides of which were crowded with colorful buoys.

"What is it?" I asked.

"It's actually a replica of an old fishing shack," she said. "My aunt used to say it was the most painted building in America. I don't know if that's the truth, but you'll see it everywhere around here. Paintings, postcards, photographs..."

"It's cool," I said.

She smiled. "When you were six, you said it looked like the house of an old sea witch. You were terrified of it."

"Really? I don't remember."

"Oh yeah. You hated it. Used to cover your eyes whenever we had to walk past it."

"Well, I like it now. I can see why so many people want

to paint it. It looks like a little window into another time or something. Can you go inside it?"

"Huh, I'm not sure," Mom said, shrugging. "I don't think so."

"They should have a gift shop where they only sell paintings of it, and when you step inside, it's just hundreds of them up on the walls," I said. "Very meta."

Mom laughed. "Very meta, indeed."

Breakfast was amazing; we ended up splitting half the scramble and half the pancakes, which was a good thing, because they were probably the best pancakes I'd ever had in my life. Afterward, we were both squinting and yawning from exhaustion and decided to go right back to the cottage for "double naps," as Mom dubbed them. We spent a few minutes changing the sheets on the beds, then collapsed in our respective bedrooms. I usually didn't take naps because I just tossed and turned and eventually got up even more tired than I had been, but I swear the second my head hit the pillow, I was sound asleep.

woke up with a start what felt like days later, hot and stuffy and absolutely disoriented. I had no idea where I was. I flailed around in bed until I found my phone. It was noon, I'd slept for about two hours, and I was gradually remembering everything—the airplane, the car ride, the breakfast, the cottage. I groaned and stretched and sluggishly pulled myself out of bed, opening the curtains to let a little light into the room.

I peeked my head into Mom's room, but her bed was empty. The cottage was quiet and still; I thought she might be outside reading or running errands. I went into the tiny bathroom and turned on the shower. The tub was wet already, so she must have showered not too long ago.

It felt absolutely amazing under the water, washing off the filth of the airplane and the clingy heat of the morning. I kept the shower as cool as I could stand it, and when I was done, I stood dripping on the bath mat. I towel-dried my hair, put a tampon in, and threw on some shorts and a T-shirt. My hair was already curling, so I scrunched it some more and decided to let it air-dry. That was one thing about Jennica that always bugged me. She had *great* hair. My hair was unruly and impossible to do anything with. Jennica could roll around in a dumpster and come out looking like she'd just had a professional blowout.

Okay. Enough thinking about Jennica.

I went downstairs. Mom wasn't in the living room or on the front porch or the back porch, and then I realized the rental car wasn't there, so she must have gone out somewhere. I paused in front of the fan in the living room and wondered what I should do. Probably get a head start on those summer reading books. But that meant I would have to read. So. No.

Mom had opened up the windows in the enclosed porch, and the result was actually nice: A cross breeze ran through the house, keeping it pretty cool. Which was good, because I hadn't actually seen any air conditioners.

I let myself onto the front porch, where Mom had left an almost empty coffee mug and a copy of today's *Boston Herald* on the small coffee table. She must have napped for only twenty minutes or so—that was her signature move. She often said there wasn't much that couldn't be cured by a nice twenty-minute nap. I sat down on the porch swing and picked up the paper, leafing absentmindedly through it until I reached an interesting article about ten pages in.

MAKE SURE TO LOOK UP
THIS SUMMER!

The New England skies are set to provide an action-packed stage for us this summer, thanks to the reappearance of the Kit-Hale comet. Starting tonight, you'll be able to see this bright comet for just about two months. The last time the Kit-Hale comet lit up our skies was twenty-eight years ago, also during the summer months. Its appearance will be marked by an increase in meteor activity. Get ready to make plenty of wishes, because you'll see these "shooting stars" all summer long.

I'd never seen a comet before! And I knew it was silly, but it felt kind of nice, like New England was welcoming me to its shores with my own private sky show.

I dropped the paper onto the porch swing and then, because I couldn't think of anything else to do, went back upstairs and unpacked my suitcase. I might as well get comfy since the cottage was going to be my home for the next two months. I folded all my shirts and shorts and placed them into the empty dresser, then I sorted my underwear and socks and bathing suits into the other drawers. When I was done, I slid my suitcase under the bed, arranged my toiletries on the top of the dresser, and tossed the summer reading books onto the comforter. Curious, I took the first one off the stack and unwrapped it.

The Great Gatsby.

It looked like a really old copy, with a tattered dust jacket and yellowed pages. I knew it was one of Miriam's favorite books; this one had probably been hers. I opened to the title page, but there was no inscription. I brought it up to my nose and inhaled deeply. The sweet smell of old books. Even I had to admit, there was nothing quite like it.

I tossed the book onto the bed and moved to one of the bedroom's three windows. It overlooked the front yard, and if I looked across the water, I could see Motif No. 1. It really was kind of a cool building—something about it felt old-fashioned, like it had been cut and pasted from a distant time. It was weird to think that my parents had actually met here, twenty-eight years ago, against the same exact backdrop. The water, the houses, Motif No. 1...I doubted much had changed about Rockport in those twenty-eight years. It was one of those towns that felt like time had just kind of stood still....

Wait. Twenty-eight years...

Was there any chance my parents had seen the same astronomical phenomenon I was about to witness? I'd have to ask Miriam when she returned.

I went back downstairs with *The Great Gatsby* and settled myself on the back porch to read it.

Miriam got home about an hour later, letting herself in the

front door and pouring a glass of water in the kitchen before joining me.

"Hope you weren't nervous," she said, collapsing on the love seat. "I just wanted to drop off the rental car. I took a cab back. Next step is to see if the station wagon actually runs."

"Maybe that should have been your *first* step," I pointed out.

"Oh," she said with a laugh. "You're probably right."

"I've just been reading," I said, holding up *The Great Gatsby* as evidence. "I'm beginning to think the green light is a metaphor for something."

Mom smiled. "That was my copy," she said, taking a great gulp of water. "You better be nice to it."

"I'm always nice to books," I said. "Oh, hey—I saw that thing in the paper, about the comet and the meteors."

"Kit-Hale!" Mom said excitedly. "You know, the summer I met your father, that comet was all anyone could talk about."

"That's what I was going to ask you! If you saw it."

"You couldn't miss it. It lit up the sky every night. And the meteors were out of this world." She winked. "Pardon the pun."

"That's really cool that it's happening again."

"I can't wait to see it. Don't tell your father, okay? I want it to be a surprise when he gets here."

I didn't say anything right away. Mom leaned back on the couch and closed her eyes, resting the glass of water on her forehead.

It just made me wonder, that was all—why did she want to surprise Dad? If they were getting a divorce, why did she care about things like surprising him?

After a moment, Mom took the glass away from her forehead, put it down on the coffee table, and went outside to see if the station wagon would start. I followed her, having nothing else to do, and as I stood on the porch, jokingly crossing my fingers as the car groaned sickly and eventually turned over, I realized that this was it—this was my summer. No Jennica, no Josh, no Cecilia, no Dad, no Los Angeles, no bookstore, just Mom and me and this cottage and the comet and this town I didn't really know the first thing about. It felt a little scary, and for the first time since Mom had mentioned this trip, I felt an unpleasant feeling tightening around my chest....

I was trapped.

I was trapped here.

The car coughed out a great gust of black smoke, then it seemed to settle down into an almost steady purr. I watched Mom poke around in the glove compartment for the registration or something, then she got out and walked over to me. "Needs an oil change," she said. "Want to come for a ride? It will be boring."

"No, I think I'll explore a little," I said.

"Here," she said, handing me a fairly crumpled and ancient-looking twenty-dollar bill. "Take this. Found it in the dash. Probably the oldest currency in circulation. Buy yourself some candy. Oh, and there's a set of spare keys on the counter.

Bearskin Neck is that way. Don't go *too* far. Keep your phone on you. Be safe. Etcetera, etcetera."

"I will, Mom."

"Love you," she said, and kissed me on the cheek before getting back into the car. I waved as she backed it out of the driveway.

I stared after her for a few moments, my fingers finding the moonstone ring; the surface was impossibly cool in this heat, and outside, in direct sunlight, the stone was anything but white. It was made up of a hundred different colors. I rubbed it, feeling how smooth it was, then went inside to find the keys and a purse.

A few minutes later I was on the road, wondering what the heck Bearskin Neck was and whether I wanted to go somewhere with such a sinister name, but as it turned out, I was basically already there. A three-minute walk and I was standing in front of a weathered old sign explaining how the area got its name:

NAMED FROM A BEAR CAUGHT BY THE TIDE AND KILLED IN 1700.

1700. That was a *long* time ago.

Poor bear.

I started walking down the road, which was surprisingly crowded with people. It was a narrow street, with no cars on it, flanked by rows of gift stores and art galleries. I passed a general store, a couple of T-shirt stores, and a place called the Fudgery, where I made a mental note to stop in some time.

There were also little restaurants, small seafood places that looked like they couldn't hold more than ten or fifteen people at a time. I passed a toy store, a crystal shop, an old-fashioned place called the Country Store, and a store called China Gifts International. Every place looked like it had been there for ages, giving the whole street a sort of timeless, vintage feel— just like Motif No. 1.

I walked all the way to the end of the road, where a long jetty began. It was made up of huge rocks, and people were walking out to the very end of it. The harbor was to my right, and beyond that, the cottage. To my left, the rest of Rockport, and right in front of me, past the jetty, was the open ocean.

I took a deep breath, filling my lungs with the salty air, and let it out slowly.

Two months to go.

You could survive two months of anything, really.

Especially if you didn't have a choice.

motif no. 1

Miriam stopped at the grocery store on her way home from the auto shop, and she made gazpacho and salad for dinner. We ate on the front porch, side by side on the swing, our legs not quite touching the ground. Mom had read my mind about the Fudgery and picked up a thick hunk of fudge for dessert; it was melty and delicious by the time we ate it. It was eight when we finished cleaning up; Mom yawned incessantly as she washed dishes at the sink.

"I think it's going to be an early night for me," she said.

"It's only five o'clock in California," I replied. I'd started doing that, obsessively comparing the time change, checking the clock and wondering what Dad was doing, what Josh was doing, what Cece was doing.

(And what Jennica was doing. And what Lara was doing. And what Jennica and Lara were doing *together*.)

"I know, but I slept on an airplane last night, so I think I deserve some horizontal shut-eye," she explained.

I didn't feel tired at all. And it didn't *look* like night, either—the sky was a pale purple, and although the sun had gone down, everything was still lit in a delicate, dusty glow.

"Don't you want to see the comet?" I asked.

"We have all summer to see the comet."

Obviously, there would be no changing her mind.

As soon as the last dish was dried and put away, she kissed me on the top of my head and mumbled a good night before shuffling upstairs to bed.

I sat down at the kitchen table and checked my phone. No new messages. Out of a bad habit, I scrolled down until I found Jennica's name, then clicked through to see the last message she'd ever sent me:

You are totally overreacting!!!

As it turned out, I *wasn't* overreacting, because we hadn't spoken since that day.

I groaned and turned off my phone. I was antsy and kind of sad and kind of lonely and kind of grumpy, and because I didn't want to be *any* of those things, I found my shoes and put them on, grabbed the spare keys, and let myself out of the house.

I left my phone on the kitchen table.

I felt instantly better.

It had cooled a little outside, or at least the humidity had settled down a bit, so it was still warm but no longer oppressively hot. I started walking aimlessly, and before I really realized it, I was heading down the T-Wharf. I could see across the water to Bearskin Neck, which was still buzzing with people, while the wharf itself was pretty empty. To my right was a small marina; a few dozen boats sat quietly in the harbor on their moorings, and the marina's porch, which featured a smattering of rocking chairs, was empty except for an older man in the rocking chair closest to me. He was half-hidden in shadow, but I could see his pure white hair and a small dog on his lap. He noticed me and gave a little wave, then gestured up at the sky.

I followed his motion and looked up, surprised to see Kit-Hale in the sky—I'd almost forgotten about it! It wasn't super bright yet, but it was *so* cool. It had a long tail that stretched out behind it and a more strongly glowing orb at its front. As I watched, a brief flash of light dashed across the sky next to it. A shooting star!

"That was a good one," the old man said. "And the comet will only get brighter in the next few weeks."

"Did you see it the last time it came around?" I asked, walking closer to him.

"Oh, yeah," he said. "I saw it once when I was real young, then again almost forty years ago. The blink of an eye when you're this old." He laughed loudly at his own joke, disturbing the small dog, which up until that point had been sleeping. It stood up on the man's lap, balancing precariously as it shook itself awake. Then it saw me and hopped down, prancing over for a pet. I knelt down in front of it and scratched behind its ears.

"That's Book," the old man said.

"Book? What a cute name."

"It's funny to go around the house yelling, 'Where's my Book? Has anyone seen that darn Book?'" The old man laughed again, and I noticed his arms were covered with tattoos. Everett would approve.

I stared upward for a few more moments, absentmindedly petting Book, laughing when the dog kept nudging its head into my palm.

"Your ring is glowing like something else," the old man said.

I looked down at my hand, the one petting Book, and he was right. In the moonlight, the moonstone ring was shining so brightly it was like a little beacon.

"Oh wow," I said. "It's a moonstone. My dad gave it to me."

"Moonstone, *ahhh*. Those stones love being out in the nighttime. They commune with the moon, you know. That's how they get their name. A beautiful stone. Good for new beginnings, new love. A fresh start. That sort of thing."

"Really?"

"I know a bit about stones," the old man said, and even when he wasn't laughing, he seemed happy, jovial, like he was always a moment away from a chuckle.

I touched the ring with my other hand, considering. New love didn't seem that plausible, but new beginnings? This entire summer was basically the definition of a new beginning. Maybe that was why Everett had given me this ring. Maybe he knew a bit about stones, too.

I got up, and Book ambled slowly back to its owner.

"Don't forget to make a wish," the old man said.

"A wish?"

"On a shooting star. Every damn one you see. Especially with that ring on."

"All right," I said, laughing. "I'll do that." I gave him a wave goodbye before I turned away, making my way back up the wharf and toward Bearskin Neck. I wanted to see Motif No. 1 up closer, to see if maybe there was a gift store or something else inside it.

I reached the Motif by slipping between two buildings about halfway down the neck. I found myself in a narrow back alley crowded with empty lobster traps and buoys leaning against every free surface.

There it was, the Motif, just a few dozen feet away, at the end of another tiny wharf. I wasn't sure I was even allowed to be back here, but there weren't any signs or anything, so I kept going, making my way along the concrete until I reached the big red building. There was a door here, but nothing to suggest a shop, and sure enough, when I tried the door, it was locked.

Bummer.

I walked along the side of the building that had all the buoys hanging from it. I found a window, but it was too dark to see anything inside. I passed another door—locked. And another—locked.

So apparently there wasn't a gift store.

I turned my attention back to the sky and gasped when I saw what was happening. There had to be *hundreds* of meteors streaking through the darkness one after another, crowding the night sky until everywhere I looked there were shooting stars.

Don't forget to make a wish, the old man had said.

I didn't really believe in things like wishing on a star, but with all the bad luck I'd experienced in my short life...Why not?

So I closed my eyes.

And promptly drew a blank.

I mean...What was I even supposed to wish for?

There were *so many* things I wanted. I wanted Jennica to dump Lara and be my friend again. I wanted Bell's Books to remain open forever and ever. I wanted my parents to get back together....

I wanted my parents to get back together.

Because if they got back together, I knew, just *knew*, everything else would work itself out.

So I squeezed my eyes shut even tighter, touched the moonstone ring for good measure, and made a wish:

I wish my parents would love each other forever.

A gentle *click* from behind me caused me to jump a mile—I opened my eyes and turned around. It took me a second to see it, but there...One of the doors in Motif No. 1 had opened. One of the locked doors. One of the closed, locked doors.

My heart was beating a mile a minute. For a weird second, my whole body went numb. I couldn't feel my fingers. But after a moment, when nothing else happened, I felt the feeling rushing back.

How the heck had the door opened?

I took a step closer to it, trying to peer into the darkness within, but I couldn't see anything. I fished around in my pocket for my cell phone, then remembered I hadn't brought it with me, so I couldn't use its flashlight.

I stepped closer, right up next to the door, and let my eyes adjust to the darkness.

I couldn't see much without a flashlight, but to be fair, it didn't seem like there was much of anything *to* see. The building was definitely empty, except for a few boxes or crates at the far end. I took another step inside, then another, but as my eyes adjusted more, the darkness only revealed more and more of nothing much at all.

Shrugging, I turned around—

—and ran directly into a person.

I screamed. They screamed. We kept screaming for at least five seconds, and then we shut up at the same time, because we both realized neither one of us was trying to kill the other one. As soon as I stopped screaming, I looked up at the intruder's face—there was just enough light to see that it was a girl, about my age. I was so relieved I started laughing.

"I'm sorry," I said, still laughing. "You scared—"

"—the *crap* out of me," she finished, then dissolved into hysterics herself. Pretty soon, we were both cracking up, doubled over in the dark, semicreepy building.

I laughed until I couldn't breathe anymore, then the two of us stumbled back out into the night and sat down on the edge of the wharf with our feet dangling just inches from the water.

"Were you trying to sneak in?" I asked when I had finally calmed down enough to breathe again.

"Sort of," she admitted. "I'm meeting a friend. What about you—did you pick the lock?"

"No, the door just opened!"

"Really? It's not supposed to be open; that's weird. My friend always picks the lock." She pressed a hand against her chest. "My heart is beating *so* fast."

"Me too."

She was pretty, with light eyes and long, curly, messy hair. She was wearing jean shorts and a T-shirt that looked vintage, like she'd gotten it from her mom or something, and she had a little woven, multicolored cotton backpack.

"I'm Anna," I said.

"Emmy." She stuck out her hand, and we shook awkwardly, then immediately started laughing again.

"I was *so* scared," I admitted.

"I thought you were a murderer!"

"Or a bear. For a second I thought you were a bear."

"Because of Bearskin Neck?" she guessed. "That's funny."

"You're meeting a friend out here?"

"Yeah, my friend Beckett. I mean, he's sort of my friend. I only met him at the beginning of summer."

"Do you live here?"

"I spend summers here," she said. "How come you were trying to get into the Motif?"

"Oh, I don't really know, to be honest. I was just bored. I thought there might be a gift store."

"Do you usually break into private property when you're bored?" she said, a huge grin spreading across her face.

"Not as a rule," I said. "But it's my first day here, and I've never really been on the East Coast before, so maybe this is the new East Coast me."

"Where are you from?" she asked, perking up. "Are you from California? I've *always* wanted to go to California!"

"Los Angeles."

"Ugh, I've *always* wanted to go to Los Angeles! Are there palm trees on your street?"

"Not right *on* my street, but there are tons of cactuses."

"I *love* cactuses," she said, resting her head in her hands and looking downright wistful.

"You've never been to the West Coast?"

"No, never. I think Beck has. He'll be here any minute. Oh, you should stay and meet him! If you don't have anywhere else to be."

"No, not really," I said, trying to sound casual. In truth, I was kind of pumped. I thought I was going to be doomed to a long, lonely summer, and here was someone who wanted to hang out with me! Granted, she'd almost given me a heart attack, but still. "I can hang around."

"Cool. Beck's great, you know, but it will be nice having another girl around."

"What were you guys going to do tonight? I wouldn't be getting in the way?"

"Not at all. He was supposed to teach me how to play poker." She made a face. "Can I be honest with you?"

"Sure."

"I think he sort of . . . You know. Has a crush on me."

"Well, that wouldn't surprise me. You're really pretty."

Emmy's eyes flashed in a really sweet, genuine way. "Thanks," she said. "So are you."

"So is he being weird around you or something?"

"Super weird. For the first few weeks, we just did normal things like eating ice cream and going swimming. But now he's like . . . asking if he can teach me poker and stuff."

I couldn't help it; I laughed. "That still seems sort of normal to me."

She smiled and knocked her knee against mine, and I felt a jolt in my stomach—a happy jolt. The jolt of making new friends.

"I know it *sounds* normal, but you'll see," she said. "There's just something a little dorky about it."

We both looked up at the same time. The sky had gotten a

lot darker since I went into the Motif, and the Kit-Hale comet was really visible now. The meteors seemed to have slowed down, though, and the massive shower was over.

"Did you see all the shooting stars before?" I asked.

"Yeah, I did!" she replied. "Did you make a wish? My mom is *always* telling me to wish on things. Dandelions, lucky pennies, everything. She totally believes in stuff like that."

"I did, sort of," I said.

"Me too," she admitted. "Even though I'm not *really* sure I believe in it. What did you wish for? Oh, I shouldn't have asked! You don't have to tell me. You're not supposed to tell, anyway."

I might have told her, maybe, if we both didn't hear the whistling at the same time. We turned and looked down the wharf, where a boy about our age—Beckett, I assumed—was walking toward us, his hands stuffed into his pockets, his hair longish and pretty messy. When he saw Emmy, I swear his entire face just lit up. It was like he didn't even register me as being another human. Emmy was right—he definitely had a crush on her. He was cute enough, I guess, although in a kind of familiar, seen-his-face-a-million-times-before kind of way. Not really my type. Definitely dorky.

"Hi, Beck! This is Anna," Emmy said, gesturing at me.

Beckett blinked slowly, like he was coming out of a dream, and he definitely looked at me like he was seeing me for the first time. "Oh, hi," he said. "I'm...Beckett."

He paused in a weird way just before he said his name, and I saw his eyes flash over to Emmy. He really had it bad; he couldn't even form words around her. It was kind of sweet.

"Nice to meet you," I said.

"Anna is from Los Angeles," Emmy said dreamily. "You've been to California, right, Beck?"

"Yeah, San Francisco," Beck said. He dropped his backpack onto the ground, then took a seat (somewhat reluctantly) on my other side. (Emmy was all the way at the end of the wharf, so if he tried to sit next to her, he would have fallen into the water.) "How did you guys meet?"

"Anna broke into the Motif!"

"Really?" Beck said, raising an eyebrow. "What did you use?"

"Nothing," I admitted. "The door just opened."

He shrugged but didn't say anything else, just looked out across the harbor. He seemed upset about something—probably the simple fact of my existence, ruining his quiet one-on-one night teaching Emmy how to play poker.

Gradually the three of us turned our attention skyward, where Kit-Hale was still burning brightly.

"My friend Josh is gonna be jealous," I said, if only to break the silence that had built up among us. "He loves anything to do with space."

"It's pretty cool," Beck said, just as a meteor streaked across the sky. We all gasped—it had been a big one—then started laughing at the same time. In an instant, all weirdness had vanished from Beck, and he got back to his feet, offering his hand to me to help me up. "Let's get fudge," he said. "I'm hungry."

"Beck *loves* chocolate," Emmy said as we started back toward Bearskin Neck, leaving Motif No. 1 behind us.

"Will it still be open this late?" I asked, and even as the words left my lips, I yawned, a sudden wave of exhaustion rushing over me.

"The Fudgery stays open pretty late. Until the tourists go home, basically," Beck answered.

We reached the small storefront, and Emmy held the door open, playfully ushering Beck and me inside. The familiar smell of sugar and chocolate filled my nose, and even though I'd just had fudge for dessert, I suddenly wanted more.

Beck picked out a triple chocolate fudge while Emmy chose something called penuche walnut. I chose a caramel, and before Emmy or Beck got a chance to pay, I slid the twenty Miriam had given me across the counter.

Emmy said, "Thank you, Anna!" and she and Beck went to wait outside.

The cashier, a young girl with her frizzy hair in a ponytail, counted out my change and handed me almost seventeen dollars back.

"Oh, I think you counted wrong," I said. "You gave me too much."

She almost rolled her eyes (catching herself in the nick of time), and said, "No, this is right."

I shrugged and put the change back in my purse, then met Emmy and Beck on a bench outside.

"Thanks, Anna," Beck said.

"Their fudge is so good," Emmy said, sighing happily as the three of us sat there and ate our pieces.

People were still milling around on the neck, but it was thinning out as it got later. As we sat there, a few shop owners flipped over their OPEN signs.

"Okay, Anna," Emmy said, finishing her last bite of fudge and balling up the paper in her hand. "Very important question if we are going to hang out again. What is your favorite book of all time?"

Oh no. A question I dreaded. Did I make something up? Did I try to come up with an answer I thought *she* might like? Did I just admit that I didn't really like reading? Growing up with Miriam, I understood there was a certain type of person who simply couldn't allow someone else to not like reading. Hopefully, Emmy wasn't like that.

I settled on telling the truth:

"I don't think I've found it yet."

Emmy smiled happily; that appeared to be the right answer.

"Beckett's favorite book is *The Hobbit*," she said.

"Well, I'm reading *The Lord of the Rings* now, and that might take over," Beck said.

"I like every book," Emmy continued. "I don't think I've ever read a book I didn't like. At least something about it, you know? My aunt always tells me I should find *something* good in every book I read, even if it's just the fact that it has to end eventually."

"I'm reading *The Great Gatsby* now," I said, "but that's just a summer reading book."

"Are you kidding me?" Emmy exclaimed. She slipped her backpack off and reached into it eagerly, pulling out a copy of *The Great Gatsby* a moment later. "My aunt just gave this to me when I got here! We can read it at the same time!"

"I don't understand what the green light means," Beck mumbled.

"I think this is the same exact same copy I have," I said, taking it from her. "Except yours is in way better condition." I opened the front cover and noticed some writing underneath the jacket flap. I lifted it up.

To my little Emmy. Never be a Daisy. You're so much more. Love, Auntie

"She always writes stuff like that," Emmy said.

"I'm a really slow reader," I warned her.

"That's okay! I'll just read, like, a chapter a week. Or maybe two? I'm reading twelve other books at the same time, so I'll go slow with this one, and we can talk about it and make sure we're reading at the same pace!"

"Nerds," Beck announced loudly, but I could tell he was mostly joking.

"That sounds great," I said, handing the book back to

Emmy as I yawned again. I wasn't sure what time it was, but I knew I needed to get some sleep. "Jet lag," I explained, getting up from the bench. "I should probably head home."

"Same time tomorrow night?" Emmy said, slipping *The Great Gatsby* into her backpack. "We can meet by the Motif again."

"Sounds good," I replied.

"Bye, Anna!" she said.

"Bye, Anna," Beck echoed.

I waved goodbye to them both and started off toward the cottage, trying not to fall asleep standing up, the comet burning in the night sky above me, feeling happier than I'd felt in a really long time.

in the middle
of the ocean

M iriam woke me up at nine the next morning, proclaiming that if I slept any later, I'd never get adjusted to the time change.

"But it's *nine*," I argued, my voice croaky from sleep. "And it's *summer*."

"Well, I've been up for three hours, and I'm bored," she said. "We're going to the beach."

We basically never went to the beach back home, which was kind of funny, because we lived so close to it. But I thought the beach was one of those things you almost had to be apart from to really appreciate—if you were too close, if you could go whenever you wanted, you sometimes ended up just never going.

So I got up. I put on my bathing suit with a pair of jean shorts over it, found my baseball hat in the closet, and paused. I hadn't taken my guitar out of its case yet; it was sitting in the wicker armchair in the corner of the room. It was such a Dad thing, a present from him, that it somehow made the absence of him that much more palpable. He wasn't here. He was all the way on the other side of the country. He'd texted me in the middle of the night, a message that made my actual heart ache:

I miss you!!!!!!!!!!!!!!

Fourteen exclamation marks. I'd counted. That wasn't a coincidence; that was Everett Bell being Everett Bell.

I wrote him back now, before I went downstairs:

I miss you too Dad! Very miserable without you.
Lot of moping. Some tears.

He would laugh at that.

I took the guitar out of its case now, playing a few chords, laying it down across my bed for later.

Mom had made toast and was spreading peanut butter on a slice. She smiled when I walked into the kitchen and nudged the plate toward me. I picked out a piece with peanut butter and jam already on it, then sat down at the kitchen table.

"How did you sleep?" she asked.

"Pretty good."

"Did you go out last night? I thought I heard the door."

"Yeah, I just walked around Bearskin Neck for a little bit."

"Anything exciting happen?"

"I saw the comet. And a ton of meteors."

I decided not to tell her about Emmy and Beck just yet. She'd inevitably have a million questions I didn't know the answer to ("Where do they live?" "What do their parents do for a living?" "Do they have any pets?" "What are their deepest hopes and dreams?"), and besides, it felt nice to have a secret, something just for myself.

"Man, I used to walk around all the time after my aunt went to bed," she said with a wink. "You better not get into half the stuff I did."

"What kind of stuff?" I said.

She smiled—a dreamy, far-off smile that made it clear she wasn't going to tell me—and brought the plate of toast over to the kitchen table. She grabbed her coffee from the counter and sat down across from me.

"We'll stop at a little deli and get sandwiches for lunch," she said. "You should bring a book or something. Have you opened any more of your summer reading?"

"Not yet," I said, mouth full of toast. "Just *The Great Gatsby*."

"Ugh, I love that book," she sighed. "That was one of those books I'd read over and over again. You know, it was one of my summer reading books, too."

"Weird how in fifty years, summer reading assignments haven't changed that much," I pointed out.

"How old do you think I am, Anna?" Miriam asked

seriously, then smiled and added, "The classics are still classic, but you're right: There are plenty of contemporary books out there that deserve to be read."

"If you were a teacher, you'd make your students read, like, forty books over the summer."

"Forty would be the minimum," she said with a wink. "Fifty for extra credit."

Twenty minutes later, we were loading the station wagon with our beach gear. Aunt Dora had a small shed in her backyard with cobweb-covered beach chairs and an ancient umbrella. I shook out the chairs while Mom opened the umbrella carefully, checking for spiders. We brought a few beach towels, books, sunblock, then stopped for sandwiches a few minutes from the cottage, and were on our way.

The beach we were going to was called Wingaersheek, just down the road in Gloucester. We found a spot in the parking lot and traipsed between huge sand dunes to get to the beach. I'd never seen sand dunes this big before; they were taller than Mom, and all I wanted to do was run to the top of one—but they were fenced off.

"They've been fenced off since I was a kid," Mom said, reading my mind. "You can do damage if you walk on them."

The walkway beneath our feet was made up of planks of old wood, and it led through the dunes to the beach. Miles of soft white sand spread out in front of us. California had no shortage of beaches, but still—I had never seen one quite like this, so flat and endless and *clean*.

It was already getting hot. We lugged our stuff close to the water; I opened the beach chairs while Mom struggled with the umbrella, pushing the spiky end into the sand and twisting it downward. I slipped off my jean shorts and kicked them aside as Mom put our food in the shade under her beach chair and kicked her flip-flops into the sand. She took a deep breath and wiped the back of her hand across her forehead.

"Crap," she said, pulling off her sundress. "I'm already sweating. Let's go for a dip."

I let her take my hand and lead me down to the water, although she must have known there was little chance of getting me actually *in* it. Getting my feet wet, yes. Going in waist-deep, probably. Any deeper than that and I started to remember that I was actually a terrible swimmer. My anxiety just got the best of me. I started to think about all the things I couldn't see underneath the water (sharks, obviously, but also, I was *terrified* of jellyfish after Cecilia had been stung by one and her foot blew up to four times its normal size—she and Josh had both thought it was hilarious; I had been scarred for life). Miriam was like a fish in the water. I liked watching her cut through the waves, an actual mermaid. I was never scared something would happen to *her*. She was faster than jellyfish, and sharks would definitely know not to mess with her.

But still—it was *hot*. I was excited to feel the water, cool down a little. I marched confidently toward the waves....

Then screamed and jumped backward when the first small swell rolled over my feet.

"*Cold!*" I yelped, hopping around on the sand. "*So cold!*"

Miriam burst out laughing, watching me. She took a few steps into the water.

"*How is it so hot air but so cold water?!*" I shouted, falling backward onto my butt and scrambling like a crab to steer clear of the freezing waves.

"I don't think that was English," Mom said. The water was up to her waist now; she took a deep breath and dived into the waves, disappearing completely, the sea buttoning up around her, swallowing her whole. The ocean was darker here than in California, more green than blue. And—as I'd just discovered—very, very cold.

A few seconds went by, then Mom surfaced twenty or so feet away, farther from shore. She gave a little wave, disappeared under the water, and came up closer again, standing up and walking her way out of the swell. She held her hand out to me and pulled me up, kissing me on the cheek.

"Very dramatic," she said.

"Don't touch me; you're cold," I whined. We walked back to the beach chairs, and she grabbed a towel and tied it around her waist.

"Come on," she said. "I want to show you something."

She led me farther down the beach, away from the parking lot and our stuff. She was dry enough now from the sun that her skin was pleasantly cool, and I let her wrap her arm around my shoulders.

"I can't believe you don't like swimming," she murmured into my hair. "I've failed you as a mother."

"I have a lot of other perfectly nice qualities," I said.

"Name one," she joked, and pulled her arm away, taking my hand instead as she made a sharp left and started leading me directly into the water.

"Mom!" I said, digging my heels into the sand.

"Will you relax," she replied, rolling her eyes. "Look."

She pointed. I looked.

There was a long, wide stretch of sand leading way out into the ocean. The water lapped around the edges of it, covering some parts of it shallowly. There were people way out on the sand, just walking in the middle of the ocean, like it was totally chill and not at all death-defying.

"It's a sandbar," she said.

"It looks more like a death trap," I countered.

"It's not. I checked the tide schedule before we left the house. We have another hour before the water starts to move."

"And then..."

"This will all be covered up. Kind of cool, huh?"

It *was* kind of cool. We started walking on the sandbar, and after a few minutes, I looked back and saw how far we'd gotten from the shore.

"We used to come here all the time when I was a kid. My aunt loved this beach," Mom said.

"I'm warming up to it," I admitted.

"You get used to the water, too. It's always freezing," she said.

We kept walking, out and out and out into the water, until it felt like the shore was a mile away from us.

Jennica would love this, I wanted to say.

But I didn't. I wouldn't.

I just kept walking. Out into the middle of the ocean. Somehow, with Miriam Bell, that didn't seem like such an impossible reality.

We stayed way out on the sandbar until the water started splashing around our ankles, then we headed back to our beach chairs. Hours passed—we ate every bite of food we'd packed and reapplied sunscreen every twenty minutes (I was pale; Miriam was anal). Miriam read a book off and on and dozed off and on, and I tried to read *The Great Gatsby* but mostly thought about Bell's Books. It didn't seem real to me that we were selling it. And in some weird way, the sandbar reminded me of it. Maybe it was the way it kept going, long after you would have guessed. Maybe it was the way Miriam seemed so *happy* there, giggling and dipping her toes into the water like she might dip into the pages of a book. Whatever it was, I missed California more than ever, even though, when you sat this close to the water and looked out at the horizon, it was admittedly hard to tell what coast you were on.

Miriam was right (although I swore not to admit it to her); I *did* get used to the freezing water after a while. By necessity, mostly—it was so damn hot outside I needed frequent trips to dip my hands in the surf, scooping handfuls of water over my arms and shoulders, pressing my cold palms to my forehead happily.

When we were finally ready to leave, we were both exhausted, and the walk from the beach to the car felt endless, the beach chairs and cooler and umbrella each at least ten pounds heavier than when we'd carried them in.

"Who knew a day at the beach could be so *exhausting*," I complained when we reached the car, throwing everything into the back and leaning up against it, momentarily, to catch our breaths.

"I know," Mom agreed. "It's different in California, when we're only carrying a coffee, huh?"

"It's just such a *process*."

"You sound like your father. You know he used to hate the beach?"

"Really? But he goes surfing all the time."

"When he was your age. *Hated* it. Everything about it. Getting sand in his bathing suit. Getting his hair wet. Getting salt in his eyes. He was kind of a baby back then." She got this look for a minute, just a minute—this faraway look, like she was suddenly fourteen again and begging my dad to go to the beach with her. It sort of broke my heart. But to be fair, everything seemed to break my heart lately.

"Well, I can't promise I'll want to come to the beach with you every *day*," I said. "But maybe we can work out a once-a-week type arrangement."

"Sounds good to me," Mom said, winking before she opened the driver's side door and slipped inside.

I wanted desperately to nap when we got back to the cottage, but Mom wouldn't let me.

"That's a great way to never adjust to the time change," she said.

"Says the woman who went to sleep at eight o'clock last night."

"Eight o'clock is a perfectly respectable bedtime. Napping at four, however, is a recipe for disaster. Plus, I have big plans for the living room."

"The living room?"

"We're going to tackle one room per day until the cottage is spotless."

"I thought this was a vacation."

"It will take us two hours, *tops*. Little dusting, little vacuuming, little beating out the couch cushions. You can take that job. I think you'll find it oddly satisfying."

Actually, I *did* find it oddly satisfying (although I swore—again—not to admit it to her). I took the cushions outside to the porch and spent a few minutes banging each one against the banister, then I removed each slipcover and lugged them to the downstairs bathroom, which had an ancient washing machine and dryer stacked one on top of the other. After a few minutes staring blankly at knobs that made absolutely zero sense to me, Mom came and showed me where to put the soap, what dial controlled the water temp, and how to turn it on. (You pulled the dial toward you! But it didn't say that anywhere!)

"This washing machine is older than you are," Mom said fondly, resting her hand on it as the ancient gears inside sprang to life.

"You need a minute alone with it?" I asked, and she stuck her tongue out at me before shoving a dustrag into my hand.

"Come on. Bookcases. Now."

Look, if there's one thing you can say about me, it's that I know how to dust a bookshelf. There's no shortcut. You have to take every single one of those paper houses off the shelf, dust them individually, then take the rag across the book-dust-graveyard that's left behind on the shelf. Then you have to give it a minute. Dust resettles. Give it another wipe, then you can start putting all the books back where they go. It takes a long time if you do it right. And Miriam Bell would *know* if you did it right. So I got comfy and settled into the task at hand. Along with books, there were a half dozen old photo albums. I opened up one and leafed through it to find photos of Aunt Dora as a teenager. Why was every generation always so cooler than the ones that followed? I'd kill for Aunt Dora's wardrobe. And those cars!

I finished with the bookcase nearly forty-five minutes later. Mom rewarded me with a glass of lemonade I hadn't noticed her making, then she said she'd ordered pizza for delivery.

"Look at this place!" she said, twirling around with her arms spread out. "It's so clean! The slipcovers will be dry by the time the pizza gets here. Let's relax on the porch with our lemonades."

It was about six when we settled ourselves on the swing on the front porch. It was still oppressively hot, still sunny in a dusty, hazy way, and just getting buggy. Mom lit a citronella candle and put it on the coffee table.

"That's the thing about the West Coast," I said. "No bugs."

"Ugh, I know. I don't miss the bugs," she agreed. "But this *air*. You can't beat this air."

She was right. The sea air was really something else. Muggy and warm but a breeze that cut the heat at all the right moments, like it knew when you needed a breath of something cool. And it just tasted *cleaner* than Los Angeles. Fresher.

I put my feet up on the table and leaned my head on the back of the swing. I could feel Miriam staring at me, which usually meant she was gearing up for a lecture or some deep conversation. I just waited. She took her own time in things like that.

"How you doing, kid?" she asked finally in a soft voice that had to paddle its way through the thick air.

"What do you mean?"

"You know, we've been here for a day now. A day and a half. Things are starting to settle in a little bit. You touched the Atlantic Ocean. Walked through East Coast sand. Did your first load of laundry in a prewar washing machine. You feeling okay about everything? I haven't heard you call Jennica yet. Maybe you should try? We could both say hi?"

"Oh, I tried her earlier," I lied. "When you were in the other room. She says hi, but she was just running out to the mall, so she couldn't talk long."

Mom nodded. "Well, there will be plenty of time to talk to her, I suppose."

"Yeah, totally."

"And everything else? How's your brain, kid?"

My hands had absentmindedly gone to the moonstone ring on my finger. I twirled it around and around. The stone was cool and smooth. Had it really been only three days since Dad had come over for my birthday dinner?

I realized that Miriam was waiting for an answer. I shrugged and said, "Pretty good. I kind of miss Dad. Even though we just saw him."

Mom smiled and nodded. "Sometimes knowing you *can't* see someone makes you miss them more. Even if you just saw them."

"Do *you* miss him?" I asked carefully, keeping my tone light and conversational, not quite meeting her eyes. I couldn't stop thinking about the ride to the airport, how he'd put his hand on her leg for just a moment, how she'd called him *B*, a nickname I hadn't heard her use in so long.

I looked up when she didn't answer right away. She looked a little sad. A little hard to read. After a moment, she blinked a few times (were her eyes wet?) and said, "I think that's us."

She nodded toward the front yard, and I turned to see a beat-up Toyota Corolla come to a rest next to the curb. It had a small magnetic sign on the side of its passenger door: GEORGIE'S PIZZA. A tall, lanky teenager unfolded himself from the driver's seat, got our pizza from the back, and loped up to the house.

"Hey there," he said. He put the pizza on the coffee table and touched the brim of his baseball cap in an oddly old-fashioned gesture.

"Did the tip come through online?" Mom asked.

"Yes, ma'am, thank you," he said. He paused just a moment, like he wasn't in that much of a hurry. His eyes wandered upward to the sky, which was only just beginning to darken, just slightly. "See the comet last night?" he asked.

"It was great," I said.

"I swear, the first few meteors and my car wouldn't start for a full hour," he said, still looking up, shaking his head slowly back and forth.

Miriam and I exchanged a look; I tried not to laugh.

"I mean, to be fair, it's a shitty car," he added after a second. His eyes widened, and he finally looked back down at us. "Oh! Sorry about that. Enjoy your pizza. It's a beautiful night."

He turned quickly and headed back to his car, contorting himself inside like a puzzle. The engine spluttered when he put it into gear, and we watched with slight trepidation as it lurched away from the curb and started off down the street.

"What an odd young man," Miriam said thoughtfully.

"What book would you give him?"

"*Lost in the Funhouse*," she said immediately, not so much as a moment's hesitation. Then she looked at me, her eyes twinkling. "Don't you think?"

It was a favorite of Miriam's, a short story collection by John Barth. I'd only read the titular story. It was weird and meta, but I could see why she liked it. It was different and hard to predict, and it really got under your skin.

"What do you think he'd get out of it?" I asked.

"Isn't it obvious?" she said, opening the pizza box, pulling the first gooey, warm slice from its home.

No, it wasn't obvious at all. It wasn't obvious to anyone but you, Miriam Bell.

immediate
friends

Miriam made it to just past eight o'clock before she started yawning. We watched Kit-Hale appear in the sky and the shower of meteors that accompanied it.

"It's just like I remember," she said, her eyes wide and bright.

I tried to picture her as a teenager; I tried to picture *both* of my parents as teenagers, but I couldn't. I didn't think I'd ever even seen photos. That would have been in the midnineties, before the digital age, and most of the pictures from that time had been destroyed when a water pipe burst in my grandparents' house. The whole thing flooded. Grandma texted us a picture of Papa floating on an inner tube in the middle of the basement. It was really funny. Less funny was how many things were ruined, but Miriam didn't seem to mind that much.

"I have all the pictures right up here," she'd said, pointing to her temple.

She'd never been one for photography, anyway. Everett had taken most of my baby pictures.

On the porch, Miriam yawned loudly, the biggest yawn yet, and stretched her arms over her head. "I think I'm gonna call it a night, kid. What about you?"

"I might go for a little walk."

"I'm not sure I love your walking around at night," she said.

"Mom, it's Rockport, not Los Angeles. And I'm fourteen now. I could almost be a lifeguard, remember?"

"You have a point," she conceded. "You should go to the Country Store. Great candy selection. Hey, can I listen to that meditation app on your phone? While I fall asleep?"

"Yes, but one of these days you need to download it for yourself," I said, pulling my phone out of my pocket and handing it to her.

"I know, I know. Do it for me tomorrow, okay?"

"Okay." She was hopeless with technology.

"Don't be out too late."

"I won't."

"Stay on the wharf."

"I will."

"I love you."

Her eyes were half-closed already. She leaned toward me, and I kissed her on the cheek. She took the pizza box inside, and I stood up, stretching, pausing on the porch as I looked out over the water.

The sky was lit up with meteors. It looked like a painting,

with lights reflecting on the water and the sleepy little town half asleep and quiet and peaceful.

It was still a little early to meet Emmy and Beck, so I went to the Country Store first, as Miriam had suggested. It was a small building with old gray siding and white-trimmed windows. There was a white bench outside occupied by an uninterested ten-year-old playing on an iPhone, and the wide windows were full of candy boxes and old-fashioned games. I pushed open the door and stepped inside.

The inside of the store smelled like sugar: warm caramel and sweet saltwater taffy and bitter sticks of black licorice. One entire wall was just buckets and buckets of penny candy, and I found myself standing in front of it, completely over-whelmed with where to start.

Aunt Dora had loved saltwater taffy, I remembered, and each year on her birthday, Miriam would send her a care package full of it.

I grabbed a small bucket and dropped a few of the weirder flavors in there—cotton candy, bubble gum, birthday cake. Then, amused by all the possible strange candy options, I went on a hunt for things I had never tried before. By the time I was done, I had a selection of truly bizarre candy, including wax lips, pink bubblegum cigars, a box of candy cigarettes, a strip of brightly colored candy buttons, some sort of chocolate bar shaped like a potato (Idaho Spud!), a pack of wax bottles filled with pastel liquid, candy-coated peanuts labeled Boston Baked Beans, three candy necklaces, and three jewel-toned Ring Pops.

Satisfied with my selection, I made my way to the register.

"Quite the assortment here," the guy behind the counter said. He was around Everett's age, and he wore a T-shirt with a funny illustration of a lobster smoking over a boiling pot of water (SAY NO TO POT in white letters underneath).

"I haven't heard of half this stuff," I admitted.

"Candy cigarettes? A classic," he said, pouring everything into a bag and placing it on the scale. "Although in hindsight—a weird choice for kids."

"And the bubblegum cigar."

"And edible buttons," he said, shaking his head. "Honestly, these old candies are a trip." He handed me the bag, and I paid for it with a ten-dollar bill.

"Thanks," I said.

"I'm gonna need a full report on that chocolate potato," he replied.

"I'll make sure to come back," I said, smiling.

Motif No. 1 was just across the neck, but I took my time walking there anyway, just enjoying the night and the way the darkness had sliced through the mugginess of the day. It was still hot out, and the heat was making my fingers swell. I wasn't used to wearing jewelry, and I twisted the moonstone ring around my finger now, trying to make it more comfortable. When I got to the red building, I paused, remembering how the door had opened for me last night.

I walked up to it and tried the handle again. It turned easily under my palm, and I pushed it open and walked inside. The stale air tasted familiar to me now, and there was something else, something I hadn't noticed before. An almost metallic quality. I stuck my tongue out, just a little, like I was catching snowflakes.

My eyes adjusted more quickly to the dim light, and I walked a little farther in than I had before, unafraid now.

Voices outside pulled me out of my reverie, and I smiled to hear Emmy and Beck arguing lazily about something, Emmy's voice rising as she viciously stated her case. I walked toward the door and leaned against the doorframe, watching them.

Emmy was standing on a wooden crate, balancing with her arms out, and Beckett was sitting on the ground, his back against a pylon as he watched her, a smile on his face.

"You couldn't be more wrong if you tried," Emmy was saying. "It is honestly surprising that the Guinness Book of World Records hasn't called you to congratulate you on being the World's Wrongest Person."

"The World's Wrongest Person," Beck repeated thoughtfully. "I bet after they call me, they'll call *you*, to give you the World's Worst Grammar Award."

Emmy got very still, and her eyes narrowed to slits. I'd seen my mom make the same face at my father. It made me think maybe Emmy *did* like Beck just a little. "How dare you?" she said. "My grammar is *impeccable*." She noticed me then and relaxed immediately, jumping off the crate. "Oh, hi, Anna!"

"Hi," I said.

"Out for another midnight breaking-and-entering spree?" Beck asked, smiling.

"It was open again!" I protested. "What are you arguing about?" I closed the door to Motif No. 1 and walked over to them.

"Emmy is just very, very wrong about TV," Beck explained.

"He made me watch this *terrible* show," Emmy said. "*Salute Your Shorts*. Have you heard of it?"

"Nope," I said.

"It's so bad," Emmy said.

"It's incredible," Beck argued. "Have you seen *Hey Dude*? It's sort of like that. She doesn't like *Hey Dude*, either."

"Haven't heard of it," I said.

"Do you watch TV?" Beck said with an almost disgusted tone to his voice. "You're just like Emmy. She doesn't watch any TV."

"I watch TV!"

"Let's not fight," I said mock-seriously. "Look. I brought candy."

I set the bag down on a pylon and sat down on an empty crate. Beck immediately reached into the bag, grabbing a candy necklace and looping it around his head.

"Oh, taffy!" Emmy said, picking out a blue cotton candy piece. "Thanks, Anna!"

"Okay, Emmy, if you like TV so much, what's your favorite

show?" Beck pressed. "Do you like *Are You Afraid of the Dark?*"

"Oh, I've heard of that!" I said. "Isn't that old?"

Beck shook his head. "I can't deal with you girls, honestly."

"Sorry if Anna and I are just intellectually superior to you and can't be entertained by the same mindless drivel that holds your interest," Emmy said, rolling her eyes.

It happened so fast—Beck reached out his hand and casually pushed Emmy into the water. She hit the surface with a tremendous splash.

"I'm sorry," Beck said to me. "But it just honestly *had* to be done."

Emmy resurfaced a second later, shouting with pure fury. I jumped up from the crate.

"Shouldn't you help her?" I asked.

"She's fine," Beck said lazily. "There's a ladder. I know because she pushed me in last week. I owed her."

Emmy was letting off a truly impressive stream of expletives and making a lot of noise as she splashed toward the ladder. She pulled herself up, dripping wet and very angry.

"You are a *monster*," she said when she swung her leg onto the pier. Her hair was matted to her face, and her eyes were flashing.

"You mess with the bull, you get the horns," Beck said confidently, but I noticed he had carefully positioned himself so that I was between them.

"Oh, no you don't," I said, moving to the side. "I want no part of this."

"Beck, I'm *soaking*. What am I going to do now?" Emmy said.

"You should have thought of that eight days and three hours ago when you pushed me into the ocean in this exact spot," Beck said. We were doing a complicated dance: He kept moving to keep me in front of him; I kept moving to stay to the side.

"You've been counting the hours?" Emmy shrieked. "You actual nerd!"

"Sticks and stone," he said in a singsongy voice that frankly made *me* want to push him into the water.

"Ugh, I'm *freezing*," Emmy said.

"You should have thought of that eight days and—"

But Beck didn't have a chance to finish his sentence. Emmy moved faster than I've ever seen anyone move, darting around me to catch Beck unaware. One solid, dramatic *shove* and he disappeared over the edge.

She turned to me, smiling brilliantly, as Beck hit the water with an enormous splash.

"Care for a little nighttime swim?" she asked, winking just before she jumped off the pier herself, landing next to Beck with a genuine *whoop* of happiness.

"Emmy, this isn't *fair*," Beck complained. "It's eye for an eye. Not eye for an eye for an eye."

"All's fair in love and war," Emmy said. She executed an

impressive dead man's float on her back while Beck swam for the ladder, heaving himself up and over the side of the pier.

I sat down on the crate again and smiled weakly at him. "How's the water?"

"She got my candy necklace all wet," he mumbled sadly, sitting next to me. I scooted over to avoid getting soaked.

"I don't really swim," I said, just in case he was getting any ideas.

"Don't worry; you're not nearly as annoying as Emmy. I wouldn't push you in," Beck promised.

"Beck, come back in!" Emmy said, paddling farther out so she could see us over the side of the pier. "It's actually really refreshing."

"I'm refreshed enough," Beck said, but all the anger was gone from his voice. I watched him watching Emmy as she closed her eyes, still floating, the moonlight reflecting on her just right, her hair all spread out around her like a mermaid. It was sweet, the way he looked at her. I could tell he really liked her.

I dug around in the candy bag and found the Idaho Spud. I unwrapped it and took a bite. It was actually pretty good, with a soft marshmallow center covered in chocolate and dusted with coconut shavings.

"Are there actually *potatoes* in that?" Beck asked, swiping the wrapper to examine the ingredients.

"No, and it's surprisingly not disgusting," I said.

"I like what you've gone for here," Beck said, rooting around the bag some more. "Very weird candy choices. I approve." He took one of the wax bottles, bit off the top, drank the liquid, then popped the whole bottle into his mouth. He chewed for a couple of seconds, then nodded and said, "Disgusting. But in a very satisfying way."

Emmy was still in her dead man's float, but eventually she rolled over and swam back toward the ladder.

"Don't eat all the candy," she warned, pulling herself up rung by rung.

I got up so that she could take my seat on the crate and stepped closer to the edge of the pier as she wrung out her long hair. Great splashes of water hit the ground as I peered into the dark depths of the ocean.

"How deep is it here?" I asked.

"Not that deep," Beck said. "You can touch if you dive."

"No, thanks," I said, still looking. One thing I didn't like about the ocean was how you couldn't see the bottom. You couldn't see anything that might be around you. I'd seen photos of the Caribbean, and the sea was light turquoise and as clear as bathwater. I think I could go in water like that.

But *this* water. This water looked menacing and dark and scary and—

I was flying.

For one second, I was flying.

It took me a moment to figure out what had happened, but by then, I'd hit the surface of the water and sank quickly underneath it and it was too late to call out that I really didn't know how to swim.

I sank like a stone. Wasn't the human body supposed to be a little buoyant? Wasn't that what the air in your lungs was for?

But I'd been pushed on an exhale. I *had* no air in my lungs. And my chest was already starting to burn....

The water was freezing. Unthinkably cold. Mind-numbingly cold. The kind of cold that immediately sinks into your skin, into your bones, into your organs and sinews. I flailed my arms, and I think my hands broke the surface, but then they sank under again and I couldn't tell which way was up and which way was down, and I was scared to try to swim, because what if I swam in the wrong direction? What if I swam out to sea or deeper into the water or straight into a pylon and knocked myself out?

I was panicking. My ears filled up with the sound of *whooshing*—the whooshing of water or of my own blood in my veins, I couldn't tell. My eyes were squeezed shut, but everything seemed strangely *light*, like someone was shining a flashlight in my face.

I was going to die.

The thought came to me unbidden, and it caused a shock of panic in my chest, and I began thrashing my arms and legs out in earnest, trying to find the surface, trying to find something, a pylon to grab on to, *anything*—

And I hit something soft. Something warm...

A hand!

Arms wrapped around me, hooking me under my armpits, squeezing me tight. I felt my butt hit the sandy floor, and then we rocketed upward. When my head broke the surface, I inhaled so deeply I felt dizzy. I think I passed out for half a second, my head rolling backward and landing hard on someone's shoulder.

"You're okay," Beck said in my ear. "You're okay, Anna. I got you."

I could hear Emmy crying on the pier, and when I opened my eyes, I saw the shadowy outline of her leaning over the ladder, waiting to help me up. She was sobbing as Beck got us over to the ladder and roughly placed my hands on the lowest rung.

"You have to hold on," Beck said. "I don't think I can lift you up."

I picked up my head and made myself grab the ladder. I couldn't control my limbs properly, my legs kept giving out and my arms felt like they weighed fifty pounds each. I struggled to put one foot on the rung, then the other. I felt Beck press his body close against mine, holding us tight against the ladder so I wouldn't fall backward.

"You have to climb," he said in my ear. "I got you, okay? You won't fall."

I climbed. Slowly. One rung after another. I slipped once, halfway up, and true to his word, Beck caught me, holding on so tightly that I felt all the muscles in his body contract. I wished it were Josh instead, and I wished the hands waiting to grab onto me and pull me up were Cece's. I didn't even know these kids. They had tried to kill me. I just wanted my friends. I just wanted to be in California, I just wanted my parents to be back together, I just wanted Josh sitting at our kitchen table eating quiche and talking about books I'd never read, I just wanted Cece dragging me to the store to buy her eight millionth bathing suit. And I just wanted Jennica. I wanted to say I was sorry, to ask her what happened between us, because I didn't understand it. I didn't understand any of it, but even when I had moments of hating her, I also knew, deep down, that it hadn't been all her fault.

But no matter what I wanted, no matter who I wanted, it was Emmy's hands that wrapped around mine, and it was Beck's knee that pressed into my butt and forcefully pushed me up the last few rungs of the ladder. It was the two of them that wrestled my weak body over the side of the pier, and it was their faces I saw peering down at me anxiously as I closed my eyes and sank, momentarily, into darkness.

I could hear Emmy crying. Sobbing. It was the sound that brought me out of unconsciousness, that floated me gently back to the surface of my own reality.

"What the *hell*," I said, but my voice was weak and raspy from the salt water; I must have swallowed some without realizing.

"Anna, I'm *so, so* sorry," she cried. I felt her hands on my face, my shoulders, my arms, as she checked for cuts or injuries.

"I can't. Freaking. *Swim*." Each word was a rip in my chest, a stab of pain in my throat.

"I'm so sorry, Anna. You just looked so *wistful*; you really looked like you wanted to go in, too! You were staring at the water, and I just...I'm *so* sorry. I never should have pushed you in. I'm *so, so sorry.*"

"Give her some space, Emmy," Beck said, and through slits in my eyelids, I saw him grab her hands, pulling her back a little. I rolled onto my side and coughed up mouthfuls of seawater. My lungs were on fire. I couldn't believe I wasn't dead.

Emmy launched herself into Beck's arms, sobbing violently as he held her.

"Anna, do you think you need an ambulance?" he said seriously, gently moving Emmy aside as he leaned closer to me. "Do you need to go to the hospital?"

"No, no, I'm...I want to sit up. Will you help me up?"

He leaned over and wrapped me in a hug, then he helped me sit up and angled me so that I could lean against the crate. My lungs still burned, but my heart was slowing down, returning to its normal rhythm. I kept my eyes closed, but I could feel the two of them staring at me. One of them had their hand on my knee. I didn't know who, but it felt comforting. It felt like Miriam was there, sitting with me, waiting until I was ready to talk. When I finally opened my eyes, I saw that it was Emmy. Her eyes were red and her cheeks were streaked with tears and she looked so sad and so earnest that I couldn't help it—I laughed.

"Anna? I'm so sorry. Please, please forgive me. Please don't call the police," she said.

"The police? Don't be so dramatic," I said, smiling. My voice sounded like I'd just smoked a pack of cigarettes. "I'm sorry I yelled at you. But to be fair, you almost killed me."

"I don't know why I did that; I shouldn't have done that," she said. She was still crying a little, and she'd gotten the hiccups, which made it impossible to stay mad at her. Even if she *had* almost drowned me.

"It's okay," I said. "I'm okay." I turned to Beck. "I think you just saved my life."

His eyes were very wide. He nodded a little, but he didn't say anything.

And then we were friends.

Just like that.

Immediate friends. In the way you can maybe only be after one of you almost dies, after one of you almost kills another, after one of you saves one of your lives. Immediate, inseparable, best friends. Settling into an easy summer rhythm.

As if we'd known each other forever.

And it felt a bit like...

Luck, maybe.

Bad luck that Emmy had pushed me into the ocean, of course.

But very, very good luck that I hadn't drowned.

That Beck had saved me.

That I wouldn't have to go through an entire summer in Rockport with just my mom to keep me company.

And although I wished our friendship had started a little differently than my almost sinking to my death in a cold and unfamiliar ocean...

I'd take it.

i'm so happy
you're alive

After that, we spent every evening together. Beck worked days in his father's music shop in Gloucester ("We sell mostly guitars, but some violins and banjos, too, and it's okay because I get to play whatever I want when we don't have customers.") and Emmy spent her days with her aunt and I wasted my time lazing around the cottage, slogging my way through *The Great Gatsby* and watching old movies on VHS tapes that sometimes exploded in the VCR and took forever to extricate and carefully rewind and set right again.

Miriam somehow persuaded the local library to give her a temporary summer card, and she was on a solid book-a-day schedule, plowing her way through old mystery novels (Agatha Christie, Josephine Tey, Raymond Chandler, Dorothy Sayers), which I found literally everywhere: in the fridge, in the shower, on the front porch, on the back porch, stuck between couch cushions, on the dashboard of the car, in the VCR (?), and on every flat surface of the cottage. Once, I found seventeen paperbacks in her bed when she asked me to strip the sheets. It beat her previous record of fifteen.

"I finally have the *time*," she replied when I asked her one day, "Why all the mysteries?"

And I knew what she meant, because I similarly felt like I'd never had this much *time* before, time to do absolutely nothing, time to catch up on old rom-coms (was steadily making my way through every Sandra Bullock movie ever made) and lie on my bed staring at the ceiling and go to Wingaersheek with Mom and play guitar for hours, practicing chords until my fingers ached and then didn't ache anymore, because my calluses were properly forming now.

Two weeks passed blissfully in this way, and for some reason, I still hadn't told Mom about Emmy and Beck. She asked me what I did at night, of course, and I told her I mostly just walked and looked at the comet and thought about my feelings. Miriam *loved* thinking about her feelings, so she accepted that answer at face value and didn't press me much after that.

On the first Saturday in July, Miriam asked me if I wanted to take a ride into Gloucester with her. There was a strip of stores on Main Street that we drove to; Miriam parked the station wagon outside a vintage shop called Bananas, and we spent at least an hour digging through old party dresses and funny hats and brightly patterned shirts and too-small shoes. There were cases and cases of old costume jewelry, and every inch of the store had something interesting to look at. I found a simple blue sleeveless cotton dress with piping around the neck and at the hem and three white buttons down the bodice. When I came out of the dressing room, Miriam inhaled sharply.

"Yikes," she said. "I could have owned that same thing when I was your age."

"Really?"

"Just funny how fashions come around," she mused. "Do you like it?"

"It's cute," I said.

"Let's get it. We'll go out to a nice dinner when your father gets here."

Oh, right, Everett! I told him I'd call him today at two; I made a mental note not to forget.

Miriam found an old carpet handbag for herself, a real Mary Poppins–type thing that I just knew she was thinking would hold many, *many* books. We paid, fed the meter some more, and kept wandering down the street.

We had lunch at a little place called Passports, ducked into a few more clothing stores (I talked Miriam out of a truly heinous lime-green minidress), and finally arrived at the coup de grace: a bookstore, appropriately titled the Bookstore of Gloucester.

"Is it really *the* Bookstore of Gloucester?" I wondered, looking up at the sign. "There are no others?"

"Oh no, there's another one right over there," Miriam said, pointing. "But this one is new books; that one is used."

"And we're going in both of them?" I guessed.

"We are going in both of them."

I hadn't been in a single bookstore since Bell's Books, and as we pushed into the shop and the smell of pages and ink and nerds hit me, I felt a deep, bone-level quiver in my body. Bell's Books was closing. I had almost managed to put that fact out of my head completely, but it came rushing back now with enough strength to physically sway me on the spot.

Miriam raised an eyebrow. "Pull yourself together," she said lightly, then was gone, lost to the stacks of books, at home among her truest friends.

Even if I wanted something new to read, I couldn't allow myself to get anything. I was still struggling to make a dent in *The Great Gatsby*, and after that, it would be time to unwrap the next one of my summer reading books. But I looked around anyway, making my way slowly through the shop, somehow never once running into Miriam (I had a working theory that she could actually crawl inside a book, if it were big enough), touching my finger against the spines of various little paper bodies, waiting to see if I'd ever feel a spark, something that said: *This one! This is the one that will—finally—change your life!*

"I thought I was the only one who did that," said a voice behind me, and I turned around to see a woman a few years older than Miriam, light brown hair and red cheeks.

"Did what?" I asked, shoving my hands into my pockets.

"You have to touch the books. Acquaint yourself. It's not all about the fancy cover and the blurb on the back," she explained. She pulled a book off the shelf and held it against her chest, closing her eyes and inhaling slowly. "They'll speak to you, if you listen just right."

"You sound like my mom," I said.

The woman opened her eyes and put the book back on the shelf.

Winking at me, she said, "Your mom sounds like a smart lady."

After a half hour or so, Miriam reappeared, holding four paperbacks and looking slightly flushed, like she'd run a great distance or gotten trapped for a brief time inside a copy of Dante's *Inferno*.

We paid and headed right for the second bookstore.

This one was called Dogtown Books. and underneath that, in smaller letters, it said: USED & UNUSUAL.

"Title of your memoir," I said, nudging Miriam and pointing.

She rolled her eyes and held the door open for me.

This store smelled even *more* like Bell's Books (I had to admit, I loved how books smelled *more* like books the longer they existed), and the ache in my bones grew in size. I was almost buzzing with it. Miriam was lost in an instant, and I wished I shared her talent for being able to disappear completely, crawling down a page like the sentences were a ladder, descending into a nice story where nothing too bad ever really happened, like *Anne of Green Gables* maybe, or *Pollyanna* or *Little House on the Prairie*, something with green grass on the cover and girls in petticoats with long, flowing hair. I hadn't read any of those, but they sounded mild and soft and warm.

I sat on the floor in the art history section and pulled over-size books off the shelf that were filled with pictures of old oil paintings and watercolors and sketches. I traced my finger along the line of Picasso's *Girl in a Chemise* and wondered if there were any museums close by. I liked museums. I liked places where you had to be quiet, where there were rules, like you couldn't touch the art, and you couldn't stand too close, and you couldn't smoke or eat or drink in the exhibits. Miriam and Everett were rule breakers, but honestly, I sort of liked them. It was nice sometimes when you were just told what to do and you didn't have to decide for yourself.

Maybe that was why I thought about luck so much. Luck didn't have any rules, and I didn't like that one bit.

Miriam reappeared after a few minutes, folding herself into a seat next to me, clutching a book to her chest like she was afraid it would fly away. The books she'd gotten at the Book-store (not *the* Bookstore, as it turned out) were in her new car-pet bag, which she placed by her side as she slowly, with great reverence, turned the book she held toward me. It was a used paperback copy of David Sedaris's *Naked*. The front featured a picture of an old-fashioned pair of white boxers. We defi-nitely already had a copy of this.

"We definitely already have a copy of this," I said.

"*Look*," she said, and opened the book to the title page.

The inscription was written in black Sharpie:

To Nicholas
I'm so happy
You're alive

It was signed by David Sedaris.

When you're Miriam Bell's kid, you just knew things like what David Sedaris's signature looked like (it was little more than a scribble; the *D* of David resembled a sloppy *O*, and the rest looked like he'd sneezed while writing it).

"That's a pretty good one," I admitted.

"I wonder who Nicholas is," she said, sighing very romantically.

"I wonder why Nicholas gave this book away," I countered.

"I think it was an accident. He meant to keep it, but it ended up in a box of donations."

"And here it is."

"And here it is."

"And you're buying it."

"And I'm buying it," she agreed. "I haven't found a good one like this in a while."

"I wonder if Nicholas liked the book."

"I'm *sure* he did," she said, then rose to her feet and took her carpet bag and went to pay.

Sometimes I wished I loved *anything* as much as Miriam Bell loved books addressed to other people.

I don't even think my dad loved guitars as much, or tattoos as much as Miriam loved—

Oh crap.

My dad.

I pulled my phone out of my pocket and checked the time. It was two fifteen, and I'd totally forgotten to call him at two. I slipped out of the store and rang his number. When he picked up (after the first ring), he made his voice sound all huffy and breathy, but I knew he was kidding.

"Oh, hello, Anna Lucia," he said.

"Oh, hello, Everett Michael."

"And how are you today, Anna Lucia?"

"I'm doing very well, Everett Michael, thank you for asking."

"I assume you know what time it is?"

"Yes, Dad, I know I'm fifteen minutes late. I'm sorry. Mom's been dragging me into bookstores."

His normal voice again: "Well, that's a believable excuse. How are you, Worm?"

"Pretty good. Excited you're going to be here soon."

"Two weeks! I'm pumped. Feels like I haven't had a day off since I opened the shop. Will be nice to have a little vacation."

"Where are you staying?"

"Cute bed-and-breakfast just down the street from you. Five-minute walk. We could meet for breakfast!"

"Sure, Dad."

The door to the bookstore opened, and Miriam came out,

her carpet bag slung over her shoulder and her hand at her forehead, shielding her eyes. She saw me and nodded, then started walking to the car. I followed her.

"What else is going on? How's your mother? Is the cottage filled up with books yet?"

"It's about to get five more," I said.

"Are you talking about my books?" Miriam called over her shoulder, clutching her carpet bag protectively.

"That woman." Dad laughed.

"Insufferable," I said. And I was about to say something else, but another voice on Dad's end of the call stopped me. A female voice. I didn't hear what she said, because the sound was muffled, like Dad put his hand over the phone or pressed it against his shirt.

"One second," he mumbled, and when he spoke again, his voice was slightly strained. "Sorry, Worm. Any time for guitar lately?"

"Yeah, I've been playing a bit," I said. "Who was that?"

"Hmm? Oh, I'm at the shop. Front desk girl."

"I thought you had a front desk *guy*?"

"I do!" he said quickly. "Of course I do. That was his sister."

"He brings his sister to work with him?"

"No, his sister helps out sometimes. Sheesh, lotta questions."

"How long has she worked there?"

"She just helps out sometimes, Anna," he said, and I could tell by the change in his tone that the conversation was over. "Gotta run, okay? I have one more appointment before lunch."

"But it's only been a few minutes!"

"Right, but *you* were supposed to call me at two," he said, keeping his voice light. "Let's try again tomorrow, okay? Unless you have big plans to dig yourself out from under the mountain of books your mother seems to be constructing?"

"Sure," I said. "Tomorrow works."

"Love you; miss you."

"Love you, Dad. Miss you."

He hung up. I slipped the phone into my pocket.

"Everything all right with your dad?" Miriam asked when we got to the car. She opened the back seat door and placed her carpet bag carefully on the seat.

"Everything's fine," I said.

"You sure?" she asked, peering at me over the top of the station wagon.

No, I wasn't sure.

I wasn't sure at all.

But I bit my tongue and nodded, then I got into the car.

"I think my dad is seeing someone," I announced that night. Emmy and Beck and I were on a little beach on the side of Bearskin Neck that was opposite the Motif. It was technically a private beach, but at eight o'clock, it was totally deserted. It was a mild night, still warm enough for shorts and short sleeves but not too muggy. Emmy had brought a picnic basket (an actual, old-fashioned picnic basket!) full of cheese and crackers, and we were eating them on a blanket she'd pulled out of her backpack. Her copy of *The Great Gatsby* was lying on the blanket next to us. She'd just finished admonishing me for forgetting mine; we were supposed to compare notes.

Beck let out a slow breath of air, letting his lips vibrate against each other. "What makes you say that?" he asked.

They knew all about the divorce. Both of their parents were still together.

"I was talking to him today, and there was this woman's voice on the other end. I couldn't hear what she said, but suddenly he had to get off the phone," I explained. I was twirling the moonstone ring around my finger again. Twirl, twirl, twirl. It had become something like an always-there fidget device, and I found myself reaching for it when I was anxious or sad or just bored.

"Someone he works with?" Emmy asked.

"That's what he said."

"But you don't believe him?" she guessed.

"I've met everyone he works with. There aren't any girls. I've actually yelled at him for creating a testosterone-heavy environment. I just feel like if he finally *hired* a girl, he would have made a big deal of telling me."

"Tattoo shop, right?" Beck asked.

I nodded.

"And if he *was* seeing someone...," Emmy said gently, but then she trailed off, losing her train of thought as the sky was lit up by a short burst of dozens and dozens of meteors.

We all looked up.

Then I looked back down at the two of them, at their faces illuminated by cosmic interference. *They can't really understand*, I thought. They could try. And they *were* trying. But their parents were happily married. There was only so much they could do.

I lay down on the blanket; it was just the wide, dark sky above me. The now-familiar sight of Kit-Hale making its steady journey across the cosmos. The meteors, slowing down now, just one every other second or so.

Suddenly Beck stuck his head directly in my line of sight. The sky was blotted out with his head. He had a freckle just under his right eye. A tiny one I'd never noticed before. Everett had a freckle like that, but it was a little bigger. It made my heart ache to notice it. But then Beck pulled a silly face, pressing his nose up and sticking his tongue out so far that I could practically see into his stomach, and I laughed and rolled over and sat up again.

"Are you sad?" he asked, serious again, bumping his knee against mine. Emmy was still looking up.

"Kind of," I admitted.

"Because you want them to get back together? Your parents?"

"Of course I do. They're perfect for each other. It just doesn't make any *sense*!"

"But they're still friends," Emmy said in a dreamy, faraway voice, her eyes still trained on the sky. "They still love you. You still have them both. Why does it matter?"

I knew she didn't intend it to be mean, but it felt like an invasion of some kind, like her words were little bullets piercing my skin, sinking into my body.

"I don't want a *stepmother*," I said finally, knowing as I said it how flimsy it was, how poorly it conveyed what I really meant. Maybe the problem was, I didn't actually *know* what I really meant. I just knew I wanted them to be together. I just knew they *had* to be together. The *why* of it all seemed unimportant.

"You think one date and your dad is ready to propose?" Emmy said, still gently, still dreamily, finally looking down from the sky and over at me. Her expression changed when she saw me; her eyes got very wide and almost scared. "Oh, Anna! You're crying."

I was trying very hard *not* to cry, and it seemed like I was not succeeding, because even as she said it, I could feel the first tears escape their eye-prison and run scalding down my cheeks. *Ugh*. Great. Now I was the crier in our little group of three.

Beck retreated a microscopic amount, but Emmy threw herself into my arms, toppling me backward and landing hard on my chest, knocking the wind out of me. It was so dramatic and sudden that it actually worked; I stopped crying and started laughing, struggling to push her off me as she barnacle-suctioned to my body. Finally, Beck intervened, pulling her off me as I gasped for air.

When we were all sitting up again, she grabbed my hands and said, "Was I being a jerk?"

"No, you weren't being a jerk. You're right, of course. I'm overreacting. Even if he *has* a girlfriend. It's not really any of my business."

"I don't think you're overreacting, Anna," Beck said, his voice thoughtful and even. "I think it would be really hard for me, too, if something like this happened with my parents. Marriage is supposed to be forever, you know?"

"Till death do us part," I said bitterly.

"And then, if it's *not* forever..." He bit his lip, paused, thinking. "It's like, almost...What was the point?"

"*Beck*," Emmy said.

"No, he's right," I said. "I mean, that's exactly how it feels to me."

"I don't think a marriage has to last forever for it to be meaningful," Emmy said. "I think that's just a myth perpetuated by greeting cards and romantic comedies."

"You've seen *When Harry Met Sally* fifteen million times," Beck reminded her.

"That doesn't mean I take it as gospel."

"I think you sort of do," he mumbled under his breath. She smacked his arm.

"Anna, I'm sorry," she said. "I'm trying to understand. I'm sorry if I'm not doing a very good job."

"I've never seen *When Harry Met Sally*," I said. "But I think we have an old VHS at the house. I'll watch it."

"Ugh, it's so *romantic*," Emmy said.

"What do you mean ol—" Beck began.

"But not super realistic," Emmy continued, interrupting him. "And it might not make you feel better about your current situation. It's very pro-love-lasting-forever."

"That's okay. *Everything* is very pro-love-lasting forever," I said. I made myself another cracker with cheese and ate it in one bite.

"Well, *The Great Gatsby* isn't," Emmy said after a moment. "So maybe you should actually read it. It's cynical and dismal, and half the people die in the end."

"Spoiler alert," Beck warned.

"Okay. I'll read another chapter tomorrow," I promised.

Satisfied, Emmy had another cracker and lay down on the blanket.

The meteor shower was mostly over, but Kit-Hale was still bright in the sky. We all followed Emmy's lead, lying down, arranging ourselves like puzzle pieces, our heads almost touching.

And we *felt* like puzzle pieces. Like three sides of the same complicated shape. If you took one of us away, it somehow didn't work anymore. Something important would be missing. It would be incomplete.

I didn't tell them that, though.

I just hoped they felt it, too.

atlas moths

The next night, three bikes were waiting for me outside Motif No. 1. They were all kind of old-fashioned, with wicker baskets and wide handlebars, but they looked brand-new. Emmy and Beck were sitting on the ground but jumped up when they saw me. They were overly excited, careful in their joy, and I knew they must have talked about it before I'd gotten there—*let's do something fun for Anna, let's be super happy, let's make her feel better*.

It was a little embarrassing but also a little nice.

"We're going on a bike ride!" Emmy announced.

"Where did you get these?" I asked, touching one. It had ribbons coming out of the handlebars. Like a bike you'd see in a feel-good movie about childhood best friends.

"My aunt had them," Emmy said.

"Where are we going to go?"

"Into Gloucester," Beck said. "Have you seen the statue yet? The Man at the Wheel?"

"I've driven by it."

"It's kind of neat," Beck said. "And there's a beach there, too, but at high tide it comes right up to this stone wall. You can just jump in."

"We are *not* jumping in," Emmy clarified quickly. "Nor is anybody pushing anybody in."

"I appreciate that," I replied.

"It's just a cool bike ride," Beck said. "A cool, *dry* bike ride."

"Do you like bikes?" Emmy added hopefully.

"I can't remember the last time I rode a bike," I said. "But yeah, it sounds fun!"

"Oh great," Emmy said, her face relaxing. "Well, let's go!"

Beck led the way, then Emmy, then I brought up the rear. I was sweating within minutes, but the air felt cool as it whipped through my hair and tangled around my clothes, billowing my T-shirt out. I was beginning to feel slightly self-conscious about my style around Emmy. Or my *lack* of style. She was always dressed so casually, but just a little bit retro, too, like she had a closet full of clothes her mother had owned but never worn. Tonight she was wearing a shin-length floral skirt with buttons down the front and a white T-shirt tucked into it. The perfect white T-shirt. I felt like I could spend my entire life looking for a white T-shirt that fit me as well as the one Emmy was wearing, but I'd never, ever succeed. And if I tried to wear a skirt on a bike? I'd get it tangled around the chain in about two seconds flat. I'd end up flipping over the bike, the skirt would rip, and I'd be left naked and bruised on the sidewalk.

Emmy's skirt was flowing elegantly behind her like a freaking magazine advertisement for skirts.

Even Beck was cooler than I was. He was always wearing vintage band T-shirts or shirts for movies that had come out thirty years ago. If they *did* end up getting together, they'd be the perfect couple. I was just their awkward third-wheel friend who wore the same jean shorts and the same few shirts every time she saw them. I hadn't worn the dress Miriam had bought me at the vintage store yet. Every time I put it on, I just felt like a fake. Like someone trying to be cooler than they were.

It was kind of how I felt around my parents. Like I'd never be as *full* as they were. Full of life, full of style, full of passions and opinions and soul. Like maybe when they'd made me, they'd kept all that for themselves and left me with nothing really exceptional.

Just normal.

That's what I was.

I'd talked to my dad that afternoon, and there was no other voice on the other end of the line, just him. I didn't bring it up. Our conversation was only a tiny bit forced. But I could tell. We were avoiding the subject, tiptoeing delicately around it. He told me he'd given Leonardo DiCaprio a small tattoo that morning, which he felt very proud about since Leo rather famously didn't have any other tattoos. I asked what it was, but he'd said, "A gentleman never tells." I thought of Leo as Gatsby, the endlessly rich asshole who threw the most lavish but most emotionally empty parties. I hadn't done what I'd promised

Emmy: I hadn't read a single page that day. But I *had* watched *When Harry Met Sally*. And she'd been right: It did not make me feel better about my current situation. But I liked the end. I liked how Harry raced through the streets of New York to find Sally. And I admit: I imagined it was my dad instead. I imagined it was my dad, racing through the streets of Los Angeles to find my mom. To tell her they'd made a huge mistake. To beg her to take him back. And I imagined my mom, resisting at first, but finally relenting. Finally agreeing. *You're right. We really screwed everything up, didn't we? But it's not too late to fix it.*

By the time we reached the statue of the old man and the ship's wheel, I was covered in a thin layer of sweat. Of course Emmy looked as cool as a cucumber as she swung her leg over her bike and nudged the kickstand down. She balanced it on the sidewalk and walked to the front of the statue, but instead of looking at it, she gazed out over the water instead. It was a quiet, still night. Only a gentle lapping as the ocean brushed up against the stone wall in front of her.

I glanced over at Beck and realized he was watching her, unmoving, his feet planted on either side of his bike, his hands gripping the handlebars. An expression on his face like . . . well, like Harry. When he finally realizes he loves Sally.

I looked away so he wouldn't catch me staring and feel embarrassed. I got off my bike, hit the kickstand, and joined Emmy by the edge of the sidewalk.

"I like standing at the edge of the ocean," she said when she felt me next to her. "When you can look out in one direction and only see water. Just water. As far as the horizon. It makes me feel tiny. Like a bug."

"You feel like a bug?" Beck asked, appearing on Emmy's other side.

"You know what I mean."

"If you were a bug, what kind of bug would you be?" I asked.

"She'd be a firefly," Beck replied immediately. "I mean . . . I don't know. Never mind."

"I think you'd be a beetle, Beck," Emmy said. "You're like a beetle. Very, like . . . steady and hard."

"Oh. Thanks. Sort of."

"You're a moth, Anna," she continued. "But not like the moths we have around here, the little white ones that run into light bulbs. You're an atlas moth. Because you're quiet and unassuming and you think you're not as good as a butterfly, but when you open your wings, you're so, so beautiful."

She opened her wings then, spreading her arms out to the sea, stretching them across Beck and me, across our bodies, hitting our chests with them. I laughed and grabbed her hand. Beck didn't move. Like he was frozen. He just stared out across the water.

What she said made me feel warm, a rush of softness that blossomed in my chest. I wanted to tell her that it was really sweet, that it was the sweetest thing anyone had ever said to me, but then she'd lowered her arms again and turned around to lean against the railing, her back to the sea. Beck and I followed her lead. She was just one of those people; if she did something, you wanted to do it, too.

"Are you coming to the fireworks tomorrow, Anna?" she asked. "For the Fourth of July?"

"Oh, yeah! I forgot about that. My mom and I are going to come."

"There will be a lot of people," she said. "But maybe we can try to find each other? I'd love to meet your mom. And you can meet my aunt, too! Beck is going to come with us."

"That sounds great! I'd love to meet up. Wait, I don't even have your number."

But I realized I didn't even have my phone with me anyway. I'd never really been one of those people who were obsessed with their phone, but that summer, I'd been using it less and less. I'd stopped carrying it with me wherever I went, and I usually left it at home when I met Emmy and Beck. Since Miriam showed no signs of downloading that meditation app on her own phone, she was using mine to fall asleep basically every night. I'd go into her room when I got home and steal it back, and the cycle repeated the next night.

"Let's just meet right here. In front of the statue," Emmy suggested. "Right after the fireworks are over."

"Perfect," I said.

"They're really good fireworks," Emmy promised.

"They're pretty cool," Beck agreed.

"I've been coming to see them every year since I was born," Emmy continued. "Do you have good fireworks in California?"

"Honestly, we never really watch the fireworks back home. But it was one of the first things my mom talked about when we got here. She made me promise we'd come see the fireworks for July Fourth."

"Perfect," Emmy said, nodding appreciatively. "Then we can all meet here, okay? Don't forget."

"I won't forget."

"Should we keep riding? Beck, should we go to that park with the big rock? I think Anna will want to see that."

"Sure," Beck said. "Sure, we can do that."

He hadn't used his kickstand. He picked his bike up from the sidewalk and swung his leg over the seat.

We kept riding, the ocean on one side and the sleepy town of Gloucester on our other.

When I got home that night, after I took my phone back from Miriam's bedside table, I looked them up. Atlas moths. They were beautiful, enormous, the size of a person's hand, even bigger, sometimes. Creamy orange and white markings and short antennae shaped like ferns.

I fell asleep holding my phone; I dreamed of flying through the night sky, Emmy running underneath me and laughing, laughing....

The next day was boiling hot. The cottage felt like a sauna. We kept all the windows shut, pulling the curtains down, keeping it as dark as possible inside. We only left the front door and the back-porch door open, and we set up fans to blow a cross breeze through the house. I walked into the kitchen at lunchtime and found Miriam crawling out of the freezer. I blinked again, and she was just standing there with her feet on the linoleum and her head and shoulders stuck as far inside as she could get them. I thought it might be so hot that I was hallucinating. She had little ice crystals on her eyelashes when she pulled her head out.

"*Fork*," she said.

"Yes," I agreed.

"It is *hot*."

"Yes."

"I thought it was hot last week, on Tuesday. Remember that?"

"That was cool."

"I'm realizing that now."

"That was Arctic tundra."

"If I could time travel back to Tuesday, I'd take a jacket," she said.

"I think it's too hot to eat."

"Good, because I just checked, and we don't have any food."

"Should we go somewhere? For a walk or something?"

"That would sound nice," she said, "if I was interested in having all the skin melt off my bones."

"Fair point. Movie theater? Those are nice and cool."

"Nothing I want to see."

"Beach?"

"On July Fourth? Will be like sunbathing with a million packed sardines."

I collapsed into one of the kitchen chairs. "You're crabby."

"Yes," she said thoughtfully. She opened one of the cabinets and peeked inside. "Peanut butter and jelly?"

"Sure."

She pulled out the stuff to make the sandwiches. A line of sweat dislodged itself from the back of my skull and made its slow, languid journey down my spine, hitting every vertebra on the way down, coming to its final resting place in my butt crack. I had taken two showers already that morning, but it looked like my third was right on the horizon.

"You still want to go tonight, right?" I asked as she spread peanut butter on a slice of bread.

"Of course," she replied. "It will cool down by then."

"Hopefully."

I *still* hadn't told her about Emmy and Beck. I didn't know why. I had been meaning to. I wasn't actively keeping the information from her. But still. Every time I tried to mention it, something just...stopped me. But I guessed she would meet them tonight anyway. The cat would be out of the bag.

As if on cue, my phone started buzzing in my pocket. I slipped it out. A FaceTime from Josh. We'd talked only a few times since I'd gotten to Rockport, but that's how Josh and I were. We didn't need to be in constant communication. Same with Cecilia. We all just knew—when we needed one another, we'd be there. I thought that's how it was when you'd been friends with someone for a long time. Jennica and I had never been like that. If a day went by and I hadn't texted Jennica, she got all strange and weird the next time I saw her. I'd tried to text her more, but...Honestly, I just never liked texting.

I answered the FaceTime with the phone pointed up my nose.

When the call connected, Josh dissolved into laughter. "Gross, Anna."

"Hi, Joshy," Miriam called from the kitchen.

"Hi, Miriam! Come here, I want to show you something!"

"Did you call me just to talk to my mom?" I asked.

"Sort of, yeah," Josh said. At least he had the decency to act apologetic about it. Miriam put down the knife she was using to scoop jelly out of the jar and sat down next to me at the table. Josh was in his bedroom, sitting cross-legged on the bed. It was morning over there, nine o'clock, but Josh had always been an early riser. He'd probably been up since six. "Check this out," he said when Miriam was in the frame, and just the way he said it, I knew he was about to show her a book. I swear, Josh should have been Miriam's kid. It made way more sense than the current arrangement.

Surprise, surprise: Josh picked up a thin hardcover book from the bed next to him and showed it to the screen. It was tan, old, a vintage copy of *The Little Prince*. It had an illustration of the little prince himself on the cover, standing among flowers, with stars in the background.

Miriam whistled. "Wow. Good one."

"Just wait," Josh said.

He opened the book. On the first page, across from the inside cover, was an inscription:

> *Dec 1974*
> *Paul—"One must*
> *look with the heart"—Frannie*

"Oh wow," Miriam said.

"I know," Josh replied.

"Nerds," I whispered under my breath.

"1974," Miriam continued, choosing to ignore me. "I wasn't even born in 1974."

"I wonder if they were dating," Josh said. "Or if Frannie was trying to lock it down, you know?"

"I wonder if they're still alive," Miriam mused. "I wonder if they're still together."

"If they were ever together," Josh said.

"Don't you just think they were, though?" Miriam pressed. "Doesn't it just feel like they were together forever?"

"It does, yeah," Josh admitted, and for a moment nobody spoke, and when I glanced at Miriam, she had a dreamy expression on her face, and her words, *together forever*, seemed to have grown ten times in size, and gotten weight and mass, and were now things of their own that would live in the cottage with us, hogging the bathroom and taking up space on the shelves and wrinkling the sheets.

Together forever. Why did Miriam look so *romantic* when she said that if she was getting a divorce from the person who was supposed to be *her* together forever? If Paul and Frannie had broken up three years after she gave him that copy of *The Little Prince*, it was just like their love had never existed at all! So what was the point of it? What was the point of any of it? Love was ridiculous and absurd and a waste of time and a truly useless endeavor. That was what I should tell Emmy, if she asked for my advice about Beck again. I should tell her—it will never last. And what is the point of something that doesn't *last*?

Miriam and Josh had started discussing the finer points of *The Little Prince*, so I got up from the table and finished making the sandwiches. When I brought them back, they'd already said goodbye and hung up. I ate my sandwich wordlessly, breaking up bite-size chunks and chewing and swallowing. My throat became sluggish with peanut butter. Miriam didn't seem to notice my silence, because she was equally wrapped up in her own silence. I wondered what she was thinking about. I wondered if she ever thought I was like an atlas moth, or if she would pick another bug entirely to describe me. An inchworm, maybe. A fly.

I finished my sandwich and put my plate in the sink.

"I'm going to take a shower," I announced.

"Isn't this your fourth today?"

I was about to correct her, say it was only my third, but then I realized she was right.

She was always right.

That was the problem.

fireworks

We should ride bikes to Gloucester tonight," Miriam announced after dinner. "The traffic will be miserable."

"Do we own bikes?"

"We used to have some when I was a kid. They'd be in the shed."

"There's a shed?"

"Honey, you've seen the shed before. The beach stuff, remember?"

"Oh right," I said.

"My sweet, unobservant daughter."

We went out to the backyard, where, indeed, a small shed was tucked into the far corner of the yard (it looked vaguely familiar). It was brown and locked with an enormous and rusted padlock. Miriam had the anchor key ring, and she tried a few small keys before she found the right fit. The padlock came off in her hand. She opened the door and hung the padlock back through the loop. Then she opened the door wider, and we peeked inside.

It smelled terrible, but also not terrible. It was hard to describe the smell. It smelled like old grass and old dirt and old sweat and old air, but there was something impossibly nice and earthy to it, too. There was a ton of stuff crammed in there: a lawn mower and tennis rackets that hung from the wall and a few Hula-Hoops and a red wagon and skis in the back corner and various gardening equipment. Everything was scattered around with no rhyme or reason. And yes, there were three bikes, wedged way in the back. They looked like they hadn't been ridden in years.

"Careful of spiders," Miriam said. "There were always a lot of spiders in here."

"Yeah, this is a spider heaven," I replied. "Do you blame them? Look at all the things they can build their webs on."

"Lots of things," Miriam agreed. She picked up an old picnic basket and handed it to me. I moved it to the side.

She kept picking things apart and handing them to me, and I kept moving them until we'd created a path to the bikes. Miriam dislodged one from its home and wheeled it out to the yard. It had two flat tires. It looked like the bike Emmy had brought for me to borrow. These coastal people sure did love their beach cruisers. It was the same in Los Angeles, too.

Miriam brought out a second bike. This one had more rust than paint and two equally flat tires.

"Don't suppose there's a tire pump somewhere in here?" I

asked Mom, and lo and behold, she turned around holding a centuries-old pump.

"Hope they're just flat and don't have holes or anything," Mom said. "We probably have a patch kit somewhere in here, but the chances of my finding it are slim to spider bite."

She brought the pump out to the grass and set it down, and I helped her unscrew all the caps. It was the kind of pump you worked with your feet, so it wasn't long before all four tires were full again. She stepped back and admired her handiwork.

"These chains are rusty, but I think they'll be okay. It's not too far into town," she said.

"If we break down, we can always take a car back."

"That's the spirit."

"Did you used to ride these when you were a kid?"

"Oh god, yeah. All over the place."

"Are there any bike locks?"

"Hmm." She turned back around to look into the garden shed, moving a massive rake aside and opening a very rusty tool cabinet. She stuck her hand in and emerged with two bike locks. They even had keys sticking out of the locks. "Ta-da," she said.

"We're all set. What time are the fireworks again?"

"Nine thirty. But we can leave whenever. It will be a beautiful night. The ocean comes right up to the sidewalk. A nice breeze. I can't believe we haven't walked around by the water there yet. Oh! And if we leave now . . ." She took her phone out of her pocket and checked the time.

"We can hit the bookstores before they close?" I guessed.

"I wasn't going to say that," she said in a tone of voice that made it clear she was definitely going to say that.

"You do realize we went to both of those bookstores about fifty-six hours ago, right?"

"What are you, the official summer timekeeper?" she said, grumpily pushing past me. She closed the shed doors, locked them again, then wheeled one of the bikes around the side of the house to the front yard. I followed her.

I checked the time on my phone. It was around seven thirty. We'd get to Gloucester by eight. I was kind of nervous about introducing Emmy and Beck to my mom, to be honest. I wasn't sure why. She wasn't generally an embarrassing mom. She rarely said weird things or brought up awkward memories of me as a kid or did anything specifically *meant* to be weird.

So why was I feeling so anxious about it? Why didn't I just tell her now as she brushed dirt off her bicycle's seat? *Mom, I've made some new friends. You're going to meet them tonight.*

Why couldn't I tell her?

"Need anything from the house?" she said.

"I don't think so."

"I'll lock up."

She went inside. I played with the old and tattered ribbons hanging from my bike's handlebars. She came out a few minutes later. She'd changed from flip-flops into tennis sneakers and pulled her hair back into a ponytail. She rarely wore her hair back, and it made her look different. I stared as she came and got on her bike.

"What?" she said.

"Nothing," I said.

We started biking.

The traffic was already noticeably heavier than it usually was, and it only got worse the closer we got to Gloucester. Clearly, we'd made the right choice by taking our bikes; we flew by the slow-moving cars, and the breeze felt like a godsend, blowing my hair back and making Miriam's ponytail fly out long and wavy behind her. We did, indeed, stop by the bookstores first, then got back on our bikes and rode them closer to the water, locking them up at a bike rack near the old-man statue.

"I loved that thing when I was younger," Mom said as we walked closer to the statue. I squinted at it. It looked different from the other night. The sidewalk blossomed out in front of it in a wide circle, and there were a series of plaques around it. How had I missed those before? I guess Miriam was right: I was just a generally unobservant person.

The tide was coming in, but there were still a few feet of sand left between the rock wall and the ocean. A few people were walking down there, but it freaked me out. There wasn't *that* much space. One good wave would knock you off your feet, and then where would you go?

"She's not a fan of this," Mom said, jokingly nudging her hip against mine.

"She doesn't love it," I agreed.

"You're safe up here, kid."

Tons of people were already camped out along the wall, sitting with their legs dangling over the side, waiting for the fireworks to start. We walked for a while until we found a spot big enough for both of us to fit, then we nestled in to wait.

It was dark but still sweltering hot, although the sea breeze helped. After a minute, Miriam pulled a tiny bottle out of her purse. She opened it and had a sip, then held it out to me.

"This was my aunt's favorite thing in the whole world," she said. "We'd come down here, she'd sip a bottle, and we'd watch the fireworks. A *small* sip," she clarified when I took it from her.

I read the label. Goldschläger. Sniffed it. Cinnamon and something sharper.

I took a tiny sip and murmured my appreciation.

"Right?" Miriam said. "Okay, okay, that's enough."

She took it back from me as I tried to steal another sip. She drank most of the tiny bottle but gave me another sip toward the end. It made me feel warmer than I already was, but a good kind of warm. When it was empty, she slipped it back into her purse and rested her head on top of mine.

"I used to love watching the fireworks with my aunt," she said.

"What was she like?"

"She loved books. That's where I get it from. And she loved

the ocean, of course. And she loved that cottage. And she liked being alone. But she liked being with me, too."

"And you spent every summer with her?"

"Every single summer. My parents were busy, you know. They worked a lot. It was only me. Maybe they thought I'd be bored if I was left alone all day. Plus, my aunt was really cool. I liked being with her. She was young, she dressed funky, she loved art. We'd go to all these art shows. We'd take the train into Boston and spend the day walking around. And then I met your dad, and that was another reason to like spending the summers here."

"He lived in Gloucester, right?"

"Yup," she said, picking up her head from mine and staring out over the water. "But he'd come to Rockport almost every night. His big brother, Uncle Billy, worked in a restaurant there, so sometimes he'd drive him over and sometimes he'd just ride his bike."

"How did you meet him?"

"Just walking around Bearskin Neck, I guess. I don't remember a moment. Just...All of a sudden, he was always there. What's with the third degree?"

"Just wondering. Did you like him right away?"

"I thought he was sweet."

"But you didn't think..."

"I was going to marry him?" She laughed. "No, I did not think I was going to marry him."

I thought of the voice on the other end of the line. The woman's voice. My dad, clearly lying about who she was. Did Miriam know Everett was (probably) dating someone? Was it my place to tell her? Would she even want to know? Would she care?

She must care. Of course she would care. You don't spend so much of your life with someone and then not care what happens to them, right? Maybe it wouldn't have been something she'd readily admit to, but I *knew* Miriam would care that Everett was already dating. I knew she wouldn't like it. Because I knew they were meant to be together. I just *knew* it, and I would find a way to show it to them. I would find a way to—

Oh, okay.

As it turned out, when you never ever drank and had two tiny sips of cinnamon-scented alcohol in one hundred degree heat...

You got a teeny-tiny bit drunk.

But maybe there was something to my drunken inner monologue?

I mean... Wasn't it a little strange that my dad was flying all the way across the country to spend a week with the woman he claimed to want a divorce from? Sure, I'd be here, too, but a full *week*? It was kind of a long time.

"Ten more minutes," Mom said beside me, checking the time on her phone.

I nodded, looking up at the night sky in preparation. There was Kit-Hale, there was a long streak of a meteor flashing across the sky, and there were my hopes for my parents to get back together. Sky high. I knew I should stop thinking about it, but the thought was buzzing around in my body alongside the alcohol. There was no getting rid of it.

The fireworks started right at nine thirty, and I had to admit—they were the best fireworks I'd ever seen. And that included Disneyland. There was just something magical about the display being over the water, every explosion reflected endlessly across the surface of the ocean. I glanced at Miriam halfway through, and her face was lit up with a bright purple glow, then blue, then red. She looked beautiful. She didn't even look sweaty. My own armpits were damp and uncomfortable. I should have worn the blue cotton dress. I should try to be more like Miriam. Or more like Emmy. Or more like Jennica.

No, no. I didn't want to be anything like Jennica. I'd be like Cece: strong and confident and entirely unconcerned with what anyone else might think of me.

Once, someone in our school had drawn a picture of Cece with exaggerated arm muscles and a mullet haircut and put it up in the hallway. Cece found it, laughed, and left it hanging.

"Aren't you going to take it down?" I asked, mortified on her behalf.

"And give them the satisfaction of thinking they got to me?" she replied, flexing her arm and showing me her bicep. "Not super far off, right?"

She *was* pretty muscular. All that volleyball. But the haircut was just mean.

Still, she'd left it hanging, and when Josh had taken it down later that day, she'd made him go tape it up again.

That was Cece to a T.

Cece wouldn't feel weird about introducing her mom to her new friends. Cece would be direct and deliberate and precise.

"I have friends!" I exclaimed.

Miriam glanced over at me, one eyebrow raised.

She patted my hand with hers. "Okay, sweetheart," she said.

"No, I mean—new friends. I met new friends."

The fireworks were still exploding above us. She kept her eyes on them and inclined her face toward me, indicating that she was listening.

"That's great, honey," she said.

"They're here. At the fireworks. Do you want to meet them?"

"Of course I do. Where did you find these friends?"

"Just around Rockport. Bearskin Neck."

"I'm sure they're lovely."

The display was really ramping up; clearly, this was the grand finale. I stopped talking and just watched it. Miriam was beaming. I couldn't help it; I smiled, too. It was so bright and so loud, boom after boom after boom.

Miriam leaned over and shouted, "What are their names?"

"Emmy and Beck," I yelled back, just as another tremendous firework lit up the sky, the biggest one yet, with a *boom* that made my bones vibrate.

Miriam laughed and clapped and cupped her hands around

her mouth and gave a big whoop. Everyone around us was doing the same thing. I cheered so hard my throat hurt.

"That was awesome," Miriam said as soon as everyone quieted down. People were packing up their things, getting up, dispersing.

"We have to head back to the statue!" I said. "To meet them!"

"Lead the way, kid."

Miriam had a glossy, happy look in her eyes as we pulled ourselves to our feet and started walking back to the statue. Everything felt light, happy, like a movie. The crowd was enormous, and we clasped hands to make sure we didn't lose each other. When we got to the statue, there was a swell of people around it, reading plaques, taking selfies, milling around the sidewalk. It was hot and cramped, and I was too short to see much over everyone's heads.

"They'll be here," I said.

Miriam nodded happily, wandering away from me and closer to the water, where she put her hands on a plaque and then let her gaze wander out to sea. I heard Emmy's voice in my ear, *you're an atlas moth*, but when I turned around, she wasn't there; it was just a stranger with a glow band around his head, one of the multicolored ones that shone in the dark. He saw me looking at it, took it off his head, placed it on mine, and was gone, swallowed up into the crowd in an instant.

I felt weird. Something was happening. People were looking up, pointing up, shouting, gasping, yelling. I looked up, too, and my heart skipped in my chest, a strange flutter that made me sick to my stomach.

A million meteors. A *trillion*. Zooming across the sky so fast and so packed together that it gave the illusion of movement, like the earth was spinning too fast. I felt dizzy and tried pushing through people to find something to hold on to, but I was trapped in the sea of bodies. I couldn't do anything but stay where I was and watch as the sky exploded above me.

And then—a hand in mine.

A small, cool hand, squeezing.

Emmy. I knew it was her before I turned around, and I felt my heart leap inside me, but when I looked, it was just a little girl, too young, six or seven, and her hand was much too small to be Emmy's, of course it was. She just looked at me for a moment, and I looked at her, and then a woman scooped her up into her arms. *Sorry*, she mouthed, an apologetic smile on her face, but she was gone before I could say anything. Why wouldn't anyone just stay *still*?

And then there really *was* Emmy, a few feet away, winding her way through bodies, with Beck trailing after her. They'd come to meet me! They were really here!

I pushed toward them, muttering *excuse me, excuse me*, but when I'd reached them, they were gone. The crowd was dispersing. They'd *just* been there, but where had they gone? I spun around in a quick circle, and there was Miriam, smiling happily, her ponytail impossibly perky, impossibly full.

"Hi, kid," she said. "Find them yet?"

"No," I said. "I think maybe...I think I must have missed them."

"Oh, bummer. Did you try calling them?"

"No, I don't have their numbers."

Miriam shrugged and wrapped her arm around my shoulders. How was her arm so *cool*? I felt like I was burning up.

"The summer is long," she said. "We have plenty of time. You should invite them over for pizza sometime. I can meet them then."

I nodded. "Yeah, okay."

"We should probably get going. Or do you want to wait a few more minutes?"

"No, no, we can go," I said, because everyone was leaving, and it was obvious they weren't coming. It was obvious that I hadn't seen them at all; I'd just seen two kids who *looked* like Emmy and Beck. For whatever reason, they'd decided not to come.

And I couldn't help it—I thought of Jennica.

I thought of Jennica.

The day after school when we were supposed to meet at a diner. She'd canceled at the last minute, said she was too busy with homework. I'd gone with Josh instead. We walked in the glass door, and I saw her right away, in a booth near the back with *her*. With Lara.

We got into a huge fight that night. Over text, of course. She wouldn't answer my phone calls. She wouldn't answer any of my questions—why would you lie and say you had homework to do? Why wouldn't you just tell me you already had plans? Or tell me you had to reschedule? Do you not even want to be friends anymore?

You are totally overreacting!!!

It was the last text Jennica ever sent me. Two months ago. At school the next day, she avoided me carefully, not using the hallways where she knew I had classes, not going to her locker, sitting on the opposite side of the room during our one shared study hall.

"Weird. It just doesn't really seem like something she'd do," Cece said at lunch that day. We didn't usually sit together, but I joined her table of sporty kids out of necessity.

"Well, she did it," I said.

"Have you thought maybe your texts are a *little* bit..."

"A little bit what?"

"Sometimes you can get, you know...Just the slightest bit dramatic. Why don't you just text her back and ask if you can get together after school and talk everything through?"

"That's on her," I said angrily, snatching my phone back from Cece.

Cece didn't get it. She was too forgiving. She was practically living on another planet, one without normal social cues and interactions. One with a volleyball net and a beach but nothing else. I'd pushed her words firmly out of my mind and forgotten them until now, until that moment, with the heat pressing down around me like a blanket, with my mom waiting expectantly for me to move, with the crushing blow of yet *another* friend letting me down.

Two friends.

Whatever. It didn't matter. This didn't matter. Jennica didn't matter. Nothing mattered.

I blinked angry tears out of my eyes and followed my mom through the dispersing crowds to where we'd locked up our bikes.

Only when I'd unlocked the bike lock, only when I'd swung my leg over the seat, only when I'd slowly backed the bike out of the rack, did I see it.

Sitting on the basket.

Small and unassuming, with powder-dusted wings and a soft, impossible glow.

A little white moth.

I waved it away, and it disappeared into the night.

didn't see them for two weeks.

I avoided Bearskin Neck at night; I hardly left the house unless it was to go somewhere with Miriam, vintage shopping or book shopping or grocery shopping or back to Wingaersheek Beach. When I thought about them, I just felt embarrassed. Like I'd let it happen again. Like I'd let myself get too close to someone, rely too much on someone else. I was an idiot. I never learned. I finished *The Great Gatsby* and opened the next book, a new paperback copy of *Slaughterhouse-Five*. I was so sick of summer reading books written by white men. I was so sick of books that didn't relate at *all* to my life. I was so sick of reading book after book (not just this summer, for my entire life) that meant absolutely nothing to me. So sick of not finding the one book that—Miriam promised—would change my life forever. I'd tried *so many* books, and I just kept finishing every single one feeling irritated.

Maybe it was just more bad luck.

Bad luck woven through even the books I read, even the stories I consumed.

I read *Slaughterhouse-Five* joylessly, struggling through each page, rewarding myself with every chapter I finished. Make it to chapter two and you can watch a movie. Chapter three and you can eat lunch. Chapter four and you can go for a bike ride. But not at night. No more at night.

"Honey, it just feels like something *happened*," Miriam said one morning at breakfast, the day before my dad would arrive. "And I know you keep saying nothing happened, but you were so ... *happy*. And now you're so glum. You're like a sad, mopey machine. Can you just tell me what's going on?"

"*Slaughterhouse-Five* is the single most boring book ever written," I said.

"I don't necessarily disagree with you, but I *also* don't think this has anything to do with *Slaughterhouse-Five*. This started midway through *The Great Gatsby*."

"Do you tell time based on what books are being read?"

"It's July almost-done-with-*Miss-Pym-Disposes*," she replied. It was one of her mystery books, a novel by Josephine Tey. I'd caught her laughing out loud with it, curled up on a sofa on the back porch. *She* was certainly having one of the best summers of her life. All she did was read and cook and shop and go to the beach and beg me to take long walks with her. I did, as long as it was during the day. I didn't like being outside after eight anymore. The meteors had started to freak me out. It always felt like the sky was falling. Kit-Hale felt too much like a new permanent fixture in the universe. Like a second moon or something.

"But really," Mom continued, taking a bite of her toast and talking around it. "Are you okay, kid?"

I shrugged. "I'm not *not* okay."

"That's a start," she said. She dropped the toast onto her plate and brushed her hands against each other. "Are you excited for your dad to get here?"

I thought of the voice on the other end of the line. I resisted the urge to shrug again.

"I'm excited, yeah."

"I've been hearing you practice guitar more. Do you have something to play for him?"

"Maybe."

"It's been sounding good."

"Thanks."

"How did you like *The Great Gatsby*, anyway?"

"It was all right. I thought every character was kind of the worst."

"That might be the point."

"I figured."

Miriam took another bite of toast. "He's on a red-eye tonight, so he'll be here pretty early tomorrow. We can pick him up from the train station."

"Okay."

"I thought we could go into town today. Gloucester. If you wanted."

"Bookstores?"

"And vintage. You haven't worn that dress yet."

"I'm saving it," I said.

"For what?"

"For something special."

"Wear it today," she said. "And we'll go do something fun. I'll take you to that candy place."

"Candy House?"

"Yeah. It's been open since I was a kid, you know. My aunt used to take me. We'd get chocolate by the pound."

"Sounds like a lot of chocolate."

"It was. Come on. Come with me?"

"I don't know, Mom. I was just going to read. The quicker I get through *Slaughterhouse-Five*, the happier I'll be."

"Finish it later. We'll have a ceremonial fire in the backyard and offer it up as a sacrifice to the paperback gods."

"Really?"

"It wouldn't be the first book I've burned," Miriam said, a certain twinkle in her eye.

"All right," I said finally. "I'll get dressed."

Upstairs, I almost put on the blue dress, but something made me stop. Instead, I reached for my usual uniform of shorts and a T-shirt, then I paused to examine myself in the mirror.

I'd gotten tan in the past month. My hair had gotten longer. All the sun and the salt were doing interesting things to it, making it grittier, curlier, a little lighter. I'd stopped washing it every day. I let it tumble freely down my back. If it got sprayed with salt water, I let it air-dry in the sun.

I lifted one arm up and pressed my tongue to my skin. It tasted like salt.

"Anna!" Miriam called from downstairs. "The chocolate gods are calling, and I must go!"

I rolled my eyes but skipped downstairs to meet her.

We bought a truly obscene amount of chocolate from Candy House, which was a short drive from the cottage ("Most of this is for your dad," Mom had said. "You know how he feels about chocolate."), and then we stopped in Gloucester on the way back, hitting the two bookstores and Bananas and stopping for lunch and spending a lot of time just walking up and down Main Street.

By the time we got home, it was already evening, and Miriam made a huge salad and a batch of gazpacho for dinner. We ate it on the front porch, Mom with a frosted glass of white wine and me with lemonade, which had become something of a cottage staple, always in the fridge, always freshly made with an ancient citrus press Aunt Dora had kept in a cabinet above the fridge.

Mom was quiet. I think she'd gotten quieter as the day went on, as Everett's arrival got closer and closer. I wondered if she was regretting his coming here. I wondered if she had any idea he was dating someone. I wondered what she would think, if she knew. I wondered again if I was supposed to tell her. Did I owe it to her? Or was it none of my business? I honestly didn't know the answer. It was an impossible equation, and the variables kept changing. And I'd never been good at math anyway.

When we were done with dinner, I helped Miriam clean up the dishes, then we settled into the living room and put on a movie. Miriam was asleep within five minutes of the opening credits. She could read a book until three in the morning, but movies always put her right to sleep.

I checked the time on my phone. Almost eight. I'd been going to bed earlier and earlier, now that I had nothing to do at night, but I was wide awake. I watched a half hour of the movie before getting up for more lemonade and wandering out to the front porch for some air.

It was actually kind of a cool night; a wet, chilly breeze was blowing in across the water and raised goose bumps on my skin. I looked hard at the Motif, but it was too far away to tell if anyone was there. I took a sip of lemonade, then set the glass on the coffee table. Maybe I'd just go for a little walk. Maybe I'd just get close enough to see if they were there. I wouldn't say hi. I wouldn't announce myself. I'd just see, then I'd come back and get into bed and wake up and go get Everett. I'd just see. There wasn't any harm in that.

I started walking.

Kit-Hale was bright and large in the night sky, but there

weren't any meteors. I didn't go right to the Motif; I went back to the Country Store instead and found the same guy at the register. I brought two Idaho Spud bars up to the him, and he said:

"Aha! Back for more!"

"One for me, one for you," I said. "They're actually really good."

I took a dollar bill from my pocket, but he waved me away. "Your money's no good here," he said in a dramatic voice. "Let's do this."

We unwrapped the candy bars and took a bite at the same time, and he nodded appreciatively.

"Oh man," he said. "This is pretty excellent."

"Right?"

"Can't believe I've never tried one before," he said, popping the rest into his mouth. "I'm Shane, by the way." He held his hand out to me, and I shook it. "You local?"

"Anna. Not local, just staying here for the summer."

"Ahh, summer crowd. Well, I hope you live close. Gonna storm any minute now."

"Really?"

"I can feel it in this finger," he said, pointing to the pointer finger of his left hand. "Old soccer injury. Gets tingly before it rains."

"I better get going, then," I said.

"See you later!"

But I didn't go home.

I walked more quickly now, propelled forward by sheer curiosity and nosiness and yes, the fact that I missed them. I missed them, and I wanted to see them again.

I was wearing jean shorts and a T-shirt, and it was cool enough that I got goose bumps on my arms and legs. My hair blew around my face. I didn't run into a single other person on the way to the Motif, which lent a distinct air of creepiness to the night. The wind picked up the closer to the water I got, and by the time I reached the Motif, it had begun to rain. Thick, heavy drops of water that felt like tiny bullets on my skin. So Shane's finger was right.

The Motif was deserted. The rain was starting to pour down in earnest now. I should have gone home. The sky was opening up; the rain was falling in sheets; it was hard to see where I was going. I stumbled to the Motif, but the door was locked, of course, so I turned around, pressing my back up against it, trying to stay dry in the tiny overhang at the top of the door. A tremendous bolt of lightning lit up the sky, streaking from one end of the horizon to the other. It was followed almost immediately by a crash of thunder so loud I jumped, pushing myself against the door so hard I could have melted into it.

There weren't thunderstorms in Los Angeles. Not like this. I'd seen five, maybe six, in my entire life, and they were pale copies of the storm now raging in front of me. They were like a child's crayon rendering of a thunderstorm: nothing at all like the real thing. Gentle rain, gentle lightning, gentle thunder that made our neighbor's dog bark itself hoarse. This was violent and angry. I tried counting the seconds between the light and the sound, but they were practically on top of each other now. That meant the storm was right above me. That meant it wouldn't stop anytime soon.

My tennis sneakers were soaked and my hair was soaked and my clothes were soaked and I worried about my phone in my pocket; surely it was soaked by now, too. I braced myself to make a run for it, but what good would that do? I wouldn't be any less drenched by the time I got home, and I might slip and hurt myself—these shoes weren't exactly made for running.

So I just walked.

I stepped out from under the doorway and let the full force of the water hit me. Every time the lightning flashed across the sky, I braced myself for the crash of thunder. It was already better by the time I got home, seven seconds in between.

Miriam was standing in the doorway, lit from behind with the gentle yellow glow of the hall light. She had her phone in her hand, and when she saw me, she put her other hand over her heart.

I walked up the few steps to the porch and stood dripping in front of her.

"I was worried *sick*," she said.

"I went for a walk."

"In this?"

"It wasn't raining when I left," I said.

"Anna, I woke up, you weren't here, the door was unlocked, it's pouring rain—"

A rumble of thunder so loud and long it made my bones vibrate. Miriam looked past me and took a step onto the porch. The thunder actually seemed to calm her down.

"God, I miss storms like these," she said.

"You *like* this?"

"There's nothing like an East Coast thunderstorm."

"You don't think it's kind of ... scary?"

"Scary?" she repeated, laughing. "It's just nature. Although that doesn't mean you should go prancing around in it."

"I wasn't *prancing*."

"I called you a million times."

I took my phone out of my pocket. The screen was black. It was dripping wet.

"Oops," I said.

"Give that to me; we'll put it in rice," Miriam said, reaching for it. "Don't come inside until I get you a towel."

She disappeared into the house, and I saw the kitchen light go on. I turned around and watched the rain, so thick it looked like a gray curtain. A streak of lightning. Five seconds. Thunder.

Miriam came back a minute later holding an oversize beach towel. She held it behind me as I slipped off my shorts and T-shirt, letting them fall to the floor. I wrapped the towel around me and squeezed the ends of my hair out.

Miriam bent down and picked up my clothes and hung them over the swing, then she stepped back so I could come into the house. I kept the towel wrapped firmly around me. I was cold for the first time in what felt like ages. The house was noisy with rain. Miriam closed the front door and locked the dead bolt.

"You should get in the shower. Warm up a little. Why did you go for a walk?"

I shrugged. "I was bored. Wasn't tired."

Miriam put her hand on the side of my face and smiled sadly. "You never used to be so secretive," she said.

"What do you mean?" I asked, but I felt my ears go hot with the lie. Because I knew exactly what she meant.

"I just hope you know you can tell me anything."

"I know that," I mumbled, shrugging again slightly. I found I couldn't quite make eye contact with her.

She still had her hand on my cheek. She leaned in and kissed my forehead.

"I'm going to go to sleep. I love you, Anna."

"I love you, too."

She went upstairs. The steps creaked underneath her feet. They were familiar creaks now; I'd lived in this house long enough to know its sounds, what stairs were louder than others, what spots to avoid if I needed to get a glass of water in the middle of the night.

I waited until I heard her bedroom door shut, then I went upstairs and turned on the shower.

I stayed under the spray for a long time, but I didn't ever get quite warm enough.

quiet symphony

Miriam woke me up early the next morning, throwing shorts and a T-shirt onto the bed. I pulled them on and slipped on a Rockport sweatshirt, too; the thunderstorm had left a chill in the air, and my bedroom was cool and felt slightly damp, even though the windows had been closed for the entire night.

The morning sky was clear and brilliantly colored in swirls of lavender and baby blue, and I peeked out the front door to see that pools of water had collected in the front yard and that the street had turned into a shallow stream.

"It rained all night," Miriam said, coming up behind me with a cup of coffee in her hands. She took a sip and looked over my head. "Did you sleep okay?"

"Fine."

"Did the thunder keep you up at all?"

I shrugged. The truth was, last night felt like a strange dream, and the thunder was only a fuzzy memory. I'd fallen asleep quickly, waking up only when Miriam threw clothes at me.

"We'll leave to get your dad in ten minutes," she said.

A chilly breeze blew in from the front yard. "Is it supposed to rain again?"

"Nope. This cool spell will burn off by one or two. Enjoy it while it lasts."

She went back into the kitchen, and I shut the door and followed her, pouring myself a bowl of cereal while she sat at the table and sipped her coffee.

"I thought I'd drop you off with the car and then walk home. Give you and your dad some alone time," she said.

"If you want to. How far of a walk is it?"

"Fifteen or twenty minutes. It'll feel nice, in this breeze."

"Okay."

"We can all meet up for lunch somewhere. Anywhere you want. Or maybe your dad will want to pick."

"Sounds good." I poured oat milk into my cereal and ate it standing up at the counter.

"You look tired," Miriam noted.

"Kind of."

"Are you excited to see your dad?"

"I will be when I wake up a little."

"I don't think I slept a wink."

"How come?"

"I never used to sleep during thunderstorms. Something about...all the electricity in the air. Everything feels charged.

Crackling." She paused, sipped her coffee. "There was a huge thunderstorm when I was your age. Just like the one last night. Dramatic and loud and heavy. I was in bed, reading, trying to get tired. There was this huge crash. I thought it was part of the storm, but then I heard this wailing noise. I just lay in bed, listening to it, trying to figure out what it was....It sounded like a ghost. Or an animal." Another pause. She looked far-away, remembering. "Eventually I realized it was my aunt. She'd gotten up to get a glass of water and tripped. Fallen down the stairs. She broke her ankle. She was lucky that was all she broke. I found her howling at the bottom of the stair-case, right over there. Had to drive her to the hospital in the pouring rain. Didn't know how to drive, but I figured it out."

"Why didn't you call an ambulance?"

"Phone lines were out," she said. "No cell phones back then. Speaking of, we should leave yours in rice until tomor-row morning."

"Does that really work?"

"According to the internet: sometimes."

I finished my cereal and rinsed out the bowl in the sink. Miriam put the rest of her coffee in a to-go cup. She kissed me on the temple.

"Thank you for not breaking your ankle last night," I said.

"Little scares me more than the thought of you behind the wheel," she said seriously. "I woke up thirsty but just drank from the tap."

"I bet I'll be an excellent driver."

"In a couple of years, sure."

She didn't seem convinced.

She grabbed her purse and the anchor key ring, and we walked outside. I could feel the moisture in the air and was glad I'd grabbed a sweatshirt. It wasn't *cold*, really, but it made everything feel sort of heavy and thick, like you were pushing through the air to get to where you were going. I slid into the passenger seat of the station wagon and waited as Miriam walked around to the driver's side. She was wearing jean shorts and a light purple Henley with a raw hem. She'd cut it herself, and for a while she'd worn the extra fabric as a headband, until I'd begged her not to. It used to be my father's, so on her it was oversized and slouchy, but by cutting six or seven inches off, she'd made it slightly cropped and cool.

I wondered if you were supposed to still wear your exhusband's clothes.

But they weren't officially exes yet, I reminded myself.

They hadn't even gotten the paperwork.

It was just a few minutes to the train station. Miriam parked and turned the car off and handed me the keys.

"Tell your dad I'll see him later, okay?"

"You're not going to wait?"

"I just want this to be special. You and him. I'll see you in a few hours."

She got out of the car, and I followed her. She was wearing her biggest pair of black sunglasses, the ones that covered half her face. Her hair was piled up in a messy bun. She wore dirty white tennis sneakers and a small black cross-body purse. I thought I'd never be as cool as Miriam was, and the most annoying thing was that she wasn't even trying. She'd probably gotten dressed in the dark. She'd probably done her hair on the toilet, peeing. Nothing was fair in this entire world.

"Train should be here in five minutes," she said, holding her arms out to me. I walked into her embrace. Miriam liked to hug you like you were going off on some big adventure, like she wasn't sure when she'd see you again. She smelled like faint perfume sprayed on the day before and coffee from that morning. She kissed my hair and pulled away. "See you later, kid."

I watched her walk away for a moment, then locked the car and put the keys into my pocket. I made my way onto the train platform. Quite a few people were waiting to board the train; once it reached this station, it turned around and went back to Boston. Businesspeople in suits holding briefcases. A group of teenage girls laughing about something. A tired mom with three kids and a coffee the size of her head.

I heard the train whistle from far away. I could just see it down the track, making its way slowly toward us. It was the commuter rail, and at this time of day, it would be pretty empty, filling up with every stop it made back toward Boston.

A few minutes later and it had pulled into the station in front of me. The doors swished open, and a scattering of people got out, including Everett Bell, in jeans and a faded old band T-shirt and a pair of Ray-Bans. He had his old green utility jacket slung over his arm. He pulled a small wheeled suitcase and held a coffee in his other hand. He paused for a second on the platform, turning his face up to the sky, and took a deep breath, like he was filling his lungs with the air of this town. Then he turned, saw me, raised his coffee hand in a wave, and walked over.

"Hi, Dad."

"My Worm," he said, letting go of the suitcase and hugging me in the exact opposite way Miriam had just hugged me. Her way had been *I don't know when I'll see you next*; this way was *I'm never letting you out of my sight again.* He pulled away, holding me at arm's length. The coffee cup was empty; otherwise, he would have spilled it all over me. He spotted a trash can and let it sail through the air, sinking the shot, nothing but net. "That was a journey of epic proportions," he said. "I advise you never to take the commuter rail at such an ungodly hour, if you can help it."

"Not the best?"

"Not the best."

"But you're here now."

"And what a day," he said, holding his arms out wide, almost smacking a passing commuter in the face. I grabbed his arms and pulled them down. "Did it storm last night?"

"Yeah, how'd you know?"

"I can smell it," he said. "Smells like worms."

"Gross."

"You don't smell that? Worms and dirt."

"I don't think I know what worms smell like."

"Well, breathe it in, Worm, because now you do."

We walked to the car. Dad put his suitcase in the back seat and spent a few moments stretching before he got into the driver's seat.

"Can't believe this car is still functional," he said when I'd climbed into the passenger side. He started the engine, and we were off. He knew the way without using maps, and we were quiet as he navigated the skinny streets of Rockport, pulling up in front of the bed-and-breakfast a few minutes later. A sign out front said LANTANA HOUSE. It had a wide front porch, and it looked like a proper old New England mansion. Dad pulled the car around the back to the small parking lot, and we got out again.

"Too early to check in," he said. "I'll just drop my luggage off with the front desk. Wait here and I'll be out in a second."

I leaned against the car as he ran inside, and he was back in under a minute, somehow having both changed into shorts and dropped his suitcase off in record time. He grabbed my hand and pulled me enthusiastically away from the inn.

"What about the car?"

"It'll be fine," he called over his shoulder.

We walked down Broadway toward the water, taking a left on Mount Pleasant Street and veering right toward Bearskin Neck. When we reached the top of it, he stopped so abruptly I almost ran into him. He just stared for a moment. I couldn't tell his expression behind his sunglasses, but he was perfectly motionless, perfectly quiet, just looking.

"Wow," he said finally. "It looks exactly the same. *Exactly* the same. I used to come here every single day. I mean...Even the *stores* are the same. The Country Store! The Fudgery!"

He started pulling me again. We walked all the way down Bearskin Neck, all the way to the end, to the stone jetty, and we kept walking, picking our way carefully from rock to rock, until we'd reached the very last one, until we couldn't go any farther or end up in the ocean.

We sat down and let our legs hang over the water. He put his arm around me. The day was getting warmer already, and I felt cozy in my sweatshirt. Dad smelled like the staleness of an airplane and cheap coffee and like how I imagined *tired* would smell.

"Are you exhausted?" I asked.

"I could fall asleep right here," he replied.

"You could come back to the cottage and take a nap."

"The lady at the inn said my room would be ready soon."

The sun was bright as it reflected off the water. I squinted out as far as I could see. Fishing boats dotted the water, some of them out so early they were coming home now. I bet some of them had been out for days. The people on board would be filthy and tired and smelling of fish.

Dad glanced over at me, took off his sunglasses, and slid them onto my face. The world got pleasantly darker at once.

"You know *The Perfect Storm*?" he asked.

"The book?"

"The movie."

I shook my head. "No, it's a book. Mom once recommended it to a high school girl who hadn't gotten into the college she wanted to go to."

Everett laughed, a big belly, slightly-delusional-with-exhaustion laugh. "That sounds like your mother, yeah. Well, it was a book *and* a movie. You know what it's about?"

"A fishing thing?"

"A fishing boat that left harbor and never came back. Trapped in a storm. Never found the wreckage."

"That's terrible."

"They left from just over there. Gloucester Harbor. Ship was called the *Andrea Gail*."

"Gale," I said quietly. "That's ironic."

"Not that kind of gale," he corrected. "Gail. Like the name."

"Still."

He pushed himself up, then offered me a hand and helped me to my feet.

"I'm asleep standing up," he explained. "I'll meet you and Miriam for lunch."

We walked slowly back to the inn, back up Bearskin Neck and Broadway.

"Get in," Dad said when we reached the station wagon. "I'll drive this back to your mom's and walk back."

We were quiet on the short ride, and it was only when we pulled into the cottage's driveway that he spoke again.

"What happened to her?" he asked.

"What happened to who?"

"To the girl who didn't get into college."

"Oh. She went to her second choice. She was valedictorian. She's an astronomer now. She named some new star cluster after Miriam."

"Of course she did." Dad smiled. It was impossible to know what that smile meant. Maybe it just meant he was tired.

He put his hand to my cheek, and I smiled. Then we both got out of the car, and he walked away down the street.

Miriam was in the back room when I got home, all the windows open, a glass of lemonade on the coffee table in front of her. She was reading—of course—an old and tattered paperback copy of *The Perfect Storm*.

"Where'd you get that?" I asked her.

"Inside somewhere. Why?"

"When did you start reading it?"

"About a half hour ago. Why?"

"What made you want to read that?"

"I needed a break from Dorothy Sayers. *Why?*"

The third *why* was a bit annoyed. I shook my head. It was impossible to explain, but it was the most Miriam thing in the world to start reading a book at the exact minute my father and I started talking about it.

"Haven't you read that before?" I asked, still not answering her persistent *why*.

"Of course I have," she said. "You're being very strange about this book. How is your father?"

"He's good. Tired."

"Are those his sunglasses?"

I touched my face. I'd forgotten I was wearing them. I pushed them to the top of my head. "Yup."

"They look cute on you. Are we going to meet for lunch?"

"He wants to go to Roy Moore."

She smiled. "I could have guessed. What time?"

"One."

"Go get a book. We'll read out here together."

I didn't want to read, but I couldn't think of anything else to do, so I went and got *Slaughterhouse-Five* and brought it to the porch. I made myself comfortable on a wicker armchair (as comfortable as one can make oneself on a wicker armchair) and tried to lose myself in the writing, to reach that place Miriam always managed to reach, where the outside world melts away and your eyes glaze over and hours pass without your even noticing.

No offense to Vonnegut, but it just wasn't happening.

The plot was confusing and strange; the main character, Billy, is constantly time traveling through his life, zipping forward or winding backward, making it hard to follow and complicated to keep things straight.

I slogged my way through a chapter before my mind turned off completely and I realized I'd read five pages without retaining a single scrap of information. I backtracked until I found something vaguely familiar, then started again.

On page two I realized I'd spent the past five minutes thinking about what I'd order at lunch. I backtracked again.

I looked up and realized Miriam was watching me. She was smiling. "Still not loving that book, huh?"

"It's *terrible*."

"It's not my favorite of his," she admitted, which was about as critical of a book as she got.

"It's boring. It's confusing. It's pointless. Time travel is weird."

"Weird? How so?"

"Um, because it's impossible? But we're also obsessed with it, as a construct?"

"Well, it's in intriguing idea," she said thoughtfully. "I'd love to be able to travel in time. I'd go back and give my younger self a big old hug and maybe give her a hint or two on how things are gonna go for her."

"But if you did that, you would change the entire history of the *world*," I argued.

"Good thing it's impossible, then," she said, winking. She glanced at her watch. "Almost time to go. I think I'll change quick."

She was still wearing Dad's old Henley. I nodded as she stood and went upstairs.

She'd left her phone on the coffee table. I tapped the screen to check the time; it was twelve thirty. We'd been sitting here for a while. I guess the time flew when you were reading the same few pages of the same boring book over and over again.

I went to the kitchen for some water and peered into the receptacle that held a boatload of rice and my possibly broken phone. Poor phone. I should have left it behind, but I hadn't known it was going to rain. Everett always knew when it was going to rain. He was sort of obsessed with the weather and had no fewer than four apps on his phone to show him Doppler radar and weather patterns and predictions. He always knew if you should bring a light jacket or if you'd be fine in short sleeves. He always knew if you should take the umbrella or leave it. He always knew if the sun would come out from behind the clouds by the time you'd walked to the beach.

Miriam was more of a fly-by-the-seat-of-her-pants person, at least when it came to weather. She often underdressed or overdressed, and she never consulted an app before she decided what to wear.

Roy Moore Lobster Co. was on Bearskin Neck, so when Miriam was done changing, we set off, walking slowly, because we had plenty of time to get there. It had turned into the most beautiful day. The air felt cleaned after the storm, like the rain had filtered the very oxygen around us. And it was warm without a hint of mugginess, the perfect temperature. I'd left my sweatshirt at home. Miriam had changed into an ankle-length sundress with thin straps and a muted floral design. She took my hand in hers while we walked, and I let her, for a minute, and then pulled away.

"When you were a kid, you'd let me hold your hand forever," she said, affecting a mournful tone, pulling me close to her quickly, and kissing the side of my head.

"When I was a kid, it was your job to keep me safe. I

probably would have run right into traffic otherwise. No danger of that now."

"It's still my job to keep you safe," she replied quietly, strangely serious as she pulled away again, holding her own hands in front of her in lieu of holding mine.

She was acting a little weird. Almost...nervous. Was she nervous to see my father? Had she put on a little blush, a little lip gloss, a little mascara? Miriam rarely wore makeup. I don't think I'd seen her in blush this entire summer. She'd once told me that blush was her secret weapon, her ace in the hole, that a little blush boosted her confidence more than any other kind of makeup.

"You don't *need* makeup," she'd said when I was twelve or thirteen. "No woman *needs* makeup. But you can use it if you *want* to. There's a difference there, a huge difference, between the need and the want. You got it?"

"I think so," I'd replied, not really getting it at all.

"And it's never for anybody else," she'd continued. "If you want to wear it, you wear it for *you*. Not for them. For *you*, Anna. Always."

That I'd understood.

So why was Miriam choosing this moment to wear blush for herself? The *only* way that made sense was if she wasn't actually wearing the blush for herself at all. If she was actually wearing it for—

"Everett!"

I was so deep in my head that I hadn't realized we'd reached

Roy Moore. And there, standing in front of the small facade, squatting down to pet a small yellow lab puppy, was my father. He'd changed his shirt and was wearing an old baseball cap he'd had since he was a teenager. He took it with him whenever he went on vacation. It was a super-faded denim with an embroidered lobster on it. Basically—the perfect hat for the current situation.

"Miriam," he said warmly. He stood up, smiled at the dog's owner, then opened his arms to hug Mom. I studied that hug carefully, and it was completely free of awkwardness or hesitation. It was a nice hug. It lasted a normal amount of time. When they broke apart, he grabbed me and pulled me close to him, like it had been weeks since he'd seen me instead of just hours. "Man, it's trippy to be back here," he said when he released me.

"It's exactly the same, right?" Miriam replied.

"Exactly," he agreed. "I mean...the Fudgery? Miriam, *the Fudgery* is still here!"

She smiled. "I know. And it's still just as good."

"Your mom always got the same kind of fudge," Dad said. "Something with nuts. Very gross, if you ask me. I preferred chocolate."

"We should get some after lunch," Miriam said.

"Ugh! The Fudgery!" Dad proclaimed in lieu of a yes.

The man with the dog walked away, and my dad stared wistfully after it. He'd always wanted a dog, but Miriam was desperately allergic. Would he get one now that they weren't together? Had he had that thought when they were splitting up: *Man, now I can finally get a dog.*

"What a cutie, right?" he asked me.

"Yeah, Dad," I said, my voice just a little flat. "Super cute."

We got a table on the back patio of the restaurant, so close to the harbor you could jump into it from where we were sitting. Dad was full of energy after his nap and talked nonstop, and Miriam mostly just smiled and nodded as he updated us on the goings-on back home.

"I'm going to do a few East Coast clients while I'm out here. Isn't that cool? Little tattoo shop in Gloucester is letting me hijack their space for a couple of sessions."

"You were never able to just take a damn vacation, B," Mom said, and although her tone was light and breezy, I wondered if there was some deeper meaning there. Is that one of the reasons they broke up? Was my father a workaholic who wasn't able to ever truly relax?

Miriam was kind of a workaholic, too, at least as far as the bookstore was concerned, but she was definitely able to take steps away from it. I tried to remember the vacations we'd taken when I was younger. Was it hard to get my dad to pull away from his work?

I knew I had to stop analyzing every single thing they did and said, I knew it wasn't healthy, but...It was hard to stop. The way my dad foresaw the exact moment Miriam would drop her napkin on the floor, the way he stopped it from blowing away by stepping on it with his shoe and simultaneously handing her a fresh one from the napkin holder. The way Miriam wordlessly gave him her pot of melted butter when he finished his before her, and the way he knew she was holding it out to him and took it without even looking up to confirm. The way she reached for her water glass with her right hand while he reached for one of my fries with his right hand, the perfect mirror images of each other. Had they always been like this? Had I really never noticed before, how seamlessly they complemented each other? *How* had I missed this quiet symphony that had been happening around me for my entire life?

"Anna, you're really mulling over that fry," Dad said, hitting my fry with the one he'd stolen from me.

"Can't decide if I want ketchup or mayonnaise," I said.

"Oh, that's easy," he replied.

He plucked the fry out of my hand. He dipped it in the pot of mayonnaise, then dipped it again in the pot of ketchup.

Then he popped it into his mouth while Miriam laughed cheerfully from across the table.

Everything was confusing, and nothing made sense.

Mom made gazpacho for dinner (she had recently announced that one of her summer goals was finding the perfect gazpacho recipe, and although I was beginning to get tired of cold soup, I didn't dare tell *her* that, because it brought her so much damn *joy* to cook it every few days), and by the time she was done, there were more tomato guts on the walls of the kitchen than there were in our bowls. She and Dad drank chilled white wine, and I stuck with lemonade. We ate at the kitchen table with all the windows opened wide because the evening air was cool and made the kitchen smell like mint and seaweed and the pipe our neighbor smoked in his front yard, hoping his wife wouldn't catch him.

We were planning a beach day for tomorrow, and Miriam and Everett were ironing out logistics: what time we'd meet, how long we'd stay, who'd pick up lunch beforehand.

"Wingaersheek Beach," Dad said, finishing the last bit of

gazpacho in his bowl and leaning back in his chair. "Probably my favorite beach in the whole wide world."

"It's great," I agreed. "We went out on the sandbar. Kind of creepy, but also cool."

"The best things in life are 'kind of creepy, but also cool,'" Dad said. "The best things in life are *also* this gazpacho. Miriam, you've outdone yourself."

Mom smiled and inclined her wineglass toward him before having a sip. "Many lesser recipes came before this one. I think I've almost nailed it."

"I don't see how it can get much better."

"She put olives in one batch," I said. "That was a rough night."

"They weren't the right kind of olives," Miriam said. "I still think olives could work."

"Olives, interesting. Castelvetrano?" Everett asked.

"That's what I *should* have used," Miriam replied.

"Can never go wrong with Castelvetranos."

"Agreed," Miriam said, reaching for my bowl and stacking it on top of hers, then adding Everett's to the pile. "I'll clean up in here. Why don't you two go out on the porch and get comfortable? Or, Everett, you're probably exhausted. Do you want to get going?"

"I have a few more minutes left in me," he said. "To digest and sit and talk to my daughter."

"Kind of gross, when you put it that way," I said.

"Bodies fall into the 'kind of creepy, but also cool' category,"

Everett said, getting up from the table. I followed him onto the front porch, and we made ourselves comfortable on the swing. It wasn't quite dark enough for Kit-Hale yet. Everett leaned back against one arm of the swing, and I leaned against the other, facing him. "So," he said, "tell me everything. Are you very sick of Rockport yet?"

"Not at all," I said with a smile. "I like it here. It's kind of like the town that time forgot."

"Tell me about it."

"And it's nice not having to *do* anything. Like see people or make plans. I've been watching a lot of movies."

"What else?" He reached over and touched the moonstone ring. And I didn't know if it was that gesture, or if it was something else, but Emmy and Beck came to mind, and suddenly I missed them, a lot, and felt really, really guilty for completely avoiding them the last two weeks.

"Oh, I don't know," I said after a minute, remembering that he'd asked me a question. "I guess I sort of made some friends."

"Of course you did, because you're the coolest person in the world, and wherever you go, people are like, 'Hey, is that the coolest person in the world?' and then whoever they're with is like, 'Yeah, I think it is; let's go say hi!'"

"That's basically the exact opposite of my experience," I said.

"Well, tell me about them." He had a sip of his wine and waited, his full attention on me. That was something both he

and Miriam did: When they were listening, they were *really,
really* listening. It was almost a little exposing, like having a
spotlight aimed at your head.

"I met them around Bearskin Neck. And we've just been
hanging out. Riding bikes and playing cards and stuff."

"Can I meet them?"

"Maybe. I haven't seen them for a couple of weeks. We were
supposed to meet at the fireworks, but they didn't show up
and..."

"Ahh," Dad said, nodding his head knowingly, a gesture
that immediately irritated me.

"What do you mean *Ahh*?"

"Might I give you a *tiny* piece of feedback, Worm?"

"Okay..."

"It has come to my attention that my darling daughter, who
I love dearly and would do anything for, might tend to hold
just the *slightest* bit of a grudge."

"I have no idea what you're talking about," I said, feeling
my face flush.

He looked toward the open kitchen windows, then lowered
his voice and said, "I ran into Jennica's mom at the supermar-
ket the other day."

I looked down at my hands but didn't say anything.

"She said how nice it is that Jennica's been spending so
much time with you this summer. I said, that's strange, because
Anna's been on the East Coast for a month. She said no, no,
that can't be right, because Jennica just spent the night at

Anna's house this past Saturday." Everett put his hand on my ankle and squeezed. "Care to add any insight here, Worm?"

"I can't really speak for Jennica. I mean, it sounds like she's not being super truthful," I said, avoiding his burning eye contact.

"But it got me thinking, you know. I can't remember the last time I saw Jennica. It's been months. That's on me, for not noticing. But after that conversation with Jennica's mom, it seems like maybe something happened between you girls?"

"It's nothing," I said quickly. "Jennica doesn't want to be friends anymore and . . . Mom doesn't know, okay? Could you not say anything?"

"What happened, honey? Jennica is your best friend."

"*Was.*"

"This is kind of what I'm talking about, Anna. People make mistakes. Jennica, these new friends of yours . . . Sometimes it's worth it to give people the benefit of the doubt, to be the bigger person and just let bygones be bygones."

"You don't even know what happened. You don't even know what the bygones *are.*" I was getting angry now, raising my voice a little, but I couldn't help it. I didn't need my dad to fly all the way across the country just to sit here and give me a lecture on friendship.

"To be fair, I *did* ask you what the bygones were, and you are deciding not to tell me. So I don't have much to go on here. All I know is that Jennica has been a good friend to you. Maybe it would be worth it to extend the old olive branch?"

"I'm about to hit you over the head with the olive branch," I mumbled.

He laughed at that, then took his hand off my ankle. "I'm sorry if I'm coming on a little strong, Anna. I haven't seen you in so long; maybe I'm trying to get a whole month's worth of parenting into one makeup session."

"You don't need to parent me about this," I said, still mumbling. "I have it under control."

"Okay, no more parenting." He took a sip of wine. "Okay, just *one* more parenting. The last thing I'll say, I promise: Maybe you just give these new friends another chance. Maybe they have a perfectly good reason for not being there. Just hear 'em out, and if you don't like what they have to say, you can take the olive branch right back and throw it away for good."

"I'll think about it."

"What are you thinking about?" Miriam said, opening the front door and stepping onto the porch.

"Her unnatural hatred of olives," Everett replied, winking at me.

Miriam walked to the railing and peered up at the sky. It was almost dark enough now that you could just about see Kit-Hale. Dad hadn't noticed yet. Miriam turned around, beaming.

"Everett, you remember the summer we met? The comet?"

"Of course I do."

"Look." She pointed up. He stood and joined her next to the railing and followed her gaze.

"No way," he said.

"It's back. Can you believe it?"

"What are the odds," he said.

Staring at their backs, side by side like that, I could almost imagine them as teenagers, my age, running around Rockport and falling in love under the same comet that now blazed above them.

And I felt a weird...

A tug, almost.

In the back of my mind.

A weird sense of déjà vu that made me dizzy.

I cleared my throat loudly to ruin the moment.

Everett turned around and swayed a little on the spot.

"Whoops. I think I just hit my limit," he said.

"Go, get some sleep," Miriam commanded, taking his wineglass from him. "You want me to drive you?"

"Nah, I'll be fine walking. I want to see some more of this comet," he said. "Come here and give me a hug, Worm."

I did, and he kissed my cheek before he pulled away.

"See you bright and early," he said to Miriam. "I'll walk over. And thank you again for dinner. It was perfect."

"Anytime," she said.

We watched him walk down the road, then Miriam dumped the rest of his wine into her glass.

"What were you guys talking about?" she asked as we sat on the swing again.

"Nothing much. Catching up."

"Nice to have him here?"

"Of course."

She yawned loudly. "He seems like he's doing well."

"Sure, I guess."

"I think I need to get in bed with a book. You can probably take your phone out of the rice now."

"Maybe I'll just leave it in overnight again, to be safe."

"If you need me, you know where to find me," she said, and went inside the cottage. I listened to her walking around the first floor for a minute before she headed upstairs to her bedroom.

Kit-Hale was in full glory now, and the evening was illuminated with its glow.

My conversation with my dad had left me slightly irritated and a little thrown off. I didn't like that he'd run into Jennica's mom. I didn't like that Jennica was lying about hanging out with me. I didn't like that she'd said she slept over at my house. Where was she actually, and why was she using me as a cover? Maybe she didn't want to tell her parents that we weren't speaking, either, but I still didn't like being an excuse for her. It made me feel used and icky.

And I didn't like what my dad said about my holding grudges. I wasn't holding a grudge against Emmy and Beck; I was just giving them space. If they'd wanted to meet me at the fisherman statue, they would have been there. Not showing up sent a pretty clear message.

But Everett's voice had firmly wormed its way into my

head, and a sliver of doubt was beginning to form in my brain. Maybe I *was* overreacting? Maybe Emmy and Beck had an explanation for not being there? Maybe I *did* sometimes, occasionally, every now and then, assume the worst in people?

"Ugh," I said aloud, because as irritated as I felt with my father, I couldn't help seeing that he was right. Of course he was right. I was being ridiculous. I needed to go find Emmy and Beck.

I was up and walking before I even realized I'd told my legs to move, and I gave a wary look up at the sky, just to make sure I didn't see any storm clouds. But it was a clear night, and Kit-Hale was on full display, and the occasional meteor zoomed among the stars, and I felt absolutely certain, deep down in my belly, that Emmy and Beck would be by the Motif when I got there. I walked quickly, fidgeting as I went, nervously touching the moonstone ring, unable to be still—

And they were.

They sat cross-legged on the ground, playing cards in their hands and a draw pile between them. As I got closer, I could hear Beck laboriously going over the rules of poker for what sounded like (by the tone of his voice) the eightieth or ninetieth time.

"So a flush beats a straight," Emmy repeated carefully, her face scrunched up in concentration. "But a full house beats them both? But a straight flush beats a full house? And what about four of a kind again?"

"Four of a kind beats everything but a straight and royal

flush," I chimed in helpfully, and Emmy dropped her cards in excitement, leaped up, and dove into my arms in one fluid movement.

"Anna! Anna, I thought you went back to California! After we didn't see you at the fireworks and you never came back to the Motif, I thought you must have gone home without saying goodbye!"

"No, no, I didn't go home," I said as she pulled away. "I just...I've been really busy. I'm sorry."

Beck was getting to his feet slowly. He stuck his hands into his pockets and looked significantly less happy to see me than Emmy did.

"Hey," he said.

"Hi," I replied.

"What happened at the fireworks?" he said, and Emmy shot him a look that clearly meant *we've already talked about this and you promised not to say anything.*

"What do you mean what happened?" I asked him.

"We waited for, like, a half hour," he said.

"In front of the statue? What time did you get there? I was there right when they ended."

"We were right there," Beck said, shrugging. "Not sure what happened."

"It's fine," Emmy insisted. "It was super crowded. We just missed each other."

"I was there," I promised, and I felt that weird tug again....

Like there was something…something I could almost grab on to but couldn't quite reach.

"I know you were," she said. "I swear I saw you, but when I got to where you were standing, you'd already been swallowed by the masses. Some guy gave me his glow-in-the-dark headband, though. That was fun."

My stomach gave a weird little flip. I remembered the stranger taking the glow band off his head and putting it gently on mine. Did the same guy give another glow band to Emmy? Had we really been that close and just not found each other?

"I'm sorry," I said, mostly to her, because Beck was still acting like a jerk. "I really *was* there. But there were a lot of people. We must have missed each other, like you said."

"I'm sorry, too!" she said. "But I'm so happy you didn't go back to California!"

We both looked at Beck. After a moment, he removed his hands from his pockets and said, "I'm sorry, too, Anna. Want to play?"

He dealt me in, and we sat in a circle, playing the slowest game of poker that had probably ever been played, because Emmy was absolutely hopeless at it. She couldn't keep her mind on the game—that was the problem. I could practically see her daydreaming, losing her concentration, a million miles away as we patiently waited for her to figure out what the cards in her hand meant.

Beck played five-card draw, just like my dad, and he was

pretty good at it, too. He won the first two rounds, but in the third, I came out with four aces and crushed him. He shook his head and plucked Emmy's cards out of her hand, examining them.

"Emmy, you had two kings and two fives and one jack and you didn't draw a single card? You should have tried for a full house!" he said.

"I liked these cards. It felt like the kings were a married couple, and they have a teenage son named Jack, and then twin five-year-olds. I didn't want to split them up. Jack isn't ready to leave the house," Emmy explained.

Beck slapped his hands over his face. "You're hopeless," he mumbled through his fingers.

"Maybe Beck won't make me play poker anymore, now that you're back," Emmy said to me. She spread her legs long in front of her, stretching, reaching her arms overhead, then folding her body down over her knees. It reminded me of something Jennica would do. She'd taken gymnastics as a kid, and although she didn't do it anymore, she still stretched like a gymnast: elegantly folding and contorting her body in ways I would never be able to achieve. "Oh, did you ever finish *The Great Gatsby*?" she asked, sitting up.

I nodded. "I've moved on to *Slaughterhouse-Five*."

"I love Vonnegut!" Beck said.

"All men love Vonnegut," Emmy retorted, and she pushed Beck half-heartedly, then used his shoulder to heave herself up. I couldn't help noticing that she left her hand there just a beat too long, and he looked up at her and smiled in a way that felt quietly intimate, like I was intruding on a private moment. Then the moment was over, and Emmy was balancing on pylons, hopping from one to the next quickly. I would definitely fall right into the ocean if I tried to do that.

"I'm bored," she complained.

"We could go get fudge?" Beck suggested, fitting his playing cards back into their cardboard home.

"I'm sick of fudge," she whined.

"We could ride bikes?" I said.

"I'm sick of riding bikes."

"We could go swimming?"

"I'm sick of swimming."

"You could go home so Anna and I don't have to listen to you complaining anymore?" Beck said, and she scowled at him as he turned to smile at me.

"I wish we could do something *really* fun," she said.

"Like what?" I asked.

"Rob a bank?" Beck guessed.

"If I knew what I wanted to do, I would just tell you," Emmy said sadly, crossing her arms and sitting down on one of the higher pylons, her legs dangling a few inches from the ground.

"I know what we can do," Beck announced after a minute, standing up and swinging Emmy's backpack onto his back (a fact I tucked away for later because it seemed important—he had never carried her backpack before!).

"What?" Emmy asked.

"Just follow me, whiny-pants."

So we followed him, Emmy and I bringing up the rear as he steered us up Bearskin Neck and away from the water, just a ten-or-so-minute walk before we crossed a narrow street and found ourselves at the entrance of a small playground, with swings and a slide and a merry-go-round and a few of those plastic animals with springs for legs that you sit and bounce around on.

"Oh, I *love* swings," Emmy said, making her way to one right away, and I heard Beck whisper under his breath, "I know."

I stepped onto the merry-go-round, and Beck followed, putting his hands on one of the metal bars as I situated myself in the middle. He began to run, spinning the merry-go-round as he went, faster and faster in its endless orbit around nothing.

I laughed as Beck let go of the bar, falling backward into the sand and watching my swift journey to nowhere. When the merry-go-round finally came to a stop, I waited until the world stopped spinning, then I hopped up and joined Emmy on the swings. Beck was on the other side of the playground, attempting to complete an impressively long monkey bar course.

"*Soooo*," I said, keeping my voice low.

"So, what?" she asked, but she was already smiling, and I could tell she knew exactly what I was about to say.

"You and Beck. Did something…"

Her smile got even bigger.

"We kissed," she said.

"You kissed!" I shrieked, just a bit too loud. She shushed me frantically, but I didn't think Beck heard. "Emmy! Details!"

"Well, honestly, I think we got used to having you around. When we didn't see you for so long, we kept, like, fighting with each other. About the silliest things. Like what to do, what flavor ice cream to split, where to meet. Really, really weird fights. And then just a few nights ago, actually...I don't know how it happened. We were just kind of sitting there, watching the sky. There were all these meteors, just tons and tons, streaking past the sky. And I looked over, and he was looking at me, and he leaned over really quickly and..." She paused and smiled. "It was really nice."

"Wow. I got chills," I said, showing her my arms. "So you are..."

"I don't know. I guess so. We haven't talked about it, but we *did* kiss again last night."

"I'm happy for you," I said. "And I'm happy for Beck. He's had a crush on you forever."

Emmy laughed. "Well, we've only known each other for a couple of months, but yeah. It's kinda nice." She paused and bit her lip. "It doesn't weird you out or anything?"

"Not at all. Luckily, I like you both as friends, so there's no competition," I added.

Emmy laughed. "That's not what I meant! I just meant, I hope you don't feel like a..."

"Third wheel?" I guessed. She nodded. "Not at all. I'm just happy."

"Okay, good. Oh, and I met his brother! He's really nice. His name's Billy."

"That's my uncle's name," I said as Beck finally gave up on the monkey bars and made his way over to us.

"Jumping contest," he said, taking a seat on the open swing beside Emmy. "Losers buy the winner ice cream."

"Deal," Emmy and I agreed at once.

It was a miracle one of us didn't break a leg, and in the end, Beck won by just a hair. I walked home by myself, thinking about Emmy and Beck and how nice it was that they'd finally gotten together. I could tell they were both really, really happy. They kept looking at each other when they thought I wasn't paying attention, and by the end of the night they must have touched each other's arms a total of forty-seven million times.

I took a shower when I got home, towel-dried my hair, then changed into clean pajamas. I tried to shut the dresser drawer with my hip but bumped it too hard, sending my copy of *The Great Gatsby* tumbling off the top. I knelt down to pick it up; the dust jacket had shifted, revealing an inscription underneath the flap. The words were faded and old:

To my little Emmy. Never be a Daisy.
You're so much more. Love, Auntie

Had I somehow switched my copy of the book with Emmy's? I didn't know how I'd managed to do that. I stared at the words for another minute or so, blinking, confused, before

I realized it was so hot in my room I was already starting to sweat again.

I set the book back on my dresser and went to turn on the window fan.

To my little Emmy.

Emmy's copy of *The Great Gatsby* had been brand-new.

The book on my dresser was old and worn—definitely the copy Miriam had given me.

But I guess...I guess I was wrong about that. Because this was definitely Emmy's. I mean, it had her name in it. I'd take it to her tomorrow night.

I pulled the covers back on my bed, then hung the towel up on a hook and slipped on my pajamas. Why was I so hot all of a sudden? The fan whined in my window, but I didn't think it was actually doing anything to cool down the room.

I lay down on the bed.

I sat up again.

I had a sip of water.

Beck had a brother named Billy. That was a weird coincidence.

And I had a book in my room, given to me by my mother, that was somehow addressed to a fourteen-year-old girl I'd just met a month ago.

Another weird coincidence.

Of course, Miriam Bell did not believe in coincidences. So that was something.

I lay down on the bed.

I sat up again.

I went to take another sip of water, but the glass was empty.

I stood up shakily and made my way downstairs before I really knew what I was doing. Hand on the railing, each step careful and purposeful, like I wasn't about to completely freak out.

I would get some water. That's what I needed. I needed more water.

But when I reached the bottom of the staircase, I turned right instead of left, making my way not into the kitchen, but into the living room, where a month ago I had helped Miriam do a total deep clean of the bookcases.

I stared at them now, remembering how I'd taken each book and photo album off its shelf. I'd flipped through an album featuring shots of my great-aunt as a young girl. But there were five other albums I hadn't even touched. . . .

I wasn't sure why I thought of them now, but it was like I wasn't in control of my own body, like I was on autopilot. I turned on one of the end table lamps and stood in front of the bookcase. Everything was buzzing. My fingers, my skin, my ears. I walked over to the bookcase and pulled the first photo album off the shelf. Opened it up. I was holding my breath, I knew, but I couldn't help it. My lungs were temporarily offline. I leafed quickly through the pages.

Just my aunt Dora. A bunch of people I didn't know. Mostly

black-and-white photographs, and the kind of color ones that looked almost fake, Easter egg pastels and faded sepia.

I set the photo album on the closest armchair and chose another at random.

Dora as a teenager. Polaroids of her and her friends, of boyfriends and girlfriends, of her smiling and happy.

I set it on top of the last one.

Two more down and I had a stack of four photo albums without a single shot of my mother.

And I knew it was impossible, I knew it was just my overactive imagination, but... The next one *felt* different. Warmer. A tiny *shock* as my fingers touched its spine and pulled it slowly out of the bookcase.

I opened to the first page, and while my lungs had started working again, it was my heart's turn to take a small vacation. I felt it skip a beat in my chest, then kick into overtime, *thud thud thud thud thud*, as I stared at the very first photo in the album, a picture of my aunt Dora with...

With *Emmy*.

I closed my eyes. Breathed in through my nose. Out through my nose.

What the hell was going on?

I sat down on the floor, cross-legged, holding the photo album to my chest.

Things were not okay. Things were really, really weird.

I opened my eyes, pulled the photo album away from my

body, and stared at the photo. It was definitely Emmy. She was about the same age as she was now, maybe a year younger. Aunt Dora was a lot younger than she'd been when I'd known her. Thirty years younger, maybe. She had her arm around Emmy's shoulders, and both of them wore wide, enthusiastic smiles.

To the left of the photo was a caption. *1994, Bearskin Neck.*

My heart was actually going to explode if I couldn't get it to slow down a little.

That was obviously just a typo. There was a very logical explanation for all this. I should call Cecilia. She was the queen of logical explanations. She would know exactly what was going on. Someone was playing a prank on me! Emmy and my mom were in on it together.

Emmy and my mom.

Emmy and my mom.

Emmy *was* my mom.

I slammed the photo album shut, and the sound cut sharply through the silence of the cottage.

"You are being absolutely ridiculous, Anna," I said.

"I was about to say the same thing," Miriam said from the doorway, her voice sleepy and slow.

I jumped a mile, dropped the photo album on the floor, and shot to my feet. "Mom! You are going to give me a heart attack!"

"*You're* going to give *me* a heart attack. What on earth are you doing down here? It's the middle of the night!" she said.

She leaned against the doorframe, rubbing sleep out of her eyes.

"I'm not doing anything," I said quickly. "I couldn't sleep."

"You couldn't sleep, so you decided to...look through old photo albums?"

"No. Maybe. I guess so."

Miriam moved to the couch and sat down heavily, reaching for me. I sat next to her, and she wrapped her arms around me. "What's going on, honey?"

"Um. Did you ever have, like...a nickname?"

"A nickname?" she repeated, her voice slow and thick with sleep.

"Yeah, you know. Like how Dad calls me Worm."

"Okay, um..." She yawned loudly. "My friends used to call me Mimi. In school. Once I left high school, nobody really called me that."

"Got it. Mimi. Anything else?"

"Uncle Billy always calls me Jo. After *Little Women*. That's the book that changed his life, you know."

"I know, I know," I said. "That's it?"

"Oh. Aunt Dora called me Emmy. I don't know where that one came from, but it stuck. She never called me Miriam."

"She called you Emmy," I repeated, my voice flat and expressionless. My blood was replaced with ice water, and suddenly I wasn't hot anymore, suddenly I was freezing cold.

"Yeah, why? What made you think of this?"

My head was reeling. None of this meant anything. So

what if my great-aunt called my mom Emmy? That didn't mean anything! That wasn't weird at all! Emmy was a common name! It wasn't like I had any proof of . . .

Miriam was looking at me expectantly, waiting for an answer.

"I had . . . a dream."

"A dream?"

"A dream about you. As a teenager."

"Oh. Okay. Do you want to tell me what happened? In the dream?"

"You were just . . . walking around. Bearskin Neck. With Dad."

She smiled—dreamily, sleepily. "Yeah, we did that a lot."

Then she noticed the photo album I'd dropped onto the floor. She reached down and picked it up. A few loose photos had tumbled out. She gathered them up and made a neat little stack, then she looked through them. "Wow," she breathed. "Is that what made you want to look at these photos? The dream? Talk about a blast from the past. We were *babies*."

She held a photo out to me. I didn't want to take it. But my hand betrayed me, and I found myself reaching for it anyway.

Oh. Well, that was nice.

It was a photo of Emmy and Beck, sitting in *this very room*.

I could feel myself shaking as I turned the photo over to look at the back. *Emmy and Everett, 1994.*

I was going to barf, probably.

Miriam was totally oblivious to my plight. She was looking through the photo album with a sad smile on her face, occasionally emitting little sighs or exclamations of surprise.

I looked back at the photograph in my hand. I was so confused. This wasn't Everett? This wasn't my dad? This was *Beck*. And *none of this made any freaking sense*!

"Mom...," I started, but I trailed off, knowing neither what I wanted to ask nor how to ask it.

"Yeah, sweetie?"

"This photo..."

"Yeah?"

"Is a photo of..."

She looked up, smiling distantly. "Your father and me. Have you never seen any photos of us when we were younger? There are some gems in here."

"You and Dad," I said, nodding, trying to let the words sink in. "You and Dad in the year 1994. Okay. Okay, sure."

"Are you feeling all right, Anna? You're acting like a real weirdo tonight."

"I don't know what you're talking about I'm totally fine nothing is wrong I'm fine," I said, the words coming out in a rush, tripping and tangling.

Miriam looked at me for a minute, then blinked. "Okay. Well, I'm exhausted. Can you please go to bed? I can't sleep with you skulking all over the house."

"I'm not *skulking*," I said.

"Exactly what a skulker would say," she said. She placed the photo album on the couch next to her and stood up, holding her hand out to me.

I let her help me up. She kissed the side of my face, oblivious to the fact that I was probably going to barf or pass out or have an exploded heart or all three at once.

At the top of the stairs, she paused briefly, turning to me before going into her own bedroom. "You sure you're okay, Anna? You look like you've seen a ghost."

Not a ghost, no.

What I'd seen was the fourteen-year-old version of my mother and father, hanging out around Rockport like the rules of time were meaningless.

I forced a smile. "I'm fine."

She tapped me on my nose and went into her bedroom.

I went into the bathroom, closed the door, turned on the fan, and, finally, barfed.

timelines

Okay. So I'd been time traveling. Or Emmy and Beck had been the ones who were time traveling. Or maybe we were *all* time traveling!

I drew a timeline on a piece of paper. It was a long, straight line. On one end, it said *parents, 14*. At the other end, it said *parents, present day*. In the middle, it said *both???*

It was not a very helpful timeline.

I ate breakfast the next morning despite not feeling the least bit hungry. But I knew I had to get something into my body, especially considering I'd puked up every last bit of my stomach contents last night. I'd actually felt a little better afterward, and I fell asleep surprisingly quickly. I'd woken up around seven. Miriam was out of the house somewhere, and here I was, choking down cold cereal, feeling very confused and very overwhelmed and a little bit like maybe I'd had a massive head injury and was suffering from some internal bleeding that had led me to have a very intricate, very long hallucination.

I guess that was actually a possibility.

Underneath the timeline, I wrote *possibilities:*

1. head injury, internal bleeding
2. time travel
3.

I didn't have a third one yet.

Underneath that, I wrote *things I can't explain:*

1. why is everett called beck
2. literally anything else

I had another few bites of cereal, barely tasting it as it slid down my throat, jumping a mile when the front door opened and Miriam walked in, holding a cup of coffee from the shop down the street. I shoved the paper into my pocket.

"Oh, morning," she said. "I didn't expect to see you up already."

"Beach day," I said weakly.

"Right," she said. "I think I'll stay home for that, actually, if it's all right with you."

"Is something wrong?"

"Headache," she said, not quite meeting my eyes. I knew a lot about Miriam, and I knew that whenever she had a headache, she filled a cup with ice and carried it around with her, alternating between holding it against her temples and eating it, chip by chip, claiming that anything hot only made the pounding worse. And here she was. Drinking a hot coffee. So I wasn't sure *what* was going on, but I knew my mother's head was perfectly fine.

"I'm not sure why you're looking at me like that," she said, sitting across from me.

"I'm not looking at you like anything," I said.

"Okay, Anna," she replied.

"Okay, Miriam," I echoed her.

She smiled serenely. She picked up an old and tattered paperback that had been lying on the table. *Akata Witch.* I'm sure she'd found it somewhere in the house. I'd actually read that book when I was younger.

After a second of her reading and my attempting to force down some more cereal, she said, "I took your phone out of the rice."

"And?"

"Seems to be working fine. I turned it on and charged it. It's over there."

I put my bowl in the sink and picked up the phone from the counter, warily turning it over in my hands. There was no visible damage to it, and when I tapped the screen, it lit up instantly, showing a full battery and my backdrop—a photo of Josh, Cecilia, and me when we were in fourth grade. I slipped the phone into the pocket of my shorts and peered out the kitchen window. Dad was walking up the driveway, wearing shorts, a light blue T-shirt, flip-flops, and the denim baseball hat. Very beach-ready.

"Dad's here," I called.

"Have fun," Miriam said.

"Aren't you going to come and say hi?"

"Headache," she replied, not looking up from the book.

It wasn't worth arguing with Miriam when she got in one of her weird moods, which she was clearly in right now. I rolled my eyes and said, "See you later."

"Grab the keys," she said, her eyes still trained on the page.

I grabbed the keys from their little hook on the wall, picked up my backpack from where it sat by the door, and stepped onto the porch.

"Morning, Dad," I said.

"Ready for some sun?" he asked excitedly.

"Always."

In reality, I was *not* ready for some sun. I was not ready for literally anything. I wanted to crawl back into bed and close my eyes and try to make sense of what had happened last night. I wanted to ask my father if anyone had ever called him *Beck*. I wanted to scream, maybe. I wanted to start *Slaughterhouse-Five* from the beginning and take notes on how time travel worked. As if it were a manual.

But I couldn't do any of those things, so I pushed my feelings way down into the very bottom of my brain, then tossed the car keys to my father.

He caught them and climbed into the driver's seat. Mom and I had packed the car the night before, and the beach umbrella and chairs and towels were already in there. I got into the passenger's seat and put on my seat belt. He adjusted the rearview mirror, put on his own seat belt, and backed slowly out of the driveway.

I thought it was weird he didn't ask where Miriam was. Shouldn't he have waited for her until I told him she wasn't coming? Maybe she'd texted him.

"She has a headache," I said after a minute or two of silence.

"Hmm? Oh, your mother? Sure, Worm, that's fine," he said distractedly, patting me on the leg without looking over. "Nice to have some time just the two of us."

"Yeah, totally," I said. I studied him for another second as he drove. He looked almost... nervous? Preoccupied, certainly. Like he had a million things all fighting for attention in his mind. He cleared his throat, like he was going to say something, but then fell silent instead, his eyes hidden by his sunglasses as he drove. "Jet-lagged?" I asked him a few minutes later, when the silence in the car started to become a little deafening.

"Oh, for sure. I was up at four," he said, brightening. "Took a walk to get a coffee at five and remembered nothing opens in this damn town until six or seven. But I sat by the water for a little bit and woke up. Already looking forward to a little beach nap."

"Your favorite kind of nap," I replied.

"Can't believe I'm going back to Wingaersheek. Haven't been there in so long."

"Oh, did you go there a lot? When you were...fourteen?" I asked. If this were a crime show, I'd definitely be accused of leading the witness.

"Oh, yeah," he said. "All the time. We'd get Billy to drive us, your mother and me. A bit too far to ride our bikes. I never loved the beach, you know, but your mom did. So I learned to get over it."

"And was there anyone...else?" I asked. "That you would go with?"

"To Wingaersheek? Sometimes Billy would stay, I guess. You gonna walk out on the sandbar with me?"

"Sure, Dad."

He got quiet then, and I swore he wanted to say something he couldn't find the words for. I could tell in the way he kept clearing his throat, kept glancing out the window, at the rear-view, over at my knees but never quite at my face.

But to be fair, *I* wanted to say something I couldn't find the words for, either.

Am I traveling through time?

Am I hanging out with the teenage versions of you and Mom?

Or am I completely blowing absolutely everything out of proportion and ignoring the perfectly logical explanation for all this?

I needed to put my brain on pause. I needed to think about something else. *Anything* else. Well—almost anything else. I needed to *not* think about Emmy and Beck, and I needed to *also* not think of whatever it was that my father wanted to tell me but couldn't quite get the words out but I probably knew anyway but I didn't want to know and—

Okay.

Chill, Anna.

"I'm reading *Slaughterhouse-Five*," I said, wanting desperately to change the subject.

"Oh, I love that one. Love Vonnegut."

(Beck, at the Motif: *I love Vonnegut!* But what had Emmy said? *All men love Vonnegut.* So that didn't necessarily mean anything.)

No, stop, *Anna,* chill.

"It's awful," I said. "But I'm almost done. It's a summer reading book."

"Well, you must soldier on, then, I suppose."

"Just another chapter to go."

"How many books after that?"

"Two more."

"What else so far?"

"*The Great Gatsby.*"

"That one's not too bad. What'd you think?"

"I liked parts of it. It's very serious."

"*Very* serious."

"I think that's a requirement of summer reading books," I noted. "They have to be very serious. Written by white men. Sad endings."

"You hit the nail on the head, Worm," he announced.

And then he turned on the radio.

Almost like he didn't want to talk to me anymore.

I knew that was ridiculous, because both of my parents were basically obsessed with me and wanted to talk to me whenever possible, so it just reaffirmed my suspicions that Everett had something to tell me that he wasn't looking forward to telling me.

And *his* having such an obvious secret somehow made *my* secret fade away a little.

And of course I knew what he was going to tell me. What he didn't *want* to tell me.

He was going to tell me he was seeing someone.

And that's probably why Miriam hadn't come to the beach today. Obviously, something had happened between them. Maybe he'd told her, and they'd gotten into a fight about it? Or maybe Miriam knew he was going to tell *me* and wanted to give us privacy? Or maybe he hadn't told her at all and Mom actually, really *did* have a headache? Or maybe none of this mattered at all because we were all *traveling through time and everything else was meaningless*?!

I rolled my window down a few inches, suddenly finding it hard to breathe in the car, suddenly too hot, too cramped. I turned my face to the cool breeze and took deep, long breaths. I felt sick to my stomach. I just wanted him to turn the car around. I wanted to be alone, to spend the day by myself. I didn't want him to tell me anything, because if he told me, that made it real. And right now, it wasn't real. Right now, it was just something I'd made up. Just like I'd made up the time travel stuff. Because time travel wasn't real and neither was my parents' getting a divorce. None of it was real. None of it could be real.

"You okay, Worm?"

"Just hot."

"Oh, here." Dad turned up the AC and playfully pushed my head toward the vent.

The cool air *did* help a little.

We reached the Wingaersheek Beach parking lot a few minutes later. Everett parked the station wagon and paused a moment, then he turned to me and said, "Hey, Worm—"

"Looks like a beautiful day for the beach!" I interrupted him loudly, opening the door and practically throwing myself out of the car.

And that did it.

He looked a little disappointed as we unloaded the beach umbrella and the chairs and towels, but something in his face had changed, and I knew he wasn't going to tell me anymore. He'd try another day. His resolve was gone. We walked to the beach in silence and set up the umbrella and the chairs underneath it, and he was asleep within four seconds of sitting down.

I pulled *Slaughterhouse-Five* from my backpack and read the last chapter as quickly as I could, skimming entire paragraphs and rolling my eyes approximately three thousand times. When I was done, I put it away and pulled out the third wrapped book.

Love in the Time of Cholera.

So we were three for three with books written by now-dead men, but at least Gabriel García Márquez wasn't white. He was Colombian, I knew, and one of Miriam's favorite-ever writers.

I opened to page one and started to read.

The first line was admittedly better than anything I'd read in *The Great Gatsby* or *Slaughterhouse-Five*, and I really did make a concerted effort to keep an open mind, but the next thing I knew, Everett was shaking me gently awake, handing me a thermos, and telling me I needed to drink water before I dehydrated and he took me back to Miriam looking like a prune.

"I was *sleeping*," I mumbled, annoyed, but definitely very, very thirsty. I opened the bottle and took a long sip.

"We're the laziest bums on the beach today," Everett said. He stood up and stretched dramatically. I still had *Love in the Time of Cholera* on my lap. Dad kicked the leg of my chair. "Let's take a walk," he said. "Or I'm gonna fall right back asleep and waste the entire day."

I slipped the book into my backpack and zipped it up, then I let Everett help me to my feet. I stretched, bending over and letting my arms hang loose toward my feet. Sleeping in a beach chair is not the most comfortable option, and I felt groggy and weird after my nap, like I was floating through space, untethered and lost.

When I stood up, I saw that Everett had already started walking in the direction of the sandbar, so I shoved my backpack into the shade underneath my beach chair and jogged to catch up to him. He headed right to the water's edge, walking in until the waves were up to his knees.

"Woo!" he hollered over his shoulder. "That'll wake you up!"

I still wasn't thrilled with the freezing water of the Atlantic, but I was slowly getting used to it. I walked in up to my ankles, the water swirling and foaming around my feet as my toes clenched involuntarily with the shock of the cold. Everett sloshed his way toward the sandbar, and I trailed slowly after him, still waking up, blinking against the harsh sunlight, and wishing I'd remembered sunglasses.

We reached the sandbar and started walking out toward the open water, still a slightly weird feeling even though I'd done it now, with Miriam, at least a half dozen times. Everett walked faster, with purpose, and I had to skip to keep up with him. Twenty or thirty other people were on the sandbar, and the tide was coming in fast; we didn't have that much time to be out there.

Everett kept walking until he reached the very end of the sandbar, where the water turned deeper and deeper shades of blue as the depth increased. I imagined underwater drop-offs, sheer cliff edges, a fathomless expanse of nothing. You'd be walking along in shin-high currents and then suddenly sinking miles and miles down, all the way to the bottom of the sea. Josh would love it. Josh would dive right in. It just made me feel a little dizzy, and I grabbed Everett's hand to steady myself.

"Beautiful, isn't it?" he said.

"Yeah."

"It feels like the water's just gonna swallow you up."

"I know," I said, glancing nervously behind me, where the sandbar *was* quickly being swallowed up by the rising tide. "We should probably head back."

He turned reluctantly back to shore and nodded. "You're right. We slept too long, Worm."

He put his arm around my shoulders, and we started back to shore, sloshing through ankle-deep water as the sandbar slowly disappeared underneath us. When we got to shore and looked back, you could barely see the outline of it anymore.

"How wild is nature?" Everett said, and I laughed out loud, because it was such a perfectly Everett thing to say.

"Wild, Dad," I agreed.

We went back to our beach chairs and ate the sandwiches he'd picked up, then Everett promptly fell back asleep as I read fifty more pages of *Love in the Time of Cholera*. It was actually kind of nice, reading with Dad snoring lightly next to me, the tide coming in and the day not too blazingly hot. I'd forgotten how bad Everett was with time changes; whenever we traveled to a new time zone, his jet lag came out in full force and he would fall asleep at a moment's notice. It took his body days and days to adjust, so long sometimes that he'd finally start getting used to it right as we were about to go home again.

I read my book for so long my eyes started to go blurry, then I dropped it into my backpack and stood up, stretching. I was hungry again. What was it about the beach that made you constantly hungry?

I kicked Dad's foot gently, and he groaned and tried to roll over. The beach chair rocked dangerously, and he woke up with a start, blinking behind his sunglasses.

"Oh crap. Did I fall asleep again?"

"Affirmative."

"Beach chairs do not offer the ideal support for this old man's back," he declared, holding his hands up to me. I helped him to his feet, pulling so hard I ended up falling backward into the sand, landing on my butt. He laughed and took his turn to help me up, then stood there stretching, his joints popping as he invented some interesting new yoga poses. "Man, I'm hungry," he said after a minute. "You hungry, Worm?"

"Very," I confirmed.

"Let's get this stuff packed up. Successful beach day. Nailed it."

He held out his hand for a high five, and I obliged happily. Then we spent a few minutes folding and gathering everything, shaking off as much sand as we could before carrying it back to the car.

We found a little place to eat in Gloucester that I hadn't been to yet, a small seafood restaurant with a gift shop attached. We ate in silence, both famished, and while Everett paid the bill, I wandered next door, poking through racks of corny Gloucester-branded T-shirts and shelves packed with shot glasses and snow globes. I picked up a Man at the Wheel magnet and turned it over in my hands before sticking it back on the sheet of metal.

On a small wall crowded with T-shirts, a bright pink one caught my eye. It had *Gloucester* written across the chest in highlighter-yellow letters. I grabbed it and held it up to myself in the mirror. The pink was the perfect almost-obnoxious-but-not-quite shade, and the yellow letters looked a little retro against it. I'd gotten a Rockport sweatshirt, but I didn't have anything yet that said *Gloucester* on it. This one would look so cute with jean shorts, and it was even a softer cotton, not the usual stiff, scratchy stuff you find in cheap T-shirts.

I heard a noise behind me and turned to see Everett trying on a lime-green baseball hat, comparing it with the denim one in his hand.

"Not your color," I said.

"Are you sure, because..." He found a different angle in the mirror, studying himself. "I guess you're right. Find something good?"

He flipped the lime baseball hat back onto the shelf and pointed at the shirt in my hand. I held it up, and he caught it by its hem, rubbing the cotton between his thumb and middle finger, feeling its weight.

"Cool colors," he said.

"Should I get it?" I asked. "I don't have a Gloucester shirt yet."

"Totes," he said. "You know, when we were just getting Bell's Books started, your mom wanted to make a few pieces for it. Some merch, for the die-hard fans, you know. I suggested a hot pink not unlike this one, but I was swiftly vetoed."

"You were ahead of the times," I said. "The youths like neon."

"That was exactly my argument. But alas. Miriam wanted gray."

And she had won. Bell's Books had sold the same gray T-shirt since I was a baby. It had the outline of a book on the front left pocket, and on the back, in looping cursive: *Get lost in a book from Bell's Books*. The address underneath in smaller typed letters.

"Are you going to miss it?" I asked softly, not quite meeting my dad's eyes.

"Oh man, of *course*," he replied.

But it had never really been his thing. He'd worked there some days, of course, he'd helped to manage it, to put it all together, to keep it running smoothly, but it had always, always been Miriam's.

"Me too," I said.

"This was not an easy decision for your mom, you know."

"I know."

"In fact, we've been talking about it for quite some time."

"You might have looped me in," I said.

"Maybe, Worm. But this was always going to be your mom's decision."

"I just... It's hard knowing that it failed."

"Is that what you think?"

"Well, it *did*. It's closing. It didn't work."

"I think you need to shift your perspective a little bit there," Dad said. "The bookstore's been around for *thirteen years*. That's a big chunk of time. It's paid our bills, it's bought you new clothes, it's put food on the table.... There's not a whiff of failure there, Worm. It's just...time."

I made a noise I could only accurately describe as a har-rumph, and Dad laughed and tousled my hair. Then he dug a twenty-dollar bill out of his pocket and we bought the shirt and I tried—for at least a few seconds—to shift my perspective. I really did.

But I just couldn't seem to do it.

logical
explanations

somehow managed to trick my brain into *not* thinking about time travel for the next few hours, and by the time dinner rolled around, I had almost completely forgotten the inscription in the book and the photos in the photo album and my mother's childhood nickname.

I was being ridiculous, I told myself as my parents and I walked to dinner that evening.

There was a perfectly reasonable explanation for all this, and I was only being silly and weird because I'd just read a book about time travel and I was getting too much sun. I was probably dehydrated, like my dad had said. I needed to make a concerted effort to drink more water.

The Gloucester T-shirt turned out to be a lucky purchase; I spilled soy sauce on my clothes that night at dinner and realized when I got home that everything I owned was in various states of waiting-for-the-laundry. I ripped the tags off the shirt and slipped it on, and then I paused in front of the mirror as I decided what to do.

Miriam and Everett had suggested a game night, but if I was being honest, I was kind of parented out. Dad had been weird and jet-lagged and tired at dinner, and Miriam had been weird and quiet and distant, and I felt exhausted from an hour and a half of carrying every single part of the conversation. At one point (I timed it), Everett spent a minute and a half staring into a spoonful of egg drop soup while Miriam absentmindedly separated her salad into little piles on her plate: a pile of carrots, a pile of baby corn, a pile of water chestnuts.

"Why is baby corn so much cuter than regular corn?" Everett finally said, breaking the silence to pluck a piece of the aforementioned vegetable from Miriam's plate.

"Baby anythings are cuter than their grown-up counterparts," Miriam responded in a strangely flat, emotionless tone of voice.

"That's not true. Have you seen a baby panda? Very cute grown-up animals. Perhaps the cutest grown-up animals to ever exist. The babies, though? Terrifying. They look like miniature naked mole rats," Dad said.

I searched *baby panda* on my phone and held up a picture for the table. "Can confirm," I said.

Miriam glanced at the picture, smiled a little, and shrugged. "I stand corrected."

And that was pretty much the most they'd spoken all night.

I personally thought that even the ugly, naked mole rat panda babies had been pretty cute, but at that point I'd been too emotionally exhausted to try to argue the point.

And a game night with those two weirdos was basically the last thing I wanted to do.

What I *wanted* was to go see Emmy and Beck. To prove to myself, once and for all, that they were just two normal, *present-day*, unrelated-to-me friends.

So that's what I would do.

I went downstairs, where Miriam was half-heartedly cleaning the kitchen, running a rag over the same spot on the kitchen counters.

"Mom?"

"Oh, honey. I didn't hear you come down."

"Is everything okay? Is Dad still here?"

"He decided to walk home. Is that okay? I know you were excited to play a game."

"Oh, no, that's fine," I said. "He has a long day tomorrow."

He was going to work at the tattoo parlor. He'd told me to stop by around lunchtime and we'd get something to eat. He'd hinted heavily that I might want to arrive a teeny bit before noon to catch a glimpse of one of the clients he was tattooing. Somebody famous, obviously. But celebrity spotting was kind of the last thing on my mind at that particular moment.

"I think I'll just go for a little walk, then," I said.

"To meet your friends?" she asked.

"Yeah. My friends."

"You know, I never caught their names. At the fireworks. Too loud."

"Oh. Um. Amy and Jack."

I had absolutely no idea where I'd gotten those names from, but she seemed to believe me, because she just nodded slowly, eyes a bit unfocused, expression a bit dazed.

"I'd really like to meet them one day," she said. "Maybe this weekend?"

"Sure, yeah," I said. "Of course. I'll ask them."

"Got your phone?"

"Yup, got it."

"Don't be too late, Anna."

"I won't."

"I love you."

"Love you, Mom."

I turned to go but paused by the door. She'd gone back to wiping that same bit of the counter.

"Are you... okay?" I asked.

"Oh, I'm fine, Anna. I better just get to bed a little early, I think," she said, offering me a weak smile.

"Okay, Mom."

"Love you," she said again, an automatic response, and I could tell she didn't even hear me when I said it back to her.

I went outside, closing the door behind me, letting the night swallow me up.

I thought of everything that had happened in the last

twenty-four hours, and it made me feel…a little bit un-tethered. Light. Like a balloon that might float away at any moment.

It was funny how it came and went in waves. I'd go an entire hour without thinking about the fact that I'd been spending all summer hanging out with my parents as teenagers. I'd convinced myself it *wasn't* them, of *course* it wasn't them. Logical explanations. Reality. The fact that, you know, time travel didn't exist.

And now here I was, halfway to the Motif, and it came crashing back on me, a huge rush of weirdness that made me freeze on the spot, swaying as I let that fact sink into my brain again.

I squeezed my eyes shut, felt the moonstone ring on my finger, struggled to breathe like how they told you to in the meditation app. In. Hold. Out. Slowly.

I jumped a mile when I heard the footsteps behind me, whirling around to see…

Beck, his hand half raised to tap me on the shoulder.

"Hi, Anna!" he said.

But I found myself unable to respond. I found my mouth glued shut, my lips unwilling to separate.

And any doubt I had before, any doubt I was tricking myself into having, completely vanished.

Because *how had I never realized before that this boy was my father?* They looked *exactly alike!* Even the way he was looking at me, like he was trying to decide what planet I was from. That's how my father looked at me! In a nice way, I mean. But still.

"Anna?" he said when I didn't answer.

What I *wanted* to say was, *Do you have any idea that in about fourteen years, you'll be standing in a hospital room waiting for Emmy to give birth to me?*

What I *did* say was, "Hi, Beck."

And I must have said it super, super awkwardly, because he furrowed his brows a little and stared at me quizzically.

"Are you okay?" he asked after a moment.

"Oh, yeah, just thinking. Sorry. You caught me off guard."

On second thought, it was probably normal that I hadn't realized this fourteen-year-old boy would grow into my forty-two-year-old father.

Why would I literally ever, ever, *ever* think that?

"You seem, like, a zillion miles away," Beck said, smiling again. "Nice shirt, though. Cool colors. I was gonna get some candy; wanna come?"

Cool colors, my dad had said in the T-shirt store.

Cool colors, my fourteen-year-old dad said now.

"Sure," I said. "Yeah, okay."

We started walking. I could feel Beck looking at me.

Beck.

I couldn't think of him as my father. I *couldn't*. It felt... wrong. I mean, technically, he *wasn't* my father. Not yet. He wouldn't be my father for another fourteen years. And another fourteen years after that, *I'd* be fourteen. If the number thirteen had been unlucky, fourteen was turning out to be a downright *trip*.

"Do you...want to talk about anything?" Beck asked sort of cautiously, like he wasn't sure *he* wanted to talk about anything but he thought he needed to do the right thing and ask anyway.

"Oh, no, sorry," I said. "Everything's fine."

"You just seem..."

"Distracted, that's all."

We reached the Country Store, and Beck held the door open for me, and if I wasn't confused before, I was absolutely confused now, because it looked *exactly* the same as it had before. The only way I could tell that anything was different was by checking the prices—in my time, bulk candy had been $9.99 a pound. Now it was $3.99.

(A sudden flashback to buying fudge for Emmy and Beck and myself. I'd thought the cashier had given me the wrong change back, but no—it had just been cheaper. Because it was in the past. Because *we* were in the past. I closed my eyes and took a deep breath, suddenly dizzy.)

"I wanted to try one of those potato things," Beck said, making a beeline for the wall of plastic buckets.

I peeked at the woman behind the register. She was older, with salt-and-pepper hair and a friendly smile and kind eyes.

And I had absolutely no doubt that this was Shane's mother, because they looked *exactly* alike.

I held on to a shoulder-high gumball machine, taking deep breaths and willing myself not to pass out.

"You're being really weird," Beck observed. "Would some candy cigarettes help your situation?"

"Taffy, please."

"You got it."

He tossed some taffy into his bucket, then took everything up to the register and paid. We sat on the little white bench outside the store, and I unwrapped a bubblegum-flavored taffy while Beck chewed thoughtfully on the spud.

"I love it," he said after a few seconds of chewing.

"Thanks for the taffy."

"Feeling better?"

"Yes, definitely."

"Sugar will do that to a person."

"Should we keep walking?"

"Sure," Beck said.

I unwrapped another piece of taffy as we walked, and for some reason, the sugar *did* help.

"Where are you with your summer reading?" Beck asked after a minute.

"*Love in the Time of Cholera*. Have you read it?"

"I've only read some of his short stories. Like 'A Very Old Man with Enormous Wings.' I like that one a lot. I don't think I really *get* it, but I like it."

"My mom loves that story."

"So does Emmy. She's the one who made me read it."

Emmy—of course she'd made Beck read it. A pushy fourteen-year-old forcing her favorite works of literature down the throats of everyone she met could only grow into one adult person: my mother.

Honestly. How had I never seen it before?

I laughed out loud. "Has she told you her theory yet? That everyone has one book that will change their life?"

"Of course," Beck said. "She told me, like, five minutes after we met. 'Hi, I'm Emmy. Have you found the one book that will change your life yet?'"

I glanced over at him. He was smiling really wide. "You like her a lot, don't you?" I said.

He bit his bottom lip, then nodded. "Yeah, I guess so."

And it made me feel...sad. Because I knew how their story ended. I knew it didn't work out.

"Anna, um...Are you going to say anything?" he asked, his voice quiet and self-conscious.

"Sorry. She's...really great, Beck. I'm happy for you."

"Thanks." He bit his lip again, then glanced sideways at me. "You're sure there isn't something else you want to talk about?"

"No. Just feeling kind of quiet, I guess."

"I can do quiet," he said, smiling, tossing me another piece of taffy.

I unwrapped it, and for some reason, Everett Bell's one book popped into my head.

And knowing what Everett Bell's one book was meant I knew what *Beck's* one book was.

It was *I Capture the Castle*, a book I'd never read and knew little about, other than, at the age of twenty-one, my father would read it (at the urging of Miriam, of course) and it would change his life (exactly as she predicted it would, of course).

What would happen, I wondered, if I mentioned it to him now?

If I was somehow able to persuade him to read it *now*, instead of when he was twenty-one?

What would happen?

Would something shift in the universe? Would that tiny change in the sequence of events create a chain reaction that would lead to, like...I don't know, the third world war or something?

I stopped walking.

Abruptly.

So abruptly it was as if I'd hit a wall.

Because it had just occurred to me.

If I *was* in the past...

And, you know, all signs pointed to that being the case...

Then what exactly *would* happen if I changed things?

Could I really...*really*...mess things up?

Or was everything set in stone, immovable and unchangeable? Already plotted into existence?

If I looked at my mother in the present day and she had no scars on her arm...and then I stabbed the fourteen-year-old version of her one night while we hung out...would my present-day mother awake with a start out of sleep, one fresh new scar on her skin?

Oh.

I was going to pass out.

I sat down on the curb, and it was only when he was twenty or thirty paces in front of me that Beck even realized I'd stopped walking. He jogged back to meet me, squatting in front of me, placing his hand tentatively on my knee.

"Anna? You're being weird again," he said, and although he was smiling, I could tell he was actually concerned.

"Who, me?" I said kiddingly, lying backward in the warm grass.

From this angle, Kit-Hale was all I could see. It was so bright it almost hurt my eyes to look at it. It was—

I sat up suddenly, so quickly I got a little dizzy.

"Kit-Hale!" I exclaimed.

"What about it?" Beck asked, craning his head to look upward.

"It's the comet!"

"Yeah, so?"

"The same comet that was here when my parents were fourteen!"

"Your parents? I'm not following, Anna...."

"Um, nothing. Everything is fine. Everything is great!"

It was the comet! Of course! Whenever the comet was visible in the night sky, I time traveled backward to meet my fourteen-year-old parents! It made perfect sense!

But wait.

I'd seen the comet when I *hadn't* been time traveling, too.

I'd seen the comet with my mom and dad, and we'd been solidly in the present.

So what exactly caused me to become unhinged in the space-time continuum?

It was something I wanted to think about more, but not *now*, because now I just felt a little dizzy and a little puke-y and a little weird.

"Should we try to find Emmy?" I asked, sitting up.

"Sure," Beck said. "She's probably at the Motif. We were going to play cards again." He held his hand out to me and helped me up, and we walked the rest of the way to the Motif, where Emmy was, indeed, waiting for us, sitting on a pylon, watching the night sky, her hair wild and frizzy around her head, and she was so much my mother in that moment that it actually took my breath away.

Her bike was on the ground a few feet away from her, and when I saw it, I realized...

The bikes.

The bikes in the shed had been older, slightly rusted and dusty.

The bikes Emmy and Beck and I had rode together had been brand-new.

But they were the same bikes, of course. Separated by three-ish decades and one case of probably time travel.

Definitely time travel.

Twenty-eight. That's how many years was between fourteen-year-old Miriam and present-day, forty-two-year-old Miriam.

Twenty-eight years that were not playing by the well-established rules of time and space and linear progression.

"Guys, where *were* you?" Emmy said, seeing us, jumping up from the pylon.

Beck tossed her the bag of candy, then took a pack of cards from his back pocket and started wordlessly dealing us in.

And I couldn't help myself.

I walked up to Emmy and gave her a big hug.

I didn't think we'd hugged before, aside from right after I'd almost drowned.

"Oh!" she said, wrapping her arms around me, too. "Um, hi, Anna."

"What's the one book that will change my life?" I whispered into her hair, and she pulled away from me, looking curiously into my face.

"I don't know," she said, considering. "I don't think I've known you long enough."

But I'd seen Miriam Bell slip *The Bell Jar* to a stranger after five seconds of conversation. I'd seen Miriam Bell hand all four volumes of Elena Ferrante's Neapolitan Quartet to an eighty-four-year-old man who came back a mere week later, sobbing, pressing a bouquet of daisies into her hand. I'd seen Miriam Bell hand a bundle of young adult novels to a shy sixteen-year-old girl—*Bone Gap*, *Strange the Dreamer*, *Pet*, *Every Day*, *The Raven Boys*. I'd seen Miriam Bell pluck *The Goldfinch* out of a twenty-something-year-old woman's hands, replacing it with

Every Heart a Doorway. "Much shorter," she'd said, winking. "Much more of a punch."

So that wasn't it.

"But I'll think about it," she promised. Then, lowering her voice. "I know his. It's *I Capture the Castle*. But I don't think he's supposed to read it quite yet."

I smiled. "Yeah, I think you're right."

We sat around in a lopsided circle, and Beck divided up a stack of pennies between us. At the end of twenty minutes, we'd finished the rest of the candy and Emmy had run out of coins. Beck and I counted our piles. He'd won by five cents.

"You're pretty good," he told me, gathering up the pennies and dumping them all into a Ziploc bag. Then he smirked and added, jokingly, "For a girl."

Emmy rolled her eyes so far back in her head I was afraid they'd get stuck, then she turned to me and said, "Oh, I just started *Anne of Green Gables*. Have you read it, Anna?"

"No, but my mom loves those books."

"They're so good," she said dreamily.

"I'm on *The Return of the King*," Beck said.

"Which is basically like *Anne of Green Gables*, but with orcs," I joked. Beck dissolved into laughter, but Emmy scrunched up her face thoughtfully.

"I don't think they're like each other at all," she said.

"Have you read *Lord of the Rings*?" I asked her.

"Of course. It's good, if you ignore the blatant lack of female characters."

"I mean, it's nice that they expanded them for the movies," I said carefully, an idea occurring to me. A test: "And I really do love Liv Tyler, but it's a bummer they gave all Glorfindel's scenes to her. At least, that's what my dad says. I haven't read the books."

Emmy said, "Who's Glorfindel again? An elf?" at the same time Beck said, "Who's Liv Tyler?"

And if I had any remaining doubts about who these kids were, they disappeared now. Because it was not possible that someone who'd read *Lord of the Rings* did *not* know who Liv Tyler was.

"He's the elf who rescues the hobbits from the Nazgul," I said to Emmy. "And sorry, I was thinking of something else," I told Beck.

Beck finished putting everything away, then we said good-bye and I made my way back to the cottage slowly, Kit-Hale above me and a zillion stars visible in the night sky.

For some reason, I decided to take a detour down the wharf.

I wasn't quite ready to go home, and it was bugging me, not knowing exactly how things worked.

Could I only time travel if I started at the Motif? But, no— because Beck had found me that night on Bearskin Neck. I hadn't reached the Motif yet.

But it *did* feel like the Motif had something to do with it. Everything had started there. The night I had first tried the door to find it locked. The way it had opened by itself. That was the night I'd met...

That old man.

Your ring is glowing like something else, he'd said.

My ring.

I looked down at the moonstone now, and it *was* glowing. It always glowed more at night, as if lit from within by an impossible flame.

What else had he said?

Those stones love being out in the nighttime. They commune with the moon, you know.

And then: *Don't forget to make a wish.*

I walked faster now, down the wharf and to the line of rocking chairs where he'd been sitting. But all of them were empty. And I looked for Book, the dog, but it was nowhere to be found, either.

Don't forget to make a wish.

And I *had* made a wish, I remembered with a start. Right before I'd gone into the Motif for the first time.

I wish my parents would love each other forever.

I felt dizzy again, too hot and suddenly exhausted.

The moonstone ring was so bright on my finger that it left a trail of light in its path when I moved my hand.

I needed some sleep.

A good night's sleep.

That was important.

And water.

I needed to go home and drink water and go to sleep.

I walked slowly back up the wharf, making it home just a

few minutes later. Drank a cold glass of water standing over the kitchen sink.

And before I went into my room, I poked my head into Miriam's bedroom. She was sound asleep, curled up on her side, facing the door.

And in her sleep, I swear—

How had I never seen it before?

She looked so much younger.

Just like her fourteen-year-old self.

Just like Emmy.

old nicknames

T he next morning was mild and sunny, with a gentle breeze rolling in from the water.

I made my way to the tattoo parlor around eleven, and all I could think about as I rode my bike—*Emmy's* bike—was why he'd ever gone by *Beck*.

Beck.

Beck.

It didn't make any sense as a nickname.

But then...

B...

B.

I'd always assumed my mother's rarely used pet name for my father had stood for something cutesy like *babe* or *baby* or *buttercup*, but now...Well, maybe that hadn't been right at all.

I was a little sweaty by the time I reached the tattoo parlor, a nondescript place sandwiched between a cobbler and a deli.

The sidewalk outside smelled like an oddly satisfying mix of bagels and leather. I locked up my bike and pushed into the shop. A bell over the door announced my arrival to the only two people who were there, my dad and...

I blinked.

My dad was wiping down the arm of a very shirtless, very attractive Wallace Green. The actor. The movie star. The most famous man on the actual planet, probably.

"And you're all set, Wally," Dad said, looking up and winking quickly at me. "Let me get this wrapped up. Come over here, Anna. I want you to meet my friend."

I tried to look normal, but so often when we try to look normal we accomplish the exact opposite, so I'm sure I looked completely weird as I made my way to where my dad was wrapping Wallace Green's newly extended sleeve tattoo in cellophane.

"Um," I said.

"Wally, this is my daughter, Anna," Dad said. "Anna, this is Mr. Green."

"Mr. Green? Don't be ridiculous." Wallace Green held out his free hand, which happened to be the left. "I'm Wally, Anna. It's a pleasure to meet you."

"You're Wally," I repeated. "I'm Anna."

As far as first impressions went, I'm pretty sure I nailed it.

I took his left hand with my right, and we did a modified shake, then I resisted every urge in my actual body to whip out my cell phone and text Jennica immediately. Jennica was a *huge* Wallace Green fan. She would *scream* if she knew I was standing in front of him!

She'd made me go see his last movie on opening night. The entire theater had been packed, and we'd basically both cried from start to finish.

It was called *Luck's Fancy*, about a guy named Peter, who was convinced he was in the middle of a seven-year spell of bad luck, thanks to a broken mirror.

"Luck doesn't exist. Good *or* bad," Jennica had said afterward, after she'd stopped crying. "It's a construct meant to give reason to completely random events."

But if bad luck didn't exist, then what else explained that just a few months later it wouldn't be *me* sitting with Jennica in that diner, it would be Lara?

If luck didn't exist, why had Lara moved to our town in the first place?

If luck didn't exist, why had anything in my life turned out the way it had?

"There you go," Dad said, and Wallace Green held his wrapped arm in front of his face, admiring the fresh ink.

"This is incredible, man," he said. "Absolutely incredible. You're a true artist. A one-of-a-kind. Anna, this guy's the real deal, right here."

I wasn't sure why, but it embarrassed me a little, hearing Wallace Green shower my dad with compliments. But for his part, Everett seemed to take it all in stride. He wore a confident-but-not-cocky smile on his face as he held out a hand and helped Wallace out of his chair.

"Always a pleasure, Wally," he said.

"Let me transfer this right now so I don't forget," Wallace replied, pulling his phone out of his pocket and tapping the screen. "Done. I'll let you know when I'm back in Los Angeles. Another month or so. We'll get dinner."

"Sounds good, man," Everett said, and they hugged in a genuinely affectionate way. Then Wallace Green *turned to me and hugged me*!!

Honestly, he did it so quickly I didn't even have a chance to wrap my head around the idea—or my arms around his body. So I was sure it was a very awkward hug that made me look like a complete alien.

Then it was over, and Wallace Green told me it had been a pleasure meeting me, and then Wallace Green walked out of the store and my dad started laughing while he cleaned up his supplies.

"You look like you're going to pass out, Anna. Should you sit down?"

"That was ... Wallace Green. ..."

I sat, pointing at the door.

"Indeed."

"You just ... poked Wallace Green ... with a needle. ..."

"When you put it like that, it makes me sound like quite the sociopath." Dad laughed again.

"You guys are friends?" I asked incredulously. "He wants to go to dinner with you?"

"I believe I've told you many times how cool I am, so I don't love the tone of surprise in your voice," he said, smiling. "Hungry? I can deal with the rest of this later."

"Sure. Yeah. I guess."

He locked up the shop when we left, and we walked down the street to a little diner with old-fashioned booths and counter seating. We took two open spots at the counter, and Dad ordered a coffee.

"Cute little spot, huh?" he said as the server handed us two menus.

"Super cute."

"Everything in this town is cute," he said. "Trapped in time."

My brain, for the past ten minutes, had been buzzing with the fact that I'd just met Wallace Green, but at the phrase *trapped in time*, it went back to buzzing about Emmy and Beck and meeting my parents as fourteen-year-olds. And it made me remember....

"Hey, Dad," I said, trying to keep my voice casual, keeping my eyes on the menu.

"Yeah, Worm?"

"Did you ever have any nicknames? You know, as a kid?"

"Nicknames? Hmm. Uncle Billy called me *butthead*. Endearingly, I think."

"What did your friends call you?"

"I guess they called me *Ev* sometimes. My aunt called me *Rhett Butler*. Everett, Rhett, you know."

"That's it? Nobody called you anything else? Like... anything not obvious?"

"Not obvious? Hmm, I don't think so." He shut the menu, and I followed suit. The server came back and took our orders. Dad had a sip of his coffee, then said, "Oh, you know what? Your mother had a strange nickname for me. But it didn't start out as a nickname. Kind of a funny story."

"What was it?" I asked.

"Well, when I first met your mother, I thought she was cute right away. Like *really* cute. I thought she was basically the cutest person I'd ever seen in my life. So, obviously, I was a little shy around her. Little dweeby, you know. She went by Emmy back then, at least when she was here for the summers, because that's what her aunt called her. So she introduced herself to me as Emmy, and I said, 'Hi, I'm Everett.' She said, 'Beckett?' And I was so nervous to be talking to her that I didn't even correct her. I just said, 'Yup!'" Dad laughed, shaking his head at the memory.

"So she called you Beckett?"

"For an entire dang summer."

"When did you finally tell her what your real name was?"

"I didn't. Billy did. He picked me up one night, and your mom said, 'See you later, Beck!' and he said, 'Who the heck is Beck?'" He smiled. "We'll do some pretty wild things for love, I guess."

My heart was pounding now. "So she met your brother."

"Of course."

"And what about anyone else? Did you ever hang out with anyone else?"

"Not really. I was kind of a loner back then. Didn't have a lot of friends. And your mom was just visiting for the summers, so she didn't know many people aside from her aunt."

"Any other kids? Anyone else your age? Did you ever, like…" My heart was beating so loudly I was afraid he would hear it. My chest ached with it. I tried to force a laugh, to make myself seem nonchalant. "Did you ever save anyone from drowning?" I said it so quickly all the words toppled out on top of one another. Dad made a confused face and cocked his head.

"Did I ever… What?"

"I don't know, like—" Another forced laugh. "The ocean, right? It's right here. Just wondering if you ever…if anyone ever…Cecilia plays volleyball, you know, and she's going to get her lifeguard certification soon, and it just got me thinking. I bet it's more common than you think, you know?" I tried to laugh, but it came out as more of a choking sound. Dad wasn't looking at me; he was staring at a spot on the counter, his brows furrowed, a deep line creasing his forehead.

"It's so weird you just asked me that. I haven't thought about that in years," he said slowly, his voice soft.

"So you… So you *did*?"

"It was a long, long time ago. The summer I met your mother. We were—"

"Fourteen," I interrupted him.

"Yeah. There was a girl we hung around with. Just for

that summer. I never saw her again after that. I can't...I can't remember her name...."

"What did she look like?" I whispered, my voice strained, my heart pounding, my eyes starting to water....

Dad shook his head. "I don't remember. When I try thinking about it, there's like...this glaze over everything."

"A glaze?"

"It was a long time ago, honey." His eyes were wide and glossy, like he was lost in a daydream. But when the server came over to refill his coffee, he shook his head and smiled, wrapping his arm around me and squeezing. "That reminds me, Worm, we gotta teach you how to swim."

"Yeah," I agreed, and my head was buzzing so loudly now I was surprised I even managed to speak at all. "Yeah, Dad, we should."

I spent the rest of the day reading.

Love in the Time of Cholera was an *infuriating* book and grew only more infuriating as I got closer to the end.

It was about a man, Florentino, who falls in love with a woman, Fermina, when they are both young teenagers. After a brief affair, they are separated for two years' time, during which they write love letters to each other incessantly. But when they finally see each other again, Fermina decides she doesn't love him anymore and breaks off their correspondence.

Florentino spends the next *fifty-one years* waiting for Fermina's husband to die so he can court her again. The last chapter of the book ends with them both on a ship, finally together but both old, and it was kind of impossible to tell if they even *liked* each other that much. Plus, they kept comparing love to a plague, which was just... not very romantic.

When I finished the last page, I actually threw the book across the room, feeling suddenly, *violently* angry with it. It smashed against the wall just as Miriam entered the living room.

She looked at the book, looked at me, then laughed.

"You know, any piece of art that can elicit *that* sort of reaction from you must be a good one."

"It doesn't make any *sense*," I said. "He wastes his entire life pining away for this woman who doesn't even give him the time of day, and then they end up together anyway and they're both miserable and he says she smells like an old woman! That's not romantic!"

"Love isn't always romantic, you know," she said thoughtfully. "Sometimes it's about other things. Companionship. Familiarity. Solidarity. Friendship."

"But they have *none of those things*," I said. "The title literally says *love*, and they don't love each other at all! He sleeps with half the girls in Colombia. You don't sleep with other people if you're in love with someone else!"

"I don't think you can say something like that," she replied. "I don't think love is as simple as you're making it out to be."

I couldn't think of anything to say to that, so I just grunted loudly and crossed my arms over my chest and slunk down on the couch.

The kind of love described in that book was *pointless*. It was basically the opposite of Miriam and Everett's love. It had lasted forever, but for absolutely no reason at all. Those people didn't even *like* each other. And my parents *loved* each other, but they weren't even together anymore. Make it make sense!

Miriam crossed the living room and bent down to pick up the book. She held it in her hands for a moment, almost cradling it, then set it gently on the shelf.

"Are you done with them yet? Your summer reading books?" she asked.

"One more," I grumbled.

"Let's hope you like it a little more than this one," Miriam said, then went into the kitchen to start dinner. I heard her put on NPR, bits of it drifting out of the kitchen and across the hall to where I lay draped across the couch.

Yes, I had only one wrapped book left upstairs, but I really, *really* didn't want to read it. And that was fine. I could take a break. I had time.

I made myself get off the couch and walked into the kitchen.

"Is Dad coming over for dinner?"

"Not tonight," Mom said. "He wants to go to bed early. Try and 'kick the jet lag once and for all,' he said."

"Well, I can stay in tonight, if you want. We can play a game or something."

Mom stopped chopping the onion in front of her and turned around, smiling, her eyes rimmed in red.

"I'd really like that," she said.

"Are you crying?" I asked.

She tapped the onion with the knife, and although it made sense, and although she always cried when she chopped onions, I wasn't sure if I quite believed her.

a gradual
certainty

I met Dad for lunch again the next day, and we went to the same diner, took the same two seats at the counter, but before I even got a chance to look at the menu, before Everett even ordered a cup of coffee, he swiveled his stool in my direction, then swiveled *my* stool in his direction and cleared his throat. We were face-to-face, very close, and suddenly I knew exactly what he was going to say to me.

My stomach flip-flopped as I tried to make my face neutral, expressionless, like I didn't already know what was coming. I thought of Miriam, pretending that the reason she was crying was because of the onion, and I felt my own eyes prickle uncomfortably.

"Hey, Worm, there's something I want to talk to you about," he said, and he was so uncharacteristically serious, so un-Everett-like in his tone of voice that my flip-flopping stomach turned into a stone and sank about a foot deeper into my belly.

"Yeah, Dad?" I said, trying to keep my tone light and—I was sure—failing.

"Your mother and I have given this a lot of thought. And we both agree that honesty is the best way forward. We never want you to feel like you can't talk to us about any of this stuff, okay? Any questions you have, anything that's on your mind, we're both here for you."

"Okay," I said.

"I gave the divorce papers to your mother yesterday. She'll sign them, and then I'll take them back to Los Angeles with me. Things will be all finalized soon."

"Will we have to go to court or something? Josh had to go to court."

"No, no, definitely not," Dad said. "Your mom and I have a mediator. No lawyers. Everything is going to be super smooth. We're in total agreement about everything. Open communication. No weirdness. No fighting. This won't be like how it is in the movies, okay?"

"Okay," I replied.

"Nothing will change after this, okay?"

"You mean, nothing will change except everything that's already changed?" I said quietly.

Dad's shoulders fell slightly. He put his hands on my knees. "I know this has all been a lot for you. We both know that. I want to tell you—*we* want to tell you—how proud we are of you. You're basically the best daughter anyone could have ever asked for."

"Thanks," I mumbled.

"I want to be respectful of what you're feeling and how much you feel comfortable receiving at one time," he continued. His eyes were down, staring at his hands on my knees.

This was what I'd been waiting for. The rug pulled out from under my feet.

But also, I couldn't help smiling. He'd obviously practiced this speech.

"How much I feel comfortable receiving?" I repeated.

He shrugged and met my eyes again, smiling slyly. "I read a book, okay? I'm a cool dad."

"Okay, Cool Dad. Well... You can tell me whatever it is you have to tell me. I think I already know anyway."

He nodded. "Yeah. I've prepared for that."

"Your coworker isn't really your coworker, is she?"

"You're too smart," he said lightly. "That's your problem. You're just too smart."

"How long have you been seeing her?"

"Not long," he said. "Two months. I debated even telling you. It seemed too early. But your mom..."

"Mom knows?"

"Of course your mom knows," Dad said, suddenly serious. "She's my best friend."

And if nothing in that conversation had crushed my heart into a billion pieces as of yet...

That definitely did.

Because wasn't I *currently* not speaking to my best friend?

"Get you started with anything?" the server asked, pausing in front of us. They had shoulder-length, wavy hair and a small stud nose ring.

"I think we need a donut," Dad said. "One of the big ones. And I need some coffee. And she needs...What do you need, Worm?"

"Just a water, thanks," I mumbled.

"Worm?" the server said, leaning a bit closer to me. "That's a seriously cute nickname."

"Bookworm," I explained, trying to sound just slightly less doom-and-gloom than I was feeling.

"My father used to call me Pickle," they replied. "I thought that was pretty cute, but I think Worm takes the cake."

"Nice to meet you, Pickle," Dad said, and they smiled widely.

"And for *that*, the donut's on the house," they said, and went off to get the drinks.

That was Everett Bell in an actual nutshell.

Effortlessly nice. Effortlessly funny. Effortlessly cool.

The only thing that came effortlessly to me was being completely oblivious to anything going on around me, like my parents getting a divorce.

How had I not *known*? How had I been so completely blindsided?

The server came back with our drinks and the donut. Everett cut it into two equal slices. It felt like a very obnoxious metaphor.

"When did you know?" I asked him as he took his first bite.

He chewed, swallowed, then said carefully, "Know what?"

"That you wanted a divorce?"

"Oh." He took a sip of his coffee. "It wasn't any big thing, I guess. It was just…a mutual understanding. A gradual certainty."

"A gradual certainty," I repeated.

"I don't know, honey, it's hard to explain. It's complicated and it's sort of between your mother and me. It's a delicate thing to try to share because I want to be respectful of what *she* wants to share. Does that make sense?"

"Yeah, it makes sense," I said, filling my mouth with donut so I wouldn't have to say anything else.

But the problem was—the problem had always been—that it *didn't* make any sense. None of it made any sense.

My parents were perfect for each other. They were, as my dad had just said, best friends.

And if *they* couldn't make a relationship work…

Then what was the point of relationships at all?

I rode my bike home from the diner, stopping first at the Man at the Wheel statue, realizing as soon as it came into view why my mother and I hadn't been able to find Emmy and Beck the night of the fireworks. Why it had looked so different here than it had the night I'd ridden bikes with Emmy and

Beck. Because that had been twenty-eight years ago. They'd expanded the sidewalk since then. Added plaques. Spruced things up.

And we hadn't found them because the universe definitely would have imploded if present-day Miriam met fourteen-year-old Emmy. Instead, I'd caught just a glimpse of them at the fireworks, and I'd managed to convince myself I hadn't seen them at all. If Miriam had seen them, it would have caused a . . . what was the word? Right. Paradox. It would probably have caused a paradox. The universe breaking and crunching in on itself. Two versions of the same person couldn't exist in the same space at the same time.

Well, maybe.

To be fair, I didn't understand how any of this worked. I was confused and eager to tell someone—anyone. But who?

Cecilia was rational, calm, fact-based. She wouldn't have believed any of it. She would have gently suggested I see a doctor.

Josh was fanciful, prone to exaggeration, eager to have his great adventure, just like the characters in his favorite books. He would have believed it too eagerly. He would have been on the next plane from Los Angeles to Boston. He would have hung up on me before I could finish my first sentence.

Jennica was somewhere in the middle. Willing to listen. Diplomatic and reasonable. Tending to err on the side of reality but—like the one book that had changed her life—open to the fantastic.

Alice in Wonderland.

That was Jennica's one book.

She'd told me she used to sleep with it under her pillow when she was nine.

She'd learned "The Walrus and the Carpenter" and "You Are Old, Father William" by heart.

She'd developed a sudden and passionate love for caterpillars, mushrooms, dodo birds, rabbit holes (both figurative and literal), tiny cakes, tiny doors, and the British tradition of teatime.

She could still recall the poems and the random facts because, aside from being a bit of a nerd, she always had something like an eidetic memory.

She would make me laugh by proclaiming, in a deep bravado: *"The time has come,"* the Walrus said, *"To talk of many things."*

I planted my feet on the sidewalk and balanced my bike underneath me as I pulled my phone out of my pocket.

I opened to the last text Jennica had ever sent me.

You are totally overreacting!!!

It had been only a couple of months ago, but it felt like much, much longer than that. The anger and hurt I'd felt toward her were still there but took up less space in my body now. It wasn't this all-consuming, enormous thing it had once been. It was smaller, less obtrusive, the size of a mushroom.

(But, of course, the size of a mushroom is relative. To a human, it's fairly tiny. To a caterpillar, it's fairly enormous.)

I guess when you started time traveling, the problems you once had began to shrink. There were both three months and thirty years between them. You were left with a healthy dose of perspective.

I almost texted her then—Jennica—with the ocean spread out in front of me, reminding me how small and teensy we really were, but I couldn't quite do it.

I put my phone away and looked at the ocean instead. The water was choppy today, the blue broken up by hundreds of whitecaps. *We should go on a whale-watching tour before the summer is over*, I thought. They left out of Gloucester a few times a day, big white ships crowded with tourists carrying cameras on straps around their neck. I had seen whales before off the coast of Malibu, in Point Dume, gray whales coming so close to shore it made me nervous. Standing on the very tip of the cliff with Miriam and Everett on either side of me, the waves crashing far below us, a pod of dolphins swimming parallel to shore.

"I think I'll go wait in the car," Miriam had said, and at the time, I'd thought the tears in her eyes were from the wind. It was my thirteenth birthday, and we'd been hit hard that year by June Gloom—a freezing cold spell in the middle of the summer. It must have been fifty degrees by the water, and my own eyes were stinging red.

"Go if you want to go," Everett had replied, and although,

at the time, it hadn't registered as particularly mean to me, although he hadn't *said* it in an angry voice, I remembered it now, and it made my stomach turn. I'd spent the day consumed with the fear of bad luck, watching for broken mirrors and spilled salt and ladders leaning up against the sides of houses. I'd been so consumed with *myself* that I hadn't seen what was happening immediately around me.

I pedaled back to the cottage, trying to outrace the memory, trying to lose it in the ocean wind.

But when I got home, I found Miriam sitting at the kitchen table, a cup of coffee at her elbow. Sobbing.

She was sobbing.

Really sobbing this time.

Not cutting-an-onion-eyes-red-and-nose-sniffly.

Sobbing. Tears pouring down her cheeks. Breathing so hard she was almost gasping.

Oh.

I wasn't used to seeing my mother cry.

She almost never cried.

The most she would do was tear up, her eyes getting wet and wide as the liquid filled them but didn't quite ever spill over. Except now. Now they were spilling, tears running down her cheeks with abandon. When she pulled her hands away from her face at the sound of the door opening, she had a pool of liquid in her cupped palms. I thought of Alice, drowning in an ocean of her own tears.

I didn't know what to do.

"Shut the door, Anna," she said after a moment.

I shut the door.

"I didn't know you'd be back so early," she said.

"I'm sorry," I said.

"Don't be sorry. Come and sit down."

I walked into the kitchen carefully, like the floor was filled with land mines. I sat down across from her. But then I thought better of it. I stood up, ripped a paper towel off the rack, handed it to her. Took my seat again.

"Thank you," she said, using the paper towel to blot at her face.

"Dad told me," I said, blurting out the words without even really meaning to, spilling them onto the table, where they lay awkwardly. I resisted the urge to brush them to the floor.

"Oh, this isn't about *that*," she said.

"It isn't?"

"Not really. I mean, I guess, if I'm being a hundred percent honest, it's maybe a *little* bit about that."

"What do you mean?"

"You weren't supposed to see me like this. I'm not supposed to burden you with this," she said. She was calming down now. The tears were slowing.

"It doesn't feel like a burden," I said. "It just feels like...a conversation."

She smiled. She balled up the paper towel and held on to it in her left fist. "I signed the divorce papers," she said, and nodded in the direction of the kitchen counter, where I'd failed to notice a manila folder. Inside, I could see a small, neat stack of white papers.

"Dad told me he gave them to you."

"I didn't think it would upset me this much," she said.

"Do you . . . not want to sign them?"

"Your father and I will always love each other. We'll always be friends. We'll always be in each other's lives. But our marriage was over. It was a mutual decision. A gradual certainty," she said. She was talking slowly, carefully, picking her words one after the other, ordering them just so. I wondered if Dad had already called her, if they had practiced together the words they would both use. Mutual decision. Gradual certainty. "But still. Signing the papers. The finality of it. You don't go into a marriage expecting it to end."

My heart felt too large for my body; my chest was aching with the burden of holding it. I was here, at the kitchen table with Miriam, and I was in Malibu, at Point Dume, watching the gray whales surface and disappear under the water again, wondering why she didn't want to see this.

She was in so much pain; it was written all over her face. I wished there was some way I could help her. But aside from going back in time and stopping my parents from getting together—

Oh.

Which was a thing I could do.

Was that why all this was happening?

Was I supposed to pull my parents apart? Drive a wedge

between them that would save them the inevitable pain of heartbreak? Was I supposed to fix *this moment*—my mother holding her hand to her chest like her heart was aching just as much as mine was?

"I shouldn't be telling you all this," Mom said when I didn't reply. She got up from the table, threw out the balled-up paper towel, grabbed the manila folder off the counter, and hurried out of the room with it.

I jumped up and followed her into the living room. I didn't think she actually knew where she was going, because she just sort of stood there, not knowing what her next move should be, holding the folder to her chest like she was scared it might fly away.

"Mom?" I said.

She turned around. She'd started crying again. Whatever was left of my heart turned to dust inside my chest.

"I'm sorry," I said. "Of course you can talk to me about this. We're all in this together. The three of us. Okay?"

She nodded, a tiny nod that I almost missed. She wiped at her eyes with her sleeves. "I just feel like such a failure," she said. "I couldn't keep my marriage together. I couldn't keep the bookstore open. I've never been able to get through *War and Peace*."

The last one was meant to make me laugh, and although it didn't quite work, we both smiled.

"I haven't talked to Jennica in two and a half months," I

said, because it felt like I needed to share something, to contribute to the conversation.

"What?" Mom asked, her voice at once confused and concerned.

"We got into a fight," I said. "She started hanging out with this new girl. She started blowing me off. I guess we're just not... We're not really friends anymore."

"Oh, honey. Why didn't you tell me?"

"I don't know. I didn't know how. I didn't want you to worry about me, maybe. With everything else that was going on."

"Come here," she said, tossing the manila folder onto the coffee table and holding her arms out. I walked into her embrace, and she folded her arms around me, hugging tightly, swaying gently back and forth. "You and Jennica were such good friends. Have you tried to talk to her about it?"

She let go, and I took a couple of steps back. I shrugged. "Not really."

"Will you tell me more about what happened?"

But it was hard to talk about. It was... confusing. There wasn't one blowup, obvious fight where we'd said terrible things to each other. It was more like... a sequence of small, almost inconsequential things. I thought she'd said to get to her house at four, but she'd said three. She didn't put in equal work in our group project. I'd sat with Josh at lunch one day, and she claimed I'd left her all alone.

And then Lara got there and...

Things only went downhill from there.

"I don't know," I said. "It was just a bunch of things. Like we kept fighting about...nothing."

"That sounds really hard," Mom said gently.

"It is," I said, and it was my turn to cry now, I guess, because I could feel the tears falling down my cheeks. Mom pulled me closer, mumbling soft words into my hair.

I let her hug me until I managed to stop crying, then she pulled away and touched my still-wet cheeks. "I think you should try talking to her about all this, honey," she said. "Maybe it's worth another shot?"

"Maybe."

What I wanted to say was—maybe you and *Dad* are worth another shot? Maybe that's what we should be focusing on here? The fact that signing the divorce papers made you cry an actual river of tears in the kitchen? The fact that the linoleum was soggy with salt water and your eyes were red and swollen?

But I didn't say any of that, of course.

I just nodded.

And hugged her again.

And went upstairs.

I almost opened the last summer reading book, but I couldn't quite bring myself to do it.

I almost texted Jennica, but I couldn't quite bring myself to do it.

I took a nap instead, and I woke up to Miriam calling me downstairs for dinner.

I should have prepared for it, but when I got to the kitchen, I was surprised to see Dad, sipping a glass of white wine, his feet propped up on another chair. When he saw me, he burst out laughing.

"Bed head, much?" he said. Mom was at the stove, but she peeked over her shoulder and smiled.

I touched my hair. It did, indeed, appear to be sticking straight up, so I ran my fingers through it, flattening it where I could.

"I fell asleep," I said.

"Yeah, duh," Dad replied. He held his arms out to me, and I hugged him, feeling slightly awkward and not knowing exactly why. I looked over to the stove, where Miriam seemed to be wrestling with a large pot of slime. There were splatters of green goo on the backsplash and all across the stove.

"What's that?" I asked.

"Gazpacho," Dad answered with a wink.

"*Green* gazpacho," Mom clarified.

If I never saw another bowl of gazpacho in my entire life, I would be happy.

But alas.

Here we were.

A few minutes later, Mom had ladled everyone a helping of the potentially toxic sludge and set out bowls before us. I raised my spoon apprehensively while I tried to decide whether to tell Miriam she had a smear of the verdant liquid in her hair. I decided against it. I took a bite.

"Holy guacamole," Dad said. "Miriam, this is *incredible*."

Mom looked immensely proud of herself as she tried her first bite. "Yeah, not bad," she agreed.

Dad was closer to the truth. It was by far the best gazpacho she'd made yet. Creamy, a hint of spice, the perfect touch of umami.

"Wow," I said.

Miriam beamed.

She looked a lot better than she had before my nap. She'd changed into a simple summer dress, clipped her hair out of her face, put on a little blush.

Oh—and she was no longer sobbing.

That made a difference.

Dad didn't linger long after dinner ("Early appointment," he explained as he pulled me in for a hug), and I couldn't help noticing he and my mother barely said good night to each other. Usually, they hugged. But they always said goodbye, and Everett always thanked her for dinner, and Miriam always said you're welcome. But that night, after he hugged me, Everett slipped out the front door while Miriam was in the bathroom.

And that was how I knew what to do.

That simple thing—Dad leaving quietly, Mom not asking where he'd went when she came out of the bathroom a few seconds later—told me everything I needed to know.

highly
irregular
orbits

left the house around eight that night. Miriam was reading a book on the couch; she waved her hand over her head when I told her I was going for a walk. She'd cried again, after we'd cleaned up the kitchen together. She did it in the shower, trying to be sneaky, but I could tell when she came out. Her face looked scrubbed clean, shiny and raw, and her eyes had a glassy, blank stare to them.

I paid particular attention to the cottage when I left it. Could I tell the exact moment I stepped back in time? Could I see the house reverse age by almost thirty years—a snap of the fingers and the paint would be fresher, the driveway free of cracks and pockmarks, the tree that took up most of the front yard just a young thing now, a baby tree, planted by my great-aunt one spring day when she was bored?

I kept looking behind me, but the house stayed exactly the same. I reached the end of the street and peered into the window of the little breakfast café, the coffee shop. I paused at the beginning of Bearskin Neck, waiting, watching every tourist who passed by me. Were they dressed in present-day clothes? Were they holding cell phones? Or were they thirty years behind the times?

I wanted to test my moonstone theory, but I was beginning to think something else was behind it, too. I think it had to do with intention and situation.

I think that was part of the reason it wouldn't work at the fireworks.

The situation wasn't right.

If I disappeared in a crowd of people that big, shooting backward in time and space, somebody was bound to notice.

I kept that in mind as I spun the ring around my finger.

Nothing changed.

The people around me were the same. One little boy had an iPhone in his hands.

So, the present.

Thus I made a mental note of the first rule of time travel: I couldn't do it in front of anyone else.

Another rule: It had something to do with the ring. I maybe had to twirl the ring or touch the ring or at least *wear* the ring. And that was easy since I hadn't taken it off since Dad had given it to me.

Another rule, I thought: intention.

Whenever I'd come across Emmy and Beck, aside from the first night I had met them, I'd been out *looking* for them.

And the last rule. Maybe the most important rule of all:

This had all started when I'd made a wish on those shooting stars, while Kit-Hale glowed brilliantly in the sky above me.

And all these things, somehow, converged together to create...

A recipe for time travel.

I laughed out loud, and the little kid with the iPhone shot me a weird look.

What it also meant, I thought, as I started walking again, *was that this was probably all going to be over when Kit-Hale was gone.* Which would coincide pretty much exactly with my leaving Rockport. So I didn't think time traveling was going to be a permanent fixture in my life.

"Might as well enjoy it while it lasts," I mumbled under my breath, and I kept my head up as I walked, paying attention to see if I could spot a specific moment, a wall I walked through, a shimmer, a tilt, a shift, a flash of brightness, or a shower of shooting stars.

But I couldn't.

Nothing at all.

When I reached the Motif, I still didn't know what time it was—what *year* it was—but then I saw her, Emmy, sitting on one of the shorter pylons, her legs kicking, her body pointed out to sea.

I sat on the pylon next to her.

"Hi, Anna," she said. She seemed sad, quieter than she usually was, and she didn't look over at me when she spoke. She was watching Kit-Hale. I noticed, for the first time, how much distance it had traveled across the sky. The newspaper had run a front-page article on it the other day. It would be around for only a couple more weeks. It was known as a long-period comet, a celestial body with a highly irregular orbit, one that slingshotted it toward Earth before pulling it back out again, away and away and away. They thought it probably originated outside our solar system, a fact that had made me dizzy when I read it and that made me dizzy again now. I gripped either side of the pylon, suddenly a bit unsteady.

"Wild, huh," Emmy said, still not looking at me. Her eyes were trained upward, staring at the night sky. "Halley's comet is only visible for, like, two days or something."

"The next time it will appear is 2061," I said.

"Wow. We'll be so old," Emmy laughed. "I think I kinda remember the last time it was here, though. I was six."

"I wasn't even born yet," I replied without thinking.

Emmy laughed. "What? Of course you were. You're the same age as me."

"Oh. Right."

"I remember my aunt came to visit. It was freezing. We all bundled up in sweatshirts and coats and went outside to see it." Emmy's voice was faraway, remembering.

"I have a terrible memory," I said, instead of answering.

Emmy nodded. "Well, this one is cooler than that. Did you know they can't predict this one's orbit? It's just sort of like, *Here I am! What's up, everyone!*"

"Yeah, I know," I said, smiling, staring up at it.

We were both silent for a minute, lost in our own worlds, our eyes pointed up. Finally, Emmy turned to me, cleared her throat, and said, "Beck asked me to be his girlfriend."

All the quiet, happy feelings I'd just had were sucked out of me, like someone opening a drain in a bathtub. I watched them swirl away until there was nothing left except a big empty void.

"Oh," I said. "What did you say?"

"I said I'd think about it," she replied. She went from staring at the comet to staring at her hands, holding both of them in her lap, playing with her fingers.

"Well... What do you think you're going to do?"

"I don't know. I really like him."

"But...?"

"But... I don't live here, you know? I'm just here for the summers. So what would happen for all the other time? We just wouldn't see each other?"

"Did you ask him?"

"No. I just said we'd talk about it later." She looked up at me again. She was biting her lower lip. "What do you think I should do?"

And here it was. Had I known this moment was coming? Had I foreseen its arrival? I *was* a time traveler, after all. I should be able to predict these things.

I'd already made up my mind. What to do.

So I put on my best half frown. I concentrated on looking thoughtful but pensive. Caring but firm.

"I don't know. You guys are such good friends. It would feel too risky to me. To mess that up."

I saw Emmy's face fall by the tiniest, almost imperceptible amount.

I saw her nod, the tiniest, almost imperceptible amount.

Then she said, in the tiniest, almost imperceptible voice, "Yeah. I know."

And I couldn't help it.

I held my hand out in front of my face.

I didn't know what I was expecting, really.

I was expecting to fade away, maybe.

I was expecting to blink out of existence.

I was expecting to snuff out, like the flame of a candle when you pinched it between your fingers. The slightest *ouch*, then nothing.

But nothing happened.

Did that mean Emmy still ended up with Beck? Did that mean my parents still got married? Did that mean I was still eventually born? Could you even change the past, or was everything set in stone, written in blood, carved into the earth by an unflappable hand?

If my father remembered saving a drowning girl in the present, then clearly that *had* happened to me. Was it always *meant* to happen, then? Was there nothing I could have done to avoid it?

"Um, Anna? What are you doing?" Emmy asked.

Oh.

I was still staring at my hand.

"I think I got a, um…splinter. From the pylon."

"Oh, bummer," she said. She hopped off her own pylon then, stretching her arms up over her head. "You're probably right," she continued. "About Beck. I mean, I like him, you know. As a friend, I like him a lot. I just don't know if I want to risk that. Like you said."

A quick glance at my hand—still there!

"Yeah," I said. "I mean, you don't live here. You'll be going home soon, right?"

"Couple of weeks," she replied, nodding.

"So it's probably for the best."

"Yeah." She didn't really seem sad, just quiet, but still, I couldn't help feeling like I was crushing her heart into a million pieces.

But this was better, I told myself. This was better than the pain she would feel when it ended up not working.

This was better than Miriam's sobbing at the kitchen table in the middle of the day. This *had* to be better than that.

I looked at my hand again.

I was still solid.

Which was ironic, given that I basically felt the exact opposite of that.

I spent the next two days mostly inside. I still met Dad for lunch, because he wouldn't have taken no for an answer, but I didn't go to Bearskin Neck after dinner.

I just couldn't stand to see Emmy and Beck not together. To see what I'd done.

And I kept waiting for myself to blink out of existence. For the past to change, and for the trickle-down effects to catch me completely unaware. In the shower I eyed the drain suspiciously and imagined myself turning into liquid, tumbling out to sea, dispersing into the ocean.

Would I lose consciousness? Would it be the quick, final *snap* of closing a book, slamming a door, falling asleep?

Would nobody remember who I was? Jennica, Josh, Cece... Would their memories of me be wiped clean away?

Would my mother have other children? Would my father?

It kept me up at night, so by the time Saturday rolled around, I looked in the bathroom mirror and discovered I had purple-blue bags underneath my eyes. I touched them softly, examining myself in the mirror more closely than I'd done in a while.

I was still *me*, but the summer had undoubtedly changed me, too.

I was tanner; my hair was wilder; I ran my fingers through it and wondered how long it would take for the salt to wash out completely.

Yeah, we lived near the ocean back home, but this ocean was different. The salt of this ocean got into your clothes and your bedsheets and your shoes and yes, your hair. The salt of this ocean made the air thick and almost blue and hazy and full. The salt of this ocean was something you could smell and walk through and bite.

I snapped my teeth in the reflection, and only then did I notice Miriam standing in the doorway, watching me with a bemused expression on her face, one of her eyebrows raised.

"Dinosaur?" she asked.

"Shark," I corrected.

"You've been staring in that mirror for three hundred and sixty-eight seconds," she said. "Approximately."

"You've been counting?"

"Yes. Everything okay?"

"Yeah."

"Are you sure, Anna? Because everything doesn't *seem* okay."

I turned toward her, leaning my hip against the porcelain sink. Through my T-shirt, the ceramic was cool and smooth. Even though the cottage was small and our bedrooms were right across from each other and we ate dinner together every night, it sort of felt like I hadn't seen my mother in days. Her hair was wilder, too (and that was saying something, because her hair was pretty wild to begin with). And while she didn't seem to be tanner, something about her face had changed. Her eyes, maybe. They were wider, brighter. Less the pale lavender I'd always thought they'd been and more hazel, a light-greeny, browny, taupe-y, orangey swirl of colors. She wore an old T-shirt with holes in it, the fabric worn so thin in places that it was almost translucent.

It had belonged to my father, of course. Once upon a time.

I wondered if I suddenly blinked out of existence, would

that T-shirt melt away, too? Would Miriam Bell be left naked in the hallway outside the bathroom?

"Are you going to change your last name?" I blurted out, and she smiled sadly and leaned her body against the door-jamb. She nodded the slightest amount. I barely noticed it at all.

"I thought that might be what's on your mind," she said.

"What do you mean?"

"The divorce. I'm sure it feels real to you now that we've signed the papers."

"Am I going to change *my* last name?"

"Why on earth would you change your last name, Anna?"

"I don't know. If you wanted me to, I would."

"I would never ask you to change a single part of yourself," she said in that straightforward, super-intense way she had sometimes of saying something so intimate it made my skin crawl.

"But are you?" I persisted.

"Changing my name? I hadn't really thought about it. I've been a Bell for a long time."

"Did you ever miss being a Forrest?"

Miriam Forrest.

It didn't make sense in my brain. It didn't flow right.

"I've never missed being a Forrest," she said a few moments later. "No, I don't think I'll change my name. But maybe I should ask your father about it."

"Do you think he would want you to?"

"I think he'd probably want me to do whatever I wanted."

I nodded. "I don't want to meet this woman," I said then, quietly, looking down at the tiled floor.

"I don't want to meet her, either," Miriam said, and when I looked up at her, she was smiling. "At least, not right away."

"Don't you think it feels too *soon*?"

She crossed her arms over her chest and looked over my head, thinking. "That's a tricky question to answer. It would be too soon for me. It's the last thing on my mind right now, to be honest. But just because it would be too soon for *me* doesn't necessarily mean it's wrong. Everyone moves at their own pace. Everyone needs different things in different times. And I don't think your father went looking for this. I think sometimes things just...happen. And we either let them happen or we push them away. And I think in this case, he let it happen."

"I think it's too soon," I said. "I think it's weird."

She smiled. "I never said I didn't think it was weird. But all of this is weird, you know?"

"Yeah."

"He leaves tomorrow."

"I know."

"I can't help noticing you haven't brushed your hair in three days."

"What's the point?" I said.

"Will you tell me what else is going on? Will you give me just a little clue?"

"All of this. That's all. Nothing specific."

"Can I offer a suggestion?"

"Okay."

"Reach out to Jennica. Whatever happened, whatever didn't happen, whosever fault it was...Just let all that go. Life's too short to lose such a good friend."

I shrugged. "Maybe."

"Think about it, okay? And think about taking a shower. There's a very specific smell coming off you right now, and while I love every part of you, I could do without that."

She flashed another smile and went downstairs. I shut the bathroom door and turned on the shower. Because she had a point.

I didn't know how I felt about Dad going back home. It meant we had only about three weeks left in Rockport. And two weeks after that, I'd be back in school.

It felt like another world, never mind another state. California and Massachusetts were different planets, and right now, leaving one to return to the other felt like an impossible journey that would require a spaceship and multiple crates of freeze-dried food and a complicated space suit Miriam would have to zip me into.

I stepped into the shower and let the water wash over me, imagining it washing not just the outside of me but the inside as well, giving me a fresh start and a clean slate and a spotless soul.

I tried not to look at the drain.

Dad cooked dinner that night, against the advice of both my mother and me. While great at many things, Everett Bell was a terrible cook, and among his kitchen mishaps he had once (1) set fire to the curtains that hung on the window over the sink, (2) spilled an entire bag of flour onto the floor, (3) tried to heat a fully constructed sandwich in a toaster, and (4) added white wine *vinegar* to a saucepan of risotto instead of the requested *white wine*. That meal had been particularly inedible.

Miriam and I sat at the kitchen table, under the pretext of "visiting," but really, we were supervising the entire operation. I kept eyeing the cabinet we kept the fire extinguisher in, mentally calculating how many seconds it would take me to make a mad dash and save all our lives.

His meal of choice was a vegetable risotto. Risotto takes a long time to cook, and he concentrated diligently, adding just a bit of vegetable stock at a time, stirring constantly, never letting his attention wander.

"I've been watching YouTube tutorials," he said brightly, setting bowls in front of each of us.

Honestly, it looked incredible.

"Everett, color me impressed," Mom said.

"I figured it was about time I learned how to cook," he said, and just the way he said it, it was obvious what he meant—it was time he learned how to cook because nobody was cooking for him anymore.

Miriam smiled. "Well, it *looks* beautiful."

"Here's hoping it doesn't poison us all," I added cheerfully.

"My sweet Worm, always keeping me humble," Dad replied.

He grabbed his own bowl of risotto and joined us at the table. I spooned a bit of the rice with a few English peas and a tiny sliver of asparagus.

The moment of truth: the first bite.

Oh wow. It was—

"*Delicious*, Everett!" Mom exclaimed.

"Seriously, Dad. This is so good."

Dad was practically beaming. He had already placed his napkin across his lap, but he picked it up now and dabbed dramatically at his eyes. It was meant to be a joke, but I could tell he was *actually* starting to tear up.

"I'll see you in a couple of weeks, Dad," I said.

"I know, I know," he said, waving his hand at me, setting the napkin on his lap again. "Leave me alone. Eat your dinner. Don't look at me."

He took a sip of his water and stared at his bowl of risotto. Miriam looked over at me and winked.

Dad collected himself a few moments later. He ate a spoonful of risotto and then clapped his hands together gently. "So. Bright and early at the train station. Should I call a car?"

"Don't be ridiculous," Miriam said. "We'll drive you."

"Are you sure?" he asked, tearing up again. "Ugh, look at

me. I'm a big ball of emotion. It's just been a good trip, you know? It's been nice to be back here. See this old place again." He looked around like he meant both the cottage and the whole town of Rockport, like he was seeing past the walls of the kitchen and out over the harbor, past Bearskin Neck and the rocky jetty, out into the wild blue of the Atlantic. He wiped at his eyes again, sniffing dramatically.

"It was nice to see you, Dad," I said. "Almost as nice as it was to see Wallace Green."

Mom rolled her eyes. "Not this again."

And that was it. Our last night in Rockport together.

And as we sat there, eating the risotto and laughing and talking about Wallace Green and tattoos and old, silly inside jokes only the three of us would understand, I couldn't help wondering...

Was this it?

Was this the last time we'd be together like this? In this exact way? Sharing dinner, laughing, talking...

Would Dad eventually bring his new...

I couldn't say the word. Couldn't even think it. It felt too *weird*.

But would he bring her to family dinners?

Eventually, he would have to. If they stayed together, if years passed, if they got married...

Then obviously he would want her to be a part of our family. A fourth member of our unit. The unasked-for intruder ruining our perfect triangle.

My heart was breaking.

Again. Continuously. Still.

I choked on an English pea.

Dad leaned over and thumped me on the back.

"Thanks," I mumbled, and I pretended the tears in my eyes had nothing to do with anything else.

invisible
balloon of
despair

Mom and I waved bye to Dad from the front porch. He acted all dramatic, clutching his heart, stumbling away from us into the night. Mom held a glass of white wine and stared down the street long after we couldn't see him anymore. She'd offered to drive him back, but he'd said he needed the fresh air. I thought he probably just wanted to finally start crying away from our prying eyes.

I sat on the swing and put my feet up on the coffee table, and Miriam did the same. When I held my hand out for a taste of her wine, she chuckled softly and drained the glass herself, then she handed it to me, empty, and asked for a refill.

I went and got it for her. It felt like the least I could do. Her sadness was a palpable thing, taking up space on the porch. Going into the kitchen was a relief; walking back outside was like pressing up against an invisible balloon of despair. I navigated back to the swing and collapsed on it. I had a pointed sip of the wine and gave it back to her. She continued to stare out into the night, quiet.

"When will it be finalized?" I asked.

"Soon," she said. "I dunno. Your father is handling it all. He knows I'm not good with stuff like that."

"And the bookstore?"

"I don't want to talk about the bookstore," she said quietly.

I didn't know what else to say. I leaned my head against her shoulder, and she kissed the top of my hair.

"Are you going to be okay?" I asked her after a few minutes.

"Of course," she said with not a moment's hesitation. "We're both going to be okay. We're going to grow and learn and live and love and forge onward, two independent women marching into a brave new world." She paused, had a sip of wine, then added, "Speaking of which, have you opened your last summer reading book yet? You might like this one."

"Not likely," I said.

"You haven't liked any of them?"

"They're just *boring*," I complained. "They're all about men and how hard it is being a man and how sad men are."

She snort-laughed, and I picked up my head and looked at her. Her cheeks were red, and her eyes were bright and shining. She didn't look so sad anymore.

So maybe I was wrong about everything.

Maybe things really *were* going to be okay.

She wrapped her arm around my shoulders and pulled me

close, pressing her nose against my cheek before pulling away again.

"I think you'll like the last one," she said. "It's not like that at all."

"It isn't?"

"Nope. A totally new story."

"Is it . . ." I didn't know how to ask her what I wanted to ask her, what I'd never really asked her before.

I'd asked Emmy:

What's the one book that will change my life?

But I had never asked Miriam.

"Is it what?" she said after a moment.

"You know. Is it . . . my book? My one book?"

"Oh." She smiled. Had a sip of her wine. Looked into the glass for a moment, like she was seeing something that wasn't really there. "You know, I've been wondering when you might ask me that."

"Well, you've never said. I thought maybe . . . I didn't *have* a book or something."

"Oh, everyone has a book, Anna," she said. Another sip of wine. A long moment of silence. She played with a string on my denim shorts. "And I've thought about a lot of books for you over the years. But somehow I keep changing my mind. It's almost like . . . I don't know. Maybe I haven't known you long enough."

It was just like what Emmy had said. *I don't know. I don't think I've known you long enough.*

"But you've known me my whole life," I said.

"I know," she said, scrunching up her nose. "And I've always had this feeling. That maybe it's just something you'll find out for yourself. Maybe I'm supposed to let you get there on your own. Maybe that's why I can't quite make up my mind about it."

"Maybe."

"I'm proud of you, though," she continued. "For powering through those books. As boring as they all might have been."

"I didn't really have a choice," I pointed out. "It's homework."

"And still. You did it with minimal complaining."

"I feel like I complained a lot."

"*Nooo*," she said, her voice sarcastic and singsongy.

I knocked my shoulder against hers, and then we were quiet for a while.

Kit-Hale was out, but it seemed significantly dimmer now. If you didn't know what you were looking for, you might miss the comet altogether. It just looked like a not-overly-bright star. A faint tail behind it, a smudge against the sky.

Five or ten minutes passed, and I counted only three meteors.

"I think I'll go out for a little walk," I said. "If that's okay with you."

"Of course," she said. "Going to meet your friends?"

"Maybe," I said. "Just want to see if they're around."

"Well, have a nice time. I think I'll stay out here a little while longer."

"Okay. But you're okay?"

"I'm okay, honey," she insisted.

"I love you."

"I love you, too."

I left her on the porch, her eyes half-closed, the glass of wine in her hand. It was a mild night for a change, and I made my way to Bearskin Neck already feeling like I was leaving it, like my time was running out. Like I would fade away with Kit-Hale, returning in twenty-eight or thirty-eight or a hundred more years. If it was difficult to predict a comet's return, it would surely have been more difficult to predict the return of a fourteen-year-old girl who wouldn't have much of a reason to come back here. We were selling the cottage. Selling the car, all the furniture. Clearing out the spider-heaven shed in the backyard. Getting rid of the bikes my parents had ridden around town all those years ago. That one summer they'd made a friend they could now barely remember.

Did it bother me that I hadn't seemed to make that much of an impression on my father? That the memory of saving a girl from drowning—a memory you'd think would be loud and bright in his mind—was faded and hard to look at properly. That he couldn't describe what the girl had looked like, that he didn't realize the girl was *me*.

But I thought it made a certain amount of sense.

I thought, when I was my parents' age, this summer might feel like a dream to me, too. I might question what was real, what had really happened. I might not really remember much at all. The feeling of drowning, of being underneath all that water...

It might feel like nothing more than a particularly bad dream.

When I got to the Motif, I found only Beck there, playing a game of solitaire on the ground, his legs folded in front of him and his backpack discarded a few feet away. When he heard me coming, he looked up hopefully. When he saw it was me, his shoulders fell just a bit.

"Oh. Hey, Anna," he said.

"Hey," I replied. "Expecting someone else?"

"Not really. I just haven't seen Emmy in a few days. I thought maybe..."

"Did she say anything?"

"Nah," he said. "I think maybe I did something wrong. We kind of...kissed. I don't know if she told you."

"Yeah," I said. "She did."

My stomach felt like it was full of rocks.

I'd done it.

I'd persuaded Emmy to leave Beck.

I'd split up my parents.

"Maybe she regrets it," Beck said, shrugging.

"Do you?"

"No," he said simply. "No, I thought it was kind of nice. But I'm not the best at figuring out what girls want, I guess."

"I'm sorry," I said, and in that moment, I really was. I was sorry for everything. For interfering. For abusing the privilege of time travel. For thinking I knew what was best for two people who were at once so close to me but also—at this point— barely strangers.

"Thanks," he said. "I'm glad to see you. Sorry if it seemed like I wasn't. Where have you been, anyway?"

"With my dad," I said. "He leaves tomorrow. Back to California."

"Ah. Bummer."

"Yeah. It was nice to see him."

"It's cool that you're so close with him," he said. "My dad just kind of works a lot."

"Really? You've never told me that before," I said. And I meant *Everett* had never told me that before, but of course Beck couldn't have known that.

"Yeah, I guess I don't really talk about it a lot," Beck replied. "I don't know. It's not like he's a *bad* father. He's just...always busy. I think that's why Billy is okay with driving me places and stuff. I think he's, like...trying to compensate."

"He's a good brother," I said.

"Yeah, he is." Beck paused, started gathering up the cards in front of him. "I always thought if I ever had kids, I'd try to be different. Like...around more. You know?" He laughed, fidgeting with the cards in his hands. "Is that weird for some-one our age to think about?"

"No, I don't think it's weird at all," I said, and I had to fight the urge to throw myself into his arms, this boy who would eventually grow up and be the best father in the entire world. "I think it's really nice."

"Thanks," he said, shrugging, slightly embarrassed. "Hey, can I tell you something?"

"Sure."

"My name's not really Beck."

I tried to act surprised. "Oh?"

"Yeah. It's kind of a long story. But my name is actually Everett."

"Everett," I said. "I like that."

"But you can call me Beck, still, if you're sentimentally attached to that."

I laughed. "I like Everett," I said. "I'll call you Everett."

He smiled. He finished cleaning up the cards and slipped them back into their case, then he sat back and looked up at the sky. How many hours had we spent looking up that summer? How many hours had we spent tracing the path of a comet in the sky?

"Can I ask you for something?" I said then. "A favor?"

"Sure," Beck replied.

No. Everett.

It would take a while to get used to that.

"Will you teach me how to swim?"

"Of course!" he said immediately, his eyes lighting up. "We can start tonight, if you want?"

"I don't have a bathing suit with me," I said. "But tomorrow?"

"Totally. Let's meet at the White Wharf."

The technically private beach.

"That's perfect," I said. "Thanks, Everett. I should probably be getting home now. See you tomorrow."

"See you tomorrow, Anna."

swimming
lessons

Miriam and I were up at seven to take Dad to a seven forty-five train. He was waiting for us outside the bed-and-breakfast when we pulled up, and he slid his suitcase into the trunk before jumping into the back seat. I was sitting in the front seat, so he wrapped his arms around me from behind, then pretended his hands were my hands and fumbled with the passenger-side window, rolling it up and down as Mom chuckled quietly in the driver's seat.

When we reached the train station, he stubbornly refused to get out of the back seat. "I don't *wanna leaveeeee*," he sang, and finally, I had to drag him out. He wrapped me in a truly suffocating hug that lasted for at least thirty seconds. "I'm gonna miss you so much," he said when he finally pulled away.

"As I mentioned last night, I'm going to see you in just a couple of weeks," I said.

"Each day that passes will feel like an eternity," he said

dramatically, putting the back of his hand against his forehead as if he were a damsel in an old-fashioned movie.

"For me, too, totally," I said, laughing, as Mom placed his suitcase next to him on the asphalt.

"It was really nice seeing you, B," she said. "I'm glad you came."

They hugged, but I was barely paying attention. All I could hear, like an echo in my head, was *B, B, B, B, B*...

"My sweet baby Worm," Dad said when he and Mom pulled away from each other. "Write to me. Every day. Promise."

"I'll text you, Dad," I said.

"I want handwritten letters. Calligraphy pens. Wax seals."

"I'll see what I can do."

"Bring me back some fudge," he said, hugging me for a second time as we heard the train whistle in the distance. "That's my ride," he said, winking.

He picked up his suitcase, saluted, and made his way to the platform. He was definitely crying as the train pulled up and he stepped inside it, but he looked back anyway, giving one final wave to both of us.

"What a strange man," Mom said.

"You married him," I replied before I could stop myself, and I thought it was the wrong thing to say, I regretted it as soon as the words left my mouth, but Mom only laughed earnestly, putting her hand on my shoulder.

"Touché," she said.

We drove from the train station right to Wingaersheek,

walking out on the sandbar as far as we could go. I didn't think I could ever get sick of the feeling of standing in the middle of the ocean, of being surrounded by all that water. It made me feel small and enormous at the exact same time.

We stayed at the beach all day and stopped on the way home to get a pizza for dinner. We ate it on the front porch as the sun set slowly. Mom was exhausted and kept yawning, but I felt strangely awake and super hungry; I went for a fourth piece as Mom leaned back on the swing and closed her eyes.

"Long day," she said. "I think I'm going to take a shower and get into bed. Do some reading."

"Okay, Mom."

"You'll clean all this up?"

"Sure."

"You going out again?"

"Yeah, for a little while."

"I still need to meet these friends. Amy and . . . What was it?"

"Jack," I said.

"Right. I feel like a bad mother. Letting you galivant around with strangers all summer."

"We're hardly galivanting," I said. "And besides. Didn't you used to do the same exact thing when you were my age?"

She smiled, suddenly a million miles away, remembering.

Then she kissed me on the temple. "Night, sweetheart."

"Night."

She went inside, and I finished my slice of pizza and took the box into the house. I washed our plates and set them in the drying rack, then I paused by the kitchen windows, looking out at the darkening street.

I was still wearing my bathing suit underneath my clothes, so I grabbed the house keys and a beach towel and started walking to the White Wharf. I felt nervous. I had spent fourteen years of my life aggressively refusing to learn how to swim, and here I was, walking to the water. The very *cold* water. The very cold and *shark-infested* water.

"Get a grip," I mumbled under my breath as I ducked between two buildings to reach the small beach, where Beck was already waiting for me.

Everett.

I needed to remember that.

But it was still hard to *actually* think of this fourteen-year-old boy as my father. And he wasn't, really. He wouldn't be for quite a while.

So, although it was kind of sweet to think about it as my father teaching me to swim...

It wasn't him. Not really.

But it also *was*.

It both *was* and *wasn't*.

It was complicated.

I thought of the unhelpful timeline I'd made, my parents existing in two different places at the very same moment, my present-day father arriving back in Los Angeles after a long day of travel, taking a cab back to his house, maybe ordering in for dinner, pad thai or massaman curry from his favorite restaurant.

I wondered if *she* would be there with him, and then I tried not to wonder about it, because in reality, I didn't want to know.

"Hey!" Everett called, waving cheerfully to me. He was in swim trunks. It was funny seeing him without the many, many tattoos that would eventually adorn his body.

He'd get his first one on his eighteenth birthday.

Five little trees on the inside crook of his left arm.

For my mother.

Miriam Forrest.

It was almost sickeningly cute.

But I wondered...

Would this version of Everett Bell never actually get that tattoo?

And yet.

I was still here.

So who knew.

"Are you ready?!" Everett said when I reached him.

"I'm cold," I said.

"It's, like, ninety degrees out."

"I am *anticipating* being cold," I clarified.

"Oh right. Yeah, the water is pretty chilly. But you get used to it."

"I don't *love* the beach," I said. "Even though I basically grew up on the beach."

Everett leaned a little closer to me and conspiratorially whispered, "Honestly? Me neither. Too much sand. It gets *everywhere*. And I don't love getting my hair wet, either."

"Well, I appreciate you braving it for me."

"Anything to ensure I'll never have to save your life again," he said, smiling widely.

I pulled my T-shirt over my head and stepped out of my jean shorts. I was wearing a simple navy-blue one-piece. My hair was in a ponytail. I was already shivering.

"Do you have *goose bumps*?" Everett said, laughing. "You're ridiculous."

"And I am two seconds away from changing my mind."

"Okay, okay. Let's get in, then."

We waded into the water. Everett took me by the elbow, maybe to make me feel more confident or maybe to make sure I wouldn't turn and run away. We walked in up to our waists, and then Everett stopped and turned to me.

"The first step in learning how to swim is learning how to float," he said.

The water was still and calm, and it didn't actually feel *quite* as cold as Wingaersheek. But still, my skin was all goose bumps, and I couldn't seem to unclench my muscles.

"Let's do a quick dunk," he continued. "Rip the Band-Aid off."

"Ugh," I said.

But I let him take both of my hands, and he counted to three dramatically, staring into my eyes, and then we plunged underneath the water, the shock of it taking my breath away, taking me back to the moment Emmy had pushed me into the water.

But this was different. Everett held on to my hands tightly, and when we surfaced again, he was still holding on to me and we were both laughing and spluttering in the cold water.

We spent the next forty-five minutes in the water, me floating, Everett with his hands underneath me in case I started to sink.

As it turned out, floating wasn't quite as easy as it looked, but by the end of our session, I'd definitely gotten the hang of it.

And by the end of a *week*, I could actually swim!

I mean. It wasn't a graceful butterfly stroke or anything, but I could make my way from one end of the beach to the other, diligently plodding along, my arms slicing through the cold water, my legs kicking behind me.

"You're a regular fish," Everett said as we sat wrapped in our towels on the beach.

"I want to jump off the dock," I replied before I could talk myself out of it.

"I dunno...," he said. "The water there is deep. We haven't gone anywhere you can't touch the bottom yet."

"I'm ready."

"But I don't know if *I'm* ready," he said, seeing how serious I was. "Anna, I basically got lucky last time," he said. "That I was able to find you so quickly. The water's super dark and deep and—"

"I'm ready," I said again, jumping to my feet. "I swear."

He followed me to the Motif, if only because he had no other option; I was clearly going with or without him. The whole way, he kept up a constant barrage of all the reasons I shouldn't do it. But when I was finally standing on the edge of the pier, between two wooden pylons, ready to jump despite it all, he finally grabbed me by the shoulder.

"You're very stubborn, do you know that?" he said.

And I nodded.

Very seriously.

Because in that moment, I *did* know it.

I'd been stubborn with my mom. I'd refused to listen to what she was actually telling me about the divorce. I was convinced that *I* knew what was best for her. For both of them. That I knew more about their marriage than they did.

I'd been stubborn with my father, not letting him tell me about his new girlfriend. Not asking a *single* question about her, because I thought it was too soon. Because I had judged him based on time alone. And hadn't I learned that time was basically an arbitrary thing? Flexible and wiggly and slippery and *moving*?

I'd been stubborn with Jennica. Jealous that she'd made a new friend, refusing to even give Lara the time of day.

Stubborn with Josh and Cecilia. And more than that...I took my friends for granted. I hadn't called Josh or Cece *once* since I'd gotten to Rockport. I acted like a victim when in actuality I expected my friends to be there for me exactly when I needed them and basically disappear when I didn't.

"I know," I said finally. "I know I'm stubborn. And I'm going to work on it."

And before Everett could answer, before I could change my mind, because I could stop to give it a second thought—

I jumped.

And when I hit the water, I didn't let it take my breath away. Because I was ready for it.

I was ready for the way it swallowed me up, for the way it washed over me, for the way it surrounded me completely.

I let myself hang there, suspended in the dark, for one brief moment.

And then I kicked my legs and shot up toward the surface.

ALB

walked home smiling that night, hair wet and eyes reflecting a sky crowded with stars and the faint echo of a comet that was sticking around, for now.

The cottage was dark and quiet when I got home. I let myself in and locked the door behind me, then I got a glass of water and took it upstairs. I sat cross-legged on my bed, picking up my phone, and sent a message to my group chat with Cecilia and Josh.

> I'm sorry if I've ever been anything less than a perfect friend to you.

A blanket apology felt necessary. A blanket apology felt good.

They both texted back pretty quickly, and it was rapid-fire for a few minutes.

Cece: Are you tipsy? Did you have three sips of wine again?

Josh: Who is this? I don't have this number saved in my phone.

Me: Guys. I'm being serious.

Cece: I am also being serious.

Josh: I, as well, am being serious.

Me: I'm trying to APOLOGIZE here.

Cece: You have nothing to apologize for, dweeb.

Josh: I don't know, C, I could find a couple things for her to apologize for. Like her poor reading habits.

Cece: You're such a nerd, Joshy.

Me: I just mean, if I have ever been a shitty friend to either of you, I'm sorry. I really love you guys. Right now you're definitely pissing me off, but I DO love you.

Josh: Why don't you just marry us if you love us so much?

Cece: She's not my type.

Me: I'm deleting both your numbers from my phone.

Cece: Okayyyy, Anna. Are you actually looking for feedback here or something?

Me: Yes, feedback! Feedback is good!

Josh: I can't really think of anything.

Cece: I can. If you're sure you want to hear it…

Me: Definitely sure. This is a safe space. I'm all ears.

Cece: Okay, well…You haven't come to one of my volleyball games in a while, and that's sort of bummed me out.

Me: Totally fair point. I will come to one as soon as I'm back.

Josh: Ugh, fine, okay, I'll do one.

Josh: You kind of talk about your parents' divorce like they're the only people who have ever gotten divorced and whenever I try and give you advice because MY parents got divorced, you kind of act like I don't know what I'm talking about.

Josh: As long as we're being honest.

Josh: Now I feel like a jerk.

Me: No, no Josh, you are NOT a jerk. I'm sorry I didn't listen to you. I think sometimes I feel like my problems are the biggest problems in the entire world, and nobody could ever possibly understand them. But that's ridiculous. And I'm sorry I made you feel that way.

Josh: Apology accepted.

Cece: Ditto. Can you tell us what's going on now? Are you OK?

Me: I'm okay. I've just had a lot of time to think
in the past few weeks.

Josh: That's because you're in a tiny town in
the middle of nowhere and thinking is the only
thing to do over there.

Cece: When are you backkkkkkk?

Me: Soon. I miss you!!!!!

Cece: I miss you tooooooo.

Josh: I miss you, Anna, but I don't miss you,
Cece, because I just saw you today.

Cece: Fine, I don't miss you EITHER.

They sent a few more texts back and forth to each other, and I added a couple of emojis, then tossed my phone onto the comforter. Almost immediately, the screen lit up with a call from Josh.

"Hey," I said, bringing the phone to my ear.

"Hey. You okay?"

"Yeah. I've just been doing a lot of thinking. Like you said, tiny town."

"Yeah, well." Josh paused on the other side of the line, and I heard him shifting, getting comfortable. "I'm glad you texted. I wanted to talk to you about something, actually."

"What's up?"

"I don't know if you're gonna freak out," he said quietly. "It feels like you might."

"Um...I won't really know until you tell me."

"Right. Well. Just remember that I love you and you're one of my best friends in the world, okay?"

"You are really freaking me out now."

"It's about Jennica. Do you remember when we went to the beach, the day you left, and you told me you thought her pottery wasn't that good and I said it was good, and you were like, 'How do you even know?'"

"I do not sound like that," I said, because he'd done a truly obnoxious impression of my voice.

"You sort of do. Anyway, I didn't answer you, but the truth is…Jennica and I are…"

He trailed off.

"Oh my god," I said, realization dawning on me. "How long?"

"The week after your fight."

"The *week after*!"

"Look. You always kept Jennica, like…hidden from us."

"*Hidden?!*"

"You wanted honesty, right?"

I inhaled deeply, then said, "Yes."

"You were kind of weird with her. Like you never invited us all to hang out together, we barely even knew her. But sometimes you do that. Make new friends and don't really…share."

"Don't really *share*?"

"Sarah in second grade. Molly in third grade. Chelsea for, like, one month in fifth."

There was a long pause, and when I didn't say anything, he continued.

"I think you can kind of...take Cece and I for granted. Like we're always going to be around? Like we're not going anywhere? But that's not really fair, you know?"

"Yes," I said in a voice so quiet it was little more than a squeak. "I know."

"Then you inevitably get into these weird fights with these new people, and you never talk to them again. But, Anna, people deserve second chances. People deserve the benefit of the doubt."

"Yes," I said. "I know."

"So, Jennica. It wasn't planned or anything, I swear. I just went to the coffee shop on my break one day, and she was sitting there, looking really sad. Reading a comic, actually. Not *The Elder's Incantation*," he clarified quickly. "But a good one. So I went and said hi, and we just started talking and..." He paused again. I heard him take a big breath, let it out in a huff. "She really misses you, Anna."

"I miss her, too," I whispered.

"I wanted to tell you before but...Look, I *know* you've been going through a lot, with the divorce and stuff. And the bookstore."

"You know about the bookstore?"

"Your dad told me. I ran into him a few weeks ago."

Everett Bell never could keep a secret.

"Are you sad?" I asked him.

"Of course I am," he replied. "But I'm happy that we had it for so long."

And there it was. The question I couldn't quite answer for myself.

Was a thing just as special, just as important, if it didn't last forever?

If it ended.

"Josh?"

"Yeah?"

"I'm really happy for you and Jennica."

"Oh. Thanks. I...I like her a lot."

"You're perfect for each other," I said. "Both total nerds."

He laughed. "I'm just glad you're not mad."

"I'm not mad. And I'm sorry. Okay?"

"You should reach out to her," he said.

"I know. I will. Josh?"

"Yeah?"

"I feel really lucky that I have you. I'm sorry if I don't say that enough."

"Oh, Anna," he said. "Luck has nothing to do with it. Talk to you soon, okay?"

"Okay, Josh. Bye."

"Bye, Anna."

As soon as the call ended, I clicked into my last messages with Jennica. It was almost midnight in Rockport, which meant it was nine o'clock in California, and when I texted her, she started writing back almost immediately.

What I texted her was:

Me: I'm sorry.

The little bubbles that meant she was typing back kept starting and stopping and starting and stopping again, and at least five minutes passed before her message came through.

> **Jennica:** You said some really, really mean things to me. You made me feel like you could have other friends, but I could only be friends with you.

There was a pit in my stomach the size of a rock. A black swirling blob of darkness that cringed at her words, because I knew there was truth to them. I'd been *so jealous* of Lara. Had I even given her a chance? Or had I decided right away that I hated her?

I wrote a message back.

> **Me:** I'm sorry. I thought you were never going to talk to me again.
>
> **Jennica:** A person can have more than one friend, Anna.
>
> **Me:** I know that. I just got so mad when you told me you couldn't hang out, and then you went to the diner with Lara.
>
> **Jennica:** I went to the diner with Lara because I was planning a surprise for your birthday.

I stared at that text for a long minute. There were tears in my eyes that kept pooling up but didn't quite spill onto my cheeks.

> **Me:** I didn't know that.
> **Jennica:** Well obviously you didn't know that, it was a surprise!

I smiled, because I could almost hear Jennica saying those words aloud. She would be exasperated (Jennica was easily exasperated) but smiling. She would probably have rolled her eyes.

I sent another message.

> **Me:** I think maybe my parents' divorce messed me up more than I thought it did. I think maybe I was expecting everyone to leave me like they had left each other.
> **Jennica:** I get that. And it means a lot that you apologized. I'm sorry, too. I probably should have tried to involve you more in my friendship with Lara. I just thought you hated her.
> **Me:** I did, kind of. But that wasn't fair to Lara.
> **Jennica:** Let's get together when you get back and talk about things?
> **Me:** I'd like that.

I held the phone in my hands. Jennica sent back a thumbs-up and a smiling emoji. After a second, I typed another message.

Me: What was the surprise going to be?

She sent back another emoji: a smiley face with a funny expression, the tongue hanging out and one eye winked close. Then she wrote:

> **Jennica:** Lara's parents own a really cool butterfly and moth sanctuary. They just had a hatching of atlas moths. Lara had shown me some pictures, and I just knew you would have thought they were so beautiful.

Atlas moths.

I kept staring at those two words, blinking hard, my heart speeding up.

I didn't know what else to say, so I finally wrote back:

> **Me:** That would have been amazing. I'm sorry I ruined it.
>
> **Jennica:** You didn't ruin anything. We can see them when you get back.

A heart emoji.

A kissing-face emoji.

I sent a heart emoji back, then let my phone fall out of my hands.

Atlas moths.

I felt a little dizzy.

I felt wide awake.

I felt buzzing with energy.

I felt like such a dick.

I'd ruined a perfectly good birthday surprise with Jennica because I was jealous and stubborn, and instead of just asking why she'd gone to the diner with Lara, I'd totally blown up at her and sent her mean text after mean text after mean text.

I'd almost ruined our entire friendship.

We hadn't talked for *months*.

I looked around the small room. I'd gotten used to this room, with its wicker furniture and its ocean smell and its old-fashioned, ruffle-edged comforter. I was going to miss it. I was going to miss everything about this place. The cottage, Rockport, Gloucester. Bearskin Neck. The summer had passed by so quickly. It didn't feel like enough time here.

But on the other hand, I missed California so much. I missed our house. I missed my friends. I missed the bookstore.

The bookstore.

A stabbing pain to my heart as I realized I didn't have that much more time with it.

I'm happy that we had it for so long, Josh had said.

And I guess there was truth to that sentiment, but still—I remembered afternoons we'd gotten lost in its stacks forever, Josh and me; I remembered hours that had vanished as we'd crawled into one fantasy book and out the other, as he'd led me through Middle Earth and Discworld and Oz and Earthsea and Narnia and Wonderland and Neverland. I always liked books more when Josh was reading them to me, because then I could close my eyes and really *go* there, and the bookstore would morph and change around me and...

Well, of course the bookstore hadn't changed at all.

I knew that now.

Of course it was just an ordinary, normal, obeying-the-laws-of-physics store, where the ceiling did not disappear into clouds and the stacks were not endless and the mystery section did not sometimes turn invisible and the fantasy section did not sometimes grow wings.

I knew that, and yet...

It had always felt like that to me.

Just as I knew Miriam Bell wasn't *really* magical, didn't *really* crawl into a person's brain while they were sleeping to figure out exactly what book she might recommend to them.

Of course her eyes did not change colors and she didn't crawl out of the freezer or cry handfuls of tears like Alice in Wonderland. Of course by dipping her finger into a sprinkling of spilled salt, she was no more dispelling the bad luck than satisfying her craving for one of life's most common minerals.

But she *was* magical, also, because she was my mom.

And the bookstore *was* magical because it was my home.

And I wished I could feel the way Josh felt; I wished I could be happy to have had it at all, but I couldn't help wondering—who would buy the empty store? What would it be next? Would they rip out the shelves Everett had made by hand and drag them off to the local landfill?

Would they take an ax to the front desk, the place where, if I closed my eyes, I could still see Miriam Bell sitting, her nose buried in a book and her eyes wandering to the long rows of bookcases to figure out what she'd read *next*?

I thought I could probably deal with anything as long as Bell's Books didn't become the next trendy weed dispensary.

Or a juice bar.

Or a coffee shop.

Los Angeles had enough of those.

I let my eyes wander around the room until they fell on the wrapped package on my dresser. The last of my summer reading.

I groaned.

If I wanted to finish it before school started, I needed to start it soon.

I leaned off the bed and grabbed it, then I settled back down against my pillow and carefully peeled the wrapping paper off.

Something small and thin fell out of the package and landed on my lap, but I was too busy looking at the book, turning it over in my hands, confused.

Because it wasn't a book.

It was almost a book. But not quite.

The binding was a soft, creamy material, smooth and supple under my touch. There was no writing on the front or back covers. I turned it to look at the spine. In gold foil letters were the initials *ALB*. Anna Lucia Bell.

I opened it. The papers inside were thin, delicate, almost translucent when I held them up to the light. There were hundreds of pages, blank except for soft gray lines.

A journal.

A beautiful one.

I'd never seen anything quite like it.

I placed it on the bed next to me and picked up the wrapped thing that had fallen to my lap. It was long and skinny, and when I unwrapped it, I saw a turquoise blue pen, with silver details on the cap and a shiny silver clip.

I pulled off the cap. It was a fountain pen.

I put the cap back on and picked up the journal again, opening to the first page.

Because, if I knew my mother, she'd definitely addressed it to me. She wouldn't dream of not doing so.

And there, sure enough, in her loopy, pretty handwriting, was an epigraph.

> To Anna,
> Sometimes the story that will change
> your life is the one you write yourself.
> Love, Mom

I read it over a few times. I could practically hear her whispering it into my ear. It felt like she was sitting on the bed with me, her hand on my knee and a secret smile on her face. The one you couldn't quite figure out the meaning of. The one she didn't share with anyone but me.

I turned to the second page. It was pristine in its emptiness. Devoid of words. Waiting for me to tell it something.

So I lifted the pen to paper and wrote:

I really thought thirteen would be the year that changed my life.

And I kept writing until morning.

It wasn't until the first rays of dawn came slanting in through my window that I realized I was completely exhausted. I'd filled the first thirty or forty pages of the journal, but that hardly made a dent in the book at all. There must have been at least three hundred pages in it.

Once I'd started writing, I just couldn't stop. I found myself pouring everything out: the divorce, Jennica, my fourteenth birthday, the selling of the bookstore, and the trip to Rockport.

My brain felt scrubbed clean, completely empty.

It was oddly refreshing.

But now I could hardly keep my eyes open.

I closed the journal and put it on my nightstand, resting the fountain pen gently on top.

I turned the light off and rolled over, falling asleep instantly, almost before my eyes were even closed.

I didn't know how long I slept before I felt, in that strange, dreamlike state where nothing feels quite real, a weight on the edge of my bed.

I groaned.

Miriam laughed quietly.

"It's almost two in the afternoon," she said. "I was checking if you were still of this world."

"Not of this world," I replied, my voice thick with sleep. "Definitely not."

"It smells in here," she said, and I felt her stand up again and heard her cross over to the windows. She unlocked each one and opened it. It was a windy day, and the smell of the ocean drifted in immediately.

I opened my eyes and blinked at her. She had come back around to the side of my bed, and she was looking at the journal on my nightstand.

"I was wondering when you were going to get to that," she said. "An interesting choice, opening everything one at a time."

"I took the road less traveled," I said.

"And did it make all the difference?"

"I really love it, Mom. Thank you. It's perfect."

She smiled. "I had it custom-made. Little old lady up in Northern California. I have a bottle of ink, too, for the pen."

"The pen is really cool. It took me a second to figure out how to use it."

"I think everyone should have a fountain pen," she said.

"Thanks," I said again. "It's the best."

She dug my hand out from under the covers and looked at the moonstone ring Dad had given me. She rubbed a finger across the stone and smiled. "Couldn't let your father have *all* the glory."

"Never," I agreed.

"Are you hungry? You must be hungry. Let's go for a walk and get something to eat."

"Give me a few minutes," I said, and she nodded and kissed my forehead and left me alone.

I got dressed and brushed my teeth, examining my hair in the mirror for a brief moment before determining it was beyond saving.

Miriam was waiting by the front door, and she burst out laughing when I came down the stairs.

"What?" I said.

"You look like you're sleepwalking," she replied, making grabby hands for my hair and smoothing down the mess as best as she could.

"Ouch," I complained.

"Please, for the love of god," she said, and grabbed a sun hat from a pegboard by the door. She set it on my head. "Much better."

I adjusted it so it felt comfortable and shrugged. "Fine by me."

"How late were you up last night?" she asked, opening the front door and shooing me out first.

"Let's just say the sun and I said *hi* to each other."

"You were writing?"

"I was writing," I confirmed.

She shut the door, locked it, and slipped the keys into her purse. "I used to journal a lot. It helps. Gets all the feelings out."

"How come you don't anymore?"

"It's been a while," she agreed. "Maybe I'll have to start up again."

It was a warm day, and I was glad to have the sun hat. Miriam put on her enormous sunglasses and took my hand. She held it until our palms got too sweaty, then she made a big show of wiping off the sweat on her jean shorts.

"What a day, huh?" she said. "I'm gonna miss days like these."

"Every day in Los Angeles is like this," I pointed out.

"No, I don't mean the weather. I just mean...There's something about the East Coast, honey. Something you can't find anywhere else."

"There's something about the West Coast, too," I retorted, somewhat petulantly.

"Of course there is," she replied. "That's why we live there."

We reached Hula Moon, and Mom started to open the door, but I caught her by the arm.

"Wait a second," I said. My heart kicked up a beat as she paused, waiting for me to speak. I hadn't really planned this, but so many thoughts had spilled out of me when I was journaling. Everything felt so raw and immediate. I took a deep breath and began. "It's been really hard for me to understand why you and Dad are getting a divorce. Sometimes I think it's even harder because you guys are still so *nice* to each other. You both *like* each other so much. Like maybe it would be easier if you hated each other, like Josh's parents. If you would just scream and fight and yell at each other once in a while."

Miriam's shoulders softened. She took my hand and led me away from the door to Hula Moon to a little bench a few feet away. We sat.

"Oh, honey," she said. "We *do* fight. We *did* fight. We just made a promise to never, ever do it in front of you. And you're right. We like each other a lot. I don't think that's ever going to change. There are no enemies here. There's just love and a lot of history and a lot of life."

I nodded. "Well, I guess I just wanted to ask you... If you had to do it all over again, if you could go back in time, would you still marry Dad? Let's say I wasn't even a factor. Let's say you were going to end up with me no matter what. Would you still pick him? Or... Knowing what you know now, would you have done things differently?"

She closed her eyes and tilted her face up to the sky, thinking. A small smile spread across her face. When she opened her eyes again, they were wet with tears that didn't quite spill out onto her cheeks. The classic Miriam crying-but-not-crying.

"I wouldn't change a thing," she said, and I could tell by the tone of her voice that she wasn't lying. I could tell she really, really meant it.

I wrapped my arms around her. "Okay, good," I said.

She hugged me close and kissed my cheek three times.

"I love you, Anna," she said.

"I love you, too, Mom."

"We need to eat now, okay? My stomach is a nonstop grumble factory."

I laughed and pulled away from her, nodding. "Yeah, it's kind of ruining the moment."

We stood up and went inside the café. A table was open next to the wide windows, and we didn't speak much as we ate, just looked out over the water, each lost in our own private worlds.

In my mother's private world: probably thoughts about books and gazpacho and how to cry without really crying.

In my private world: a sinking feeling that I had managed to split up two people who never should have been split up.

And that if I'd just managed to step away from myself for a moment...

I probably would have been able to see that.

But I saw it now.

That was the important part.

I saw it now.

two realities
at the same
time

went out to find Emmy after dinner.

Miriam had settled onto the couch with a book, and I had a wild idea.

I had no idea if it would work or not.

I started walking, but not toward the Motif.

Instead, I turned right outside the cottage, where Atlantic Avenue looped backward, away from the harbor. I then took a right onto Norwood Avenue. I was behind the cottage now, but the blocks were wide here, so I couldn't even see it; there were four or five houses between us.

I looked around me. There wasn't another soul in sight.

This was the perfect spot.

I looked up, found Kit-Hale in the sky above me, then twisted the moonstone ring around my finger.

Intention: *I want to see Emmy.*

Nothing happened.

Or nothing *noticeable* happened, anyway.

But I'd done everything right according to the rules of time travel, and there was nothing to do now but see if it had worked.

I made a big loop, walking from Norwood Avenue to Clark Avenue, turning right when I reached Atlantic again.

And there was the cottage.

And the car in the driveway was brand-new.

It was Aunt Dora's station wagon, but *brand-new*.

Which meant...

I had time traveled.

"Holy shit," I mumbled under my breath, all of a sudden frozen to the ground, unable to move.

Other things about the house were different, too, of course.

The tree in the front yard.

It was smaller, just like I thought it would be.

The cottage's paint looked fresher. The porch swing hadn't been installed yet. The grass was neatly cut.

The front door was wide open, and as I watched, a shadow passed by it and walked into the kitchen.

I could see her through the windows. Emmy. Pouring herself a glass of water.

I made myself move again. I made myself go up to the front door. I made myself knock on the siding, and just a moment later she popped her head around the corner.

"Anna!" she exclaimed. "Oh my god, *hi!*"

She opened the screen door and motioned for me to come in, and one of the freakier experiences of my life was walking into that house, twenty-eight years in the past.

It was almost exactly the same, but different in strange, subtle ways. It was like looking at two pictures, both slightly transparent, one held up over the other. Two realities at the same time. A stack of books on the couch that my mom was working her way through, but they were Aunt Dora's books now, not my mom's. A bowl of limes Miriam used for her gazpacho replaced with a bottle of Aunt Dora's favorite liqueur, Disaronno. My shoes kicked off by the door replaced with Emmy's. My mom. Mom.

I threw my arms around her, hugging her tightly.

"Sorry I haven't been out much," she said, laughing, hugging me back. "Aunt Dora got a cold. A cold in the middle of summer! She has the worst luck—I swear, next she's gonna break her ankle." She pulled away and squinted at me. "How did you know where I lived?"

"Beck told me," I said, catching myself in the nick of time—I'd almost called him Everett. "Sorry your aunt's sick."

"She's feeling much better now. Do you want to go for a walk or something?"

"Sure. Yeah. That sounds great."

Being in the cottage was making me sort of dizzy. Disoriented.

"Let me just go tell her," Emmy said, and she sprinted up the stairs to Aunt Dora's bedroom. Which was now my mom's bedroom. Which was just too weird to think about.

I went and waited on the front porch, watching a flurry of meteors streak across the sky.

Emmy came out a minute later, and we started walking down the street, in the general direction of Bearskin Neck.

"So," she said after a few seconds. "You saw Beck?"

"A couple of times," I said. "He taught me how to swim."

"Oh really? That's cool."

"Yeah."

"How is he?"

"He's okay. I think he misses you."

"Oh," she said. "Yeah, I guess I miss him, too."

"Look, Emmy. Can I be honest with you?"

"Of course."

"I gave you terrible advice. There's no reason why you shouldn't be with Beck now, if that's what you want to do. All that other stuff, the distance and everything, you can figure that out later. You know?"

When she didn't answer right away, I looked over at her. She was smiling. A dreamy smile that made my heart skip a beat.

"I don't think it was *terrible* advice, Anna," she said after a moment. "You brought up some interesting points, you know? And I think it was helpful—to kind of step back and look at things from every angle."

"And that's what you did? Looked at things from every angle?"

"Just about," she said.

"And..."

She laughed. "And I figured out that I really like Beck. And

I think I want to see what happens. If we keep . . . heading in a certain direction."

"A certain direction?"

"A kissing direction," she clarified.

"Oh!" I laughed. We'd reached the Motif by that point, but Beck wasn't there. It was completely deserted.

"I guess I should have tried to find him before now," Emmy said, walking slowly over to a pylon and resting her elbows on it. "But I think I just needed some time. You know?"

Some time.

Yes, Emmy, I knew exactly what you meant.

"We could try to find him now?" I suggested. "Or if you'd rather be alone, I could—"

"No," she interrupted. "Don't be silly. Stay with me. Let's go look for him."

Since he wasn't at the Motif, we walked to the end of Bearskin Neck, down to the jetty, then back, peeking into the Fudgery and the Country Store, where Shane's mom was working on a crossword puzzle at the register. And when we didn't find him at any of those places, we paused in front of the Pewter Shop, an old-fashioned red building near the entrance of Bearskin Neck, and considered our options.

"Maybe he didn't come out tonight," Emmy said, but he'd been out every other night that week, and I just had a feeling . . .

"I know one other place we can check," I said.

So we started walking again, and although I knew I couldn't put that kind of pressure on myself, it sort of felt like the entire fate of the universe—or at least my existence within said universe—rested on my shoulders. I walked so quickly that Emmy had to keep skipping to catch up with me, and when we finally got to the small playground, I let out an enormous sigh of relief. Because there he was. Lying on his back in the middle of the merry-go-round.

"Beck!" Emmy shouted. She wasted no time running toward him, and I swear he jumped a mile when he heard her voice.

I decided to give them just a minute, so I bent down and made a big show of tying my shoes. First one, then the other, and then, when I saw they were still whispering together, heads close, I untied both of the laces again.

The next time I looked up, I saw Emmy lean over and give Beck just the tiniest, quickest kiss. I thought he might explode with happiness.

My heart felt too big for my chest; my blood couldn't circulate properly.

I pulled myself to my feet, gripping the gate in the metal fence to steady myself. The subsequent rattling was loud in the quiet of the night, and both of them looked over at me, remembering they weren't alone.

"Oh—hey, guys," I said. "Needed to tie my shoe."

"Come here, weirdo," Emmy said, laughing.

But I couldn't move. I could only look at them, look at *her*. My mom.

In fourteen years, when the girl before me was twenty-eight, she would give birth to me in a hospital in Los Angeles, a city she had always wanted to go to. The boy next to her would bring donuts and coffee to all the doctors and nurses the next day. He would cry when he looked into my eyes for the first time. She would read a book whenever I fell asleep, whispering the sentences aloud to me in hopes I'd fall in love with words the way she had.

And then, thirteen years after that, they would break up. They would get divorced in a way that was sometimes okay and sometimes sad and sometimes hard and sometimes confusing. They would commit to Friday dinners. He would get a house close to her house. They would always try to do the right thing for their daughter. For me.

Did it matter, then, that their marriage didn't last forever? That love sometimes lasted only twenty-eight-ish years instead of eternally?

But my parents still loved each other. I knew that. I knew it in the way my mother cried at the kitchen table and the way my father threw himself into work, even when he was, technically, on vacation.

They still loved each other. But I knew, also, that love changed. Love evolved and morphed and shifted and grew, and sometimes, after a few decades, it didn't look quite the same as it looked on a quiet, warm night, in a soft, sleepy town, in an empty playground, on an unmoving merry-go-round.

But that didn't mean it was less important.

That didn't mean it should never have existed at all.

Emmy hopped lightly to her feet and walked over to where I stood, still gripping the fence, still unable to move.

"Is everything okay?" she asked.

I nodded and took her hand in mine.

"You should definitely date him," I said. "You should get married."

She laughed loudly, a sharp noise that sounded like bells to me, that had always sounded safe and warm and bright to me. The sound of my mother's laughter.

"I think you're getting a little bit ahead of yourself," she said.

"Who's getting ahead of themselves?" Beck called.

"Come on," Emmy insisted. She pulled my hand.

I went with her.

déjà vu

A week passed in the blink of an eye. In hot, muggy days and still, quiet nights. In games of Scrabble with Miriam on the porch and games of poker with Emmy and Beck in various places around Bearskin Neck. When I told them that I was leaving in just three days, Emmy teared up (but didn't cry, of course) and Beck didn't answer right away, just chewed on his upper lip and shuffled the cards for much longer than he needed to.

I played guitar a lot.

I wrote in my journal a lot.

It felt really nice to have a place to dump all my feelings, to unload my brain before I went to bed for the night. Miriam gave me the bottle of ink and showed me how to refill the fountain pen. The ink bottle was glass and shaped sort of like a gemstone; it looked really nice on my bedside table. Together, the three pieces—journal, pen, ink bottle—felt important. A nightly ritual that scraped my brain clean before I went to sleep.

I talked to my father every day. He was planning a big outing for when I got back to Los Angeles. Acting like it had been years since we'd seen each other, of course.

And he didn't mention his new girlfriend.

I appreciated that.

I wasn't ready to talk about her yet.

Miriam and I went to Wingaersheek Beach on the Thursday before our Sunday flight.

Miriam was in a quiet, introspective mood. She'd gotten a real estate agent in the past week and listed the cottage for sale. I knew it was tough for her to let it go, but there was no way we could keep it.

We had planned a huge tag sale for tomorrow and Saturday. Anything left over on Saturday evening, we'd drive to the local thrift store.

It was all happening so quickly, and the beach felt like the last calm before the storm.

The storm of the tag sale (which had already been quite a lot of work to pull together), the storm of saying goodbye to Emmy and Beck, the storm of leaving Rockport.

The storm of everything.

It was a beautiful day. Not that muggy, not that hot. The perfect beach-day temperature.

We hauled everything out to a spot by the water and collapsed in our beach chairs. All this stuff—the beach chairs, the towels, the umbrella—would be in the tag sale tomorrow.

In a weird way, I would miss it all.

In a weird way, I knew Miriam would, too.

Even something as small as a beach towel could end up feeling so strangely sentimental.

"You need a minute alone with that?" Miriam asked, and I realized I'd been holding the beach towel up to my cheek, as if it were a security blanket.

"We're not selling this one," I declared. "This one is coming home with us."

"Deal," she said. She stretched her arms over her head. "Look at this, Anna. I'm going to miss this."

"We can come back, you know," I said. "I checked the rental prices for the cottages around here, and they're not that bad."

"Next summer?" she said, her voice full of hope.

"Definitely," I agreed.

She reached over and took my hand. "Come on. Let's walk out on the sandbar."

It would be one of the things I missed most. Striding out into the middle of the ocean. Surrounded by the unknown. Feet and ankles and shins wet with salt water. The breeze whipping my hair around my face, and the sun beating down on my shoulders. Feeling like a regular mermaid or a goddess of the sea.

I took a deep breath of the salt air and tried to commit this moment to memory.

I would write about it tonight.

To remember forever.

But more important, to remember *now*.

We'd never had a tag sale before, and I hadn't realized how much *work* they were. After we got home from the beach, we hung flyers all over the neighborhood, even putting up a few in Bearskin Neck so the tourists would see.

We went and bought little white stickers and put price tags on hundreds of things.

And we kept a lot, too.

Miriam filled shipping boxes with books, photographs, little trinkets she couldn't part with. I slipped the beach towel into one of them, and Miriam shook her head, smiling, but allowed it.

We took the boxes to the post office in groups of two and three at a time and sent them all to Dad, in case they arrived before we got home.

"I can't just *leave* this," Miriam would say.

Sometimes, I agreed, and we packed it up.

Sometimes, in the case of a particularly random object, like a citrus press or a soap dish, I would gently talk her out of it.

It mostly worked.

On Friday morning, we woke up super early to set up everything on the front lawn.

On the flyers, we'd written *Early birds will be hit with water balloons!* but a few of them still showed up before seven anyway, loitering on the sidewalk out front while we finished getting things ready.

"East Coast people take tag sales *very* seriously," Miriam whispered to me.

"I can see that," I replied. "You should have let me make the water balloons."

She snorted and wrapped her arm around my shoulders, squeezing me toward her.

So many people came.

We were selling the inside furniture, too (anyone who bought something had to come back and take it away before Saturday night), so we had people traipsing through the cottage pretty much nonstop. We'd put all our stuff into one closet that was off-limits, including my journal, but I still wandered around the house warily, making sure nobody touched my things.

I was exhausted by the time five o'clock rolled around. Exhausted and so, so hungry. We dragged our bodies to Hula Moon and ate there, since even the thought of ordering take-out was too tiring to comprehend.

"We did good today," Mom said after we'd gotten our food and shoved it into our faces in silence for a good five minutes.

"How good?"

"Three thousand, eight hundred, and fourteen dollars. And twenty-five cents," she said through a mouthful of food.

I dropped my fork, and it clattered against my plate noisily. "Um, *what*?"

"I counted when you were in the bathroom," she said, patting the side of her purse happily. "People *love* wicker furniture. Who would have thought?!"

"Wow," I said. "We could buy—"

"So many books," she interrupted. "I know."

"Not what I was going to say."

What I was *really* wondering was how many months of bookstore rent that could pay. Two? One? I didn't know much about Los Angeles rent, but I knew it was a lot.

Miriam seemed to read my mind. She had a bite of her dinner (she'd ordered gazpacho, which, honestly, she was going to turn into a tomato one of these days) and stared out the window. We were at our usual table by the water. She swallowed, dabbed at her mouth with her napkin, and said, "Who knows what the next adventure will be?"

"What do you mean?" I asked, just a little grumpily.

"I mean after the bookstore," she said softly. "You know, it's really all I've done for the last thirteen years of my life. It's not the worst idea for me to have a little change."

I shrugged but didn't answer. Mostly because I didn't know what to say. It hadn't really clicked for me that she might *want* to sell the bookstore.

"Maybe I'll start one of those book boxes. You know, where you send people one book a month," she mused. "Or maybe I'll start an online book club! Or maybe I'll finally give in and help run the library bookstore. You know how much I love the library bookstore."

"Yeah, I know."

"Maybe I'll still go to estate sales. I could sell rare books online." She took a bite of gazpacho.

"Sure."

"Or maybe I'll take a real right turn and go into mushroom farming or something."

"Mushroom farming?"

"Probably not," she acquiesced. "No experience."

"But you're...okay? With the bookstore closing?"

"Why are you so convinced I'm going to crumble into sadness over here?" she asked, and although she kept her tone light, I knew she was serious by the way she put down her spoon and gave me her undivided attention.

"I don't know," I admitted.

"Is it because *you're* crumbling into sadness?" she asked, and the way she said it, so bluntly, staring directly into my eyes, it made me feel like she was slicing me open and peering into my brain. It wasn't a great feeling.

"I wouldn't use the term *crumbling*," I mumbled.

"But you wouldn't dispute the statement altogether?"

I shrugged.

She nodded and held her arm out to me. I placed my hand in hers, and she held it on the table, rubbing my knuckles gently.

"I know the past few months...the past year, maybe... They haven't been the easiest for you, Anna. There have been a lot of changes. Both externally and...internally."

I snatched my hand back and felt my cheeks redden. "Oh my god," I whispered. "Are you talking about my *period*?"

"I'm not *not* talking about your period," she said, and winked at me over the top of her water glass. She had a sip and then set it back on the table. "I think sometimes I view you as a little more grown up than you are. Maybe I haven't done the best job of checking in."

"I'm fine," I said. "Honestly."

"I wouldn't expect you to be *fine*," she said thoughtfully. "You know, when I was your age—"

"I know," I interrupted her.

"What do you mean *you know*?"

"I mean, I know what you were like when you were my age."

She tilted her head. "What do you mean?" she repeated. "What do you mean by that?"

I couldn't help the smallest grin from spreading across my lips. "Oh, you know. I can just imagine."

She narrowed her eyes. There was something in her expression, something almost, almost clicking into place. She looked out the window, and I saw her gaze land on Motif No. 1. She squinted hard at it, then looked back to me, then looked over at it again, her mouth hanging just slightly open, just the tiniest bit.

"Is something wrong?" I asked.

"No, I just...had the weirdest déjà vu," she said.

"Oh?"

I took a sip of my water. She looked out the window again, then shook her head, finally shrugging and turning back to the table.

"It's gone now," she said.

I couldn't help smiling wider as we went back to our meal.

Emmy and Beck were by the Motif that night, using one of the waist-high pylons to play a rousing game of war. They didn't notice me as I walked up to them, and I stuck to the shadows, which, sure, was kind of creepy, but I just wanted to watch them for a moment. I just wanted to see what they were like when they thought nobody else was around.

"Beck, you're *cheating*!" Emmy called out as they finished the game. She spun around on her heels dramatically, then leaned up against a pylon and crossed her arms over her chest.

"I'm sorry you're terrible at war," Beck said, gathering up the cards. "I really, really am."

It was hard to keep thinking of him as *Everett* when Emmy still called him Beck.

Emmy stuck her tongue out at him, but she was smiling, and eventually she uncrossed her arms and sat down on the ground, using the pylon for back support.

Beck gathered the last of the playing cards and slipped them into their case. He placed them on a pylon and then sat down across from Emmy, so close their knees just about touched.

"What do you want to do now?" he asked.

"Let's wait for Anna," Emmy said. "I bet she'll be here soon."

It was a tiny thrill to hear Emmy say my name. She said it almost exactly how Miriam said my name—which made sense, considering they were the same person—but there was something slightly different. I wasn't Emmy's daughter. I was just a friend she'd known for about two months, a girl who'd almost scared her to death in the empty building behind us. So when she said my name, there wasn't much history behind it.

When Miriam said my name, it was a heavy, full, weighted thing. A deep, big, sticky thing.

Plus, Miriam was just a bit more dramatic than Emmy. And that was saying something, because Emmy was already pretty dramatic.

Beck swung his legs around so that they were hanging over the water. Emmy did the same. Their backs were to me now, and I got a little closer, still sticking to the shadows, but close enough to hear their voices before the words were swept out to sea.

"Do you think we'll ever see this comet again?" Emmy asked. She was looking upward. So much of our summer had been spent looking up.

"Hard to say," Beck replied. "They aren't really sure when it'll come back."

"Nerd."

"You asked."

Emmy slid a few inches over, snaking her arm around Beck's waist. He was more awkward than she was. He raised an arm like he wanted to run his hand through her hair, but he couldn't quite stick the landing. He just sort of patted her on the shoulder instead. I smiled. Emmy laid her head against him.

"It's a nice night, huh," she said.

"Yeah."

A few minutes of quiet. I was just about to announce myself when Emmy slid away from Beck again, turning to face him, looking imploringly into his eyes.

"What do you think is going to happen when this summer's over?" she asked.

"What do you mean?"

"When I go back home. Are we still going to . . . you know."

"Oh. I hadn't really thought about it."

"You hadn't?"

"I mean, I guess I just . . ." Beck trailed off and shrugged. "I guess I'm just not worried about it."

"You aren't?"

"No. Are you?"

"A little. I don't know."

Emmy pulled one of her legs up, letting the other one continue dangling over the water. Beck put his hand on her ankle and spoke to her foot, not her face. "I've never really had a girlfriend before," he said.

"Me neither."

"So I don't really know how this is going to work. But I *do* know that I'm not worried about it. We can talk on the phone a lot. And we're not *that* far away. You can come visit your aunt on some weekends. I can ask Billy to drive me to you. Maybe I could even take the bus. We can figure it out."

"We could write letters to each other," Emmy said. "Like in the old days."

Beck laughed. "Yeah, we could totally do that."

Emmy put her hand over Beck's hand and didn't look at him when she said, "I like you a lot, Beckett."

"I like you a lot, too," he said. Then he lifted his hand and ran it through his hair, suddenly self-conscious. "Um. I have to tell you something."

"What?" Emmy asked.

"This is going to sound really weird. But... My name isn't actually Beckett."

"Um, *what*?"

"Yeah, I know. See, when we first met, I thought you were really... I mean, I don't know, I thought you were cute or whatever"—Emmy beamed—"and you misheard me. When I introduced myself. You thought I said *Beckett*, but I really said *Everett*. And I just didn't want to correct you. I should have, obviously, because it's my *name*, but... I didn't."

"So your name isn't Beckett," she said.

"No. It's Everett."

She said it a few times, trying it on for size, then she smiled softly and said, "You know, I never thought you looked like a Beckett."

Beck—Everett—laughed. "Really?"

"Yeah. Something about it didn't quite fit. But Everett . . . I like that."

"Thanks," Everett said.

"You know," Emmy continued. "You can call me Miriam if you want to. Only my aunt really calls me Emmy."

"I like Emmy," Everett said. "I like Miriam, too."

"I like both," Emmy said. "Sometimes it's kind of like a game. When I'm here, I'm almost a different person. But when I go home now, I'll have you here, and I'll be there, and it's almost like these two worlds are . . ." She mimicked a collision with her hands crashing into her, sound effects and all.

"I get it," Everett said. "I like Miriam. Miriam."

Miriam smiled. Everett smiled.

My parents, aged fourteen, sitting underneath a dimly glowing comet, leaned in and kissed each other.

I slipped away quietly.

I'd take a walk around Bearskin Neck and give them a little privacy.

I saw them for the last time on Saturday night, after the second day of the tag sale, where pretty much everything that wasn't bolted to the floor ended up selling. Mom and I had pizza for dinner, and the real estate agent came over to discuss a few things. I spent a little while packing upstairs, pausing when I reached the vintage blue dress.

I'd never worn it.

Why hadn't I worn it?

I pulled it over my head now, contorting my arms around my back to reach the zipper. It stuck a little, but I got it on after a minute. I looked at myself in the bathroom mirror, turning this way and that to see every angle.

It fit nicely. Better than I remembered. It hit just above my knees. I fingered the white buttons on the front and realized, as I continued to stare at myself in the mirror, that I actually looked like her. My mom. I looked like my mom, aged fourteen. Wild hair and tan skin and short sundress and something just behind her smile, like she was part of a joke you'd never understand.

And I'd always thought she was the epitome of cool, my mom.

And I'd always thought I was as boring and unspecial as one could be.

So what did it mean that I saw her now? That I looked in the mirror and saw pieces of her mixed with pieces of my father mixed with pieces of my grandparents mixed even with a piece of Uncle Billy and Aunt Dora and yes—of course, obviously—Emmy and Beck.

When I went downstairs a few minutes later, Miriam saw me, and her eyes widened.

"Oh, Anna," she said. "You look beautiful."

"Thanks, Mom," I said, surprised to find that I actually believed her.

"I'd forgotten about that dress."

"Me too."

"Don't be long, okay? Early flight."

"I won't," I said.

"Hey, Anna?" she asked, and I paused with my hand on the doorknob.

"Yeah?"

"Where do you go?" she asked, her words careful and quiet.

"Just around," I said. "Nowhere special. To Bearskin Neck, mostly."

She nodded, her eyes unfocused. She had the same look on her face that she'd had in the diner. Like she was so close to figuring it out, to remembering. . . . But she couldn't quite make the memory fit.

I guess that made sense.

It wouldn't have been the most obvious thing, to connect a girl you'd only known for a couple of months when you were fourteen to the daughter you had decades later.

I smiled at her. "Love you, Mom."

She snapped out of it and smiled back. "I love you, too, Anna. Like a really big, incredibly weird amount. Okay?"

"Okay," I agreed.

I let myself outside, feeling the profundity of every moment.

This was the last time I would leave this cottage to go meet my teenage parents.

This was the last night I'd spend in Rockport.

This was the last time I'd ever see Kit-Hale, now just a faint outline in the night sky, hardly noticeable among the stars.

When I really stopped and thought about it, I considered myself *very* adept at time traveling.

I'd managed to go back and forth all summer long, and I hadn't created a single paradox that resulted in the entire world exploding or collapsing into ruin!

I didn't think I'd even changed anything.

Except...

Wait.

There *was* one thing.

When I had asked my father about nicknames and he'd told me that Miriam had called him *Beckett* for an entire summer, he'd said Billy was the one who'd finally spilled the beans.

But last night...

Last night I'd hid in the shadows as a fourteen-year-old Everett told a fourteen-year-old Miriam his real name.

So that meant...

I *could* change the past. I *had* changed the past. Or I'd at least assisted in said change.

Which meant...I could have winked out of existence after all.

And I hadn't.

Not even when I'd told Emmy to break up with Beck.

Not even when she *had*.

Which meant...

Which meant my parents were always going to end up together.

Which meant my parents were always going to end up divorced.

So *had* my wish come true after all?

I wish my parents would love each other forever.

I twisted the moonstone ring around my finger, then glanced at the way it shone in the moonlight.

They commune with the moon, you know, the old man had said. *That's how they get their name. A beautiful stone. Good for new beginnings, new love. A fresh start. That sort of thing.*

New love.

A new *kind* of love.

Because my parents hadn't stopped loving each other.

That was the point.

They'd *never* stop loving each other.

So my wish had come true.

I had reached the T-Wharf. With the old man's words still knocking around in my head, I turned down it now, walking fast. How come I'd never seen him again? I'd looked for him, once, but he hadn't been there. But something was nagging at the back of my mind. I just wanted to see something.

I reached the end of the wharf and peered over the low fence—and there he was. Sitting in the same rocking chair he'd been in before. His dog, Book, sprawled out on the deck next to him. His face half-hidden in shadow, just like before.

"Who are you?" I asked, in lieu of a greeting.

"Oh, hello there," he said, his voice light and amused. "It's you again."

"Who *are* you?" I repeated.

The man chuckled quietly. "Did you make plenty of wishes?"

"Just one," I said.

"Did it come true?"

"Yeah. Yeah, it did."

"Told you," he said. He raised one tattooed arm and pointed up at the sky. "Almost gone now."

But I barely heard him.

I was too busy staring at his arm, because there, nestled among a hundred other tattoos, was a line of text perfectly illuminated by the porch light.

My name is Nobody.

I heard my mother's voice in my head, as clear as day: *You're a strange man, Nobody.*

I opened my mouth to speak, but he interrupted me, still pointing upward, his voice insistent, "*Look*. Before it fades away completely."

I looked to where he pointed, to the barely there whisper of Kit-Hale above us.

Beside me, the old man sighed, and I heard the creak of the rocking chair as he shifted. "Although is anything ever *really* gone?" he asked quietly. "You know what they say about time, right?"

"What do they say?"

"It's always happening. All around us. Your past, your future. 'All time is all time.' "

"I know that quote," I said. "That's from *Slaughterhouse-Five*."

"I love Vonnegut," he replied.

"All men love Vonnegut. And who *are* you, any—"

But I didn't finish my sentence.

Because when I turned back to him—

He was gone.

The rocking chair was empty.

The dog was gone.

The old man was nowhere to be found.

For one long minute I allowed myself to stare at the empty chair, my mouth slightly ajar. My brow slightly furrowed.

And then I nodded.

Yup. That felt about right.

I walked to Bearskin Neck.

The profundity was back.

Everything felt brighter, seemed brighter, felt different.

I felt different.

It felt like a million years had passed since the first night I spent in Rockport. I felt like I knew myself more now than I had then, that in the blank pages of the journal my mother had given me I had *found* myself, writing myself down word by word, sentence by sentence.

I had never looked at myself so closely before, never taken the time to ask questions of myself, to challenge myself, to push myself.

I need to stop acting like everything is happening TO me and understand that some things are just HAPPENING, I had written that morning.

My parents' divorce. The bookstore closing. Josh and Jennica. Emmy and Beck.

I couldn't control any of those things, but I *could* control the way I reacted to them.

I reached the start of Bearskin Neck, the sign I had passed so many times that summer.

NAMED FROM A BEAR CAUGHT BY THE TIDE AND KILLED IN 1700.

This was the last time I'd pass it.

And, I mean, sure, I might come back to Rockport someday—next summer, even!—but there was something so final about *these* moments, now.

I would never be fourteen again, here again, on *this night* again.

I would never be this exact person at this exact time.

Never mind that time travel existed.

My own path was linear.

I somehow knew that, as deeply as I knew that Emmy and Beck would be waiting for me by the Motif. As deeply as I knew I'd make one more stop at the Fudgery and the Country Store, to stock up on treats for the plane ride back home. As deeply as I knew who the old man with the dog really was.

As deeply as I knew, somehow, with a sudden striking clarity, that I would be okay.

Things hadn't turned out how I wanted them to, but so often in life, you don't get to choose. You just had to work with what you had. You just had to adapt.

So I was adapting.

I twisted the moonstone ring once around my finger, for good luck.

Although, now that I thought about it...

It was time to stop blaming so much on luck.

I wasn't sure I believed in it, after all.

I glanced at the sign one more time—poor bear—then went to find my parents.

acknowledgments

There's a thread throughout *Sometime in Summer* about Miriam being able to tell, often just by looking at someone, what their "one book" is. The one book that will change their life. The one book that will offer them some insight, open some window, show them something that's never occurred to them before. The book that changed my life was *The Letters of Vincent van Gogh*—a compilation of letters the artist wrote to his brother Theo. We can't pick the book that changes our life; the book picks us. So thank you, Vincent, for choosing me. And thank you to every reader who has ever reached out to *me* to tell me that one of my books changed *their* life. It is the deepest honor and something I will never take for granted.

Thank you to everyone at Little, Brown Books for Young Readers who had a hand in bringing this story to life. To Rachel Poloski and Regan Winter for shepherding it through edits and title changes, and to Samantha Gentry for seeing it to its final form. And to Tracy Koontz and Lindsay Walter-Greaney for researching twenty-dollar bills and VHS releases of *When Harry Met Sally*.

Sometime in Summer has the perfect cover thanks to the artwork of Stephanie Singleton and the impeccable design of Karina Granda. And to Farrin Jacobs and the rest of the team at LBYR and the NOVL—thank you for making me feel so valued and safe as a writer.

To my agent, Wendy Schmalz, for our seventh book together. I think even Anna might admit that's a pretty lucky number.

This book is a love letter to Rockport and Gloucester, Massachusetts, and to family vacations and humid summers and the cold bite of the Atlantic Ocean. Thank you to my parents and my brothers for sharing those memories with me. They are some of my absolute favorites.

And to Shane—to all the magical summers we've spent together and all the rest to come.

Shane Abrahamovich

KATRINA LENO

was born on the East Coast and currently lives in Los Angeles. She is the author of six critically acclaimed novels, including *You Must Not Miss* and *Horrid*. Like Miriam, she believes everyone in the world has a book that will change their life—hers was *The Letters of Vincent van Gogh*.